Kisimba

KISIMBA

GILLIAN M MERCURIO

Copyright © 2015 by G. M. Mercurio
All rights reserved.

ISBN: 1508858233
ISBN 13: 9781508858232
Library of Congress Control Number: 2015904412
CreateSpace Independent Publishing Platform
North Charleston, South Carolina

DEDICATION

To my husband, Michael, who finally convinced me to write this novel and then patiently read it many, many times. His comments and advice were invaluable.

ACKNOWLEDGMENTS
AND AUTHOR'S NOTE

THIS NOVEL IS based on a true story. However, for reasons that will become obvious to the reader, all characters are the sole products of my imagination. Their possible resemblances to any real people, living or dead, are purely coincidental. The book describes the events that took place in Uganda in the early 1970s. Some of the political figures described were real people, and the descriptions of Kampala, the Mulago Hospital, and Entebbe at that time are, I hope, accurate. Any factual errors that might exist are mine alone. Kisimba and Hope Hospital cannot be found on any map or in any history book.

My heartfelt thanks to my dear friend Karen West, who read the entire book and made many excellent suggestions.

I also want to acknowledge the CreatSpace editorial team for their invaluable input.

Finally, to all the people I was privileged to know in Africa, thank you. You changed my life.

PART 1
DRUMBEATS

1

"So...ah...Miss Werner, is your family of the Jewish faith?"

He peered at her myopically through the thick lenses of his National Health glasses. She smoothed the gray wool skirt over her knees with damp fingers and suppressed the urge to cross her legs. It was an unseasonably warm day in London, and the room was decidedly hot with a gas fire hissing away in the fireplace.

"No, Doctor Hope. Actually my name is Penelope Drayton."

He shuffled the files on his desk and triumphantly held one up. He perused it for a long time as she held her breath. "Good, good."

Was that a look of relief that flitted across his face?

"Well, Miss Drayton, are you a child of God?"

The question was not entirely unexpected. A fourth-year female medical student who had taken an overseas elective before graduation had coached her for the interview. The student had told her to have no makeup, her hair back, boring attire (including stockings), and a demeanor appropriate for a Victorian governess.

"I was baptized and confirmed in the Church of England," she replied with practiced ease. *Please don't ask me where I attend church!*

"Hmm. Which church do you attend?"

"It has been rather difficult lately, since I'm on call so often."

That distracted him. "You do realize the Hope Medical Mission is a nondenominational ministry. In general we do rather lean toward a lower form of worship. On the other hand, we have some

— 3 —

Catholic nuns in our hospitals. Why did you not apply to one of the many missions sponsored by our...uh...Anglican friends?"

"They had no positions available, sir."

After a pause Dr. Hope looked her up and down. *He isn't eyeing my legs, is he?* He said, "I must impress upon you that our mission is to save the souls of our African brethren first and to heal their mortal bodies second."

Another silence ensued while he struggled with what she could only assume were his doubts about her.

"You are a third-year medical student, correct?"

"Correct, sir. I start my fourth year in a few months. I finish school next year in May 1971."

"So you have experience in medicine, surgery, obstetrics, and so forth?"

"Yes. Under supervision, of course."

"Well, I can't send you to Nigeria. Too dangerous. Don't have anything in Kenya at present. How about Uganda?"

She knew absolutely nothing about Uganda. Her main goal at the moment was to get out of that stuffy room.

"Yes," he mused. "Uganda. Good people there. And they definitely need another pair of hands." Then he briskly got down to business. "You will buy your airline ticket and give ten pounds a week to the mission for room and board. That's payable in advance. You will dress properly at all times in cotton dresses below the knee. You will not smoke cigarettes or imbibe alcoholic beverages. You will arrange for all necessary immunizations and obtain medication for protection against malaria. We will provide the contact telephone number and address of one of our people in Kampala. You will affirm you will support our spiritual mission and do *nothing...*" This word was a stern growl. "To compromise those endeavors. Do you understand and agree?"

"Yes, sir. Will I be working in Kampala?" *Wherever that is.*

"No, no. Most of the time you will be out in the bush at one of our rural hospitals in Kisimba some miles away. It has a beautiful chapel," he responded dreamily.

"Doctor Hope," Penny asked tentatively, "if I may ask, what is your medical specialty?"

"My dear young lady," he said condescendingly, "I am a doctor of theology."

———

Penny stepped out into the dusty North London street and drew a deep breath of diesel-permeated air. She pulled her long, unruly brown hair from its ponytail and shed the jacket of her ugly gray suit with a sigh of relief. She wished she had the nerve to remove her stockings then and there. Walking toward the Tube station to begin her long ride home, she looked briefly at the offending jacket. Without compunction she draped it over the edge of a litter bin. *Maybe someone else can use it.*

An hour later she was walking up the avenue to the little flat in Dulwich that she shared with three other women: two medical students, Liz and Diane, and a nurse called Marie. Liz was waiting for her on the doorstep, and she was laden with groceries.

"Hi. How did it go with old Hope and Grope?" she asked mischievously.

"He was just as bad as you told me. Anyway, looks as if I'm going to Uganda."

"Oh, Lord! You and that Schweitzer complex of yours. Why didn't you agree to go to Toronto with Diane and me? Modern medicine, shopping, nightlife? Ring any bells?"

"By the same token, why didn't you decide to come with me to a mission hospital in darkest Africa? After all your dad is a vicar," Penny retorted.

"Exactly! Say no more. Anyway, it just goes to show I'm smarter than you."

They laughed and climbed the stairs to the flat, each carrying a shopping bag. Once in the small kitchen, they began to unload the bread, eggs, salad, and fruit. Suddenly Liz screamed, "Oh my God! There's a giant spider in here!"

The women looked on horrified as a huge yellow spider with fat, hairy legs detached from a bunch of bananas and began to wend its indolent way across the counter.

Penny whispered nervously, "What should we do?"

"Hey. You're the tropics expert. Never mind. Hand me a glass. *Now!*"

Liz imprisoned the beast under the glass just before it skittered over the edge of the counter. A couple of legs waved at them. The glass rim wedged them at joint level.

With a determined look on her pretty face, she ordered, "Find me a sheet of cardboard."

"Cardboard?" Penny said shakily. "Where am I supposed to get that?"

"Good grief! Tear up a cereal box or something."

The scary spider was successfully trapped, and Liz and Penny descended the stairs to the street. Liz held the obscene thing in the glass.

"What now? Do we just let it go? Can we kill it?"

Liz glanced at Penny grimly. "Hell no!"

Then she threw the monster, glass, cardboard, and all across the avenue as far as she could, and the women turned, rushed into the house, and bolted the door behind them.

"Great throw, Liz," Penny said faintly.

"Thanks a lot. You were a big help, I don't think! You do know that's what you're going to be dealing with over there in Africa. Consider this your first lesson. Hell's bells, I need a drink and a ciggie! You got any?"

2

WITHIN A FORTNIGHT a large brown envelope addressed to Penny arrived at the flat in the morning post. Liz tracked her flatmate down in the hospital where she was a week into a month-long student residency in obstetrics.

"Look what came for you. Open it up. I want to see what they sent!" said Liz excitedly.

Penny tore the envelope open. Inside was a letter from Dr. Hope at the mission office; a bill for two hundred pounds; a list of contact names, addresses, and phone numbers of mission personnel in Kampala and the hospital where she would be working; a note advising her telephone service could be a little unreliable; and a small pamphlet printed on aging brown paper bearing the title, "Useful Words and Phrases in Swahili."

Ouch, Penny thought. *Two hundred pounds.*

Liz grinned and said, "Well, they seem to be efficient—at least at this end. Don't forget to take the letter to the registrar so you can get permission for leave from school."

"Thanks for reminding me. I've had so many other things to deal with. I'll also need it for my application for a travel grant. I hope I get it. I hate to ask my parents for even more money."

Penny's mother, Anne, had been less than enthusiastic to hear her plans. She herself had relatives who had relocated to South Africa and Rhodesia and had never returned for various reasons. Most were related to illness. However, after maternal exhortations to be very,

very careful, she had promised to sew a few cotton dresses for Penny to satisfy the dress code of the mission. James, her father, was a man who didn't show his emotions easily. He had impressed upon her that if she found herself in a tight spot for money on her travels, he would help—no matter what. He was also sending her a 35 mm camera, which he said was an early birthday present, with instructions to take as many photographs as possible.

"Let's have a look at that Swahili guide," Liz said.

Handy phrases filled the first few pages of the tiny booklet. These included "Hello," "How are you," "I am well, thank you," and so on. All seemed to include the word *jambo*, which Penny instantly committed to memory.

The next pages had the women convulsing with laughter. They read "The carriage awaits," "The gentleman will pay for everything," and "May I have this dance?"

"How old is this thing?" said Liz. "Oh, hang on. This is a useful one. 'Where is the toilet?' Learn that one."

Many of the Swahili words were very similar to their English counterparts. This included *daktari* for "doctor," *picha* for "photograph," and *tikiti* for "ticket." Some of the phrases were vaguely ominous such as "Help! I'm lost," "We fled from there," "Where are you taking me," and "Am I under arrest?"

"Liz, I've got to get going. I've got two in labor. Then I have to get my immunizations. Why don't you come by later and have dinner with me in the doctors' mess?"

"Nah. I've got to study, and then I have a date with Charming Charlie. I'll see you soon. OK?"

―――――

The vaccines were brutal. The worst was a large volume of antiserum against hepatitis B virus. Her behind was sore for days. The doctor warned her the cholera vaccine wasn't very effective and that she shouldn't drink water that hadn't been boiled. Then he wished her luck and gave her a prescription for antimalarial pills to take once a week starting two weeks before she left for Uganda. Penny decided not to tell her mother about that. There was no point in worrying her about tropical diseases.

Despite her earlier enthusiasm, Penny was having some doubts about her decision to apply for an elective in Africa. Liz wasn't far wrong when she talked about Penny's Schweitzer complex. As long as Penny could remember, the idea of doing heroic deeds on that continent had fascinated her. It had probably started in her Sunday school, where they began each session by singing, "Over the seas there are little brown children..." When Penny was older, she had spent hours with her mother's maiden aunt, Alice, a vigorous old lady who had been a teacher for years in both Africa and China. Penny had listened avidly to her tales of adventure and travels through the jungles and paddy fields respectively. She had trusted Alice implicitly ever since the day at lunch when Penny was ten and diffidently told Alice she hated brussels sprouts. The old lady had waved her hand at the offending vegetables and informed her she didn't have to eat them but might go hungry as a result. The additional fact that Alice claimed to be in spiritual contact with the late Sir Arthur Conan Doyle had intrigued her at the time. Although, Penny had to admit that thinking about the story now gave her pause.

As a girl, Penny had discussed with her mum, at length, her desire to become a doctor. She discovered her mother had always wanted to be a nurse, but Penny's grandfather, whom she had never met, didn't think it was proper for a woman to go to college for any reason and had put paid to that ambition. She had finally achieved her goal in part at an older age and worked for several years as a practical nurse. She had loved it and only gave it up when the work became too strenuous.

— 9 —

Penny's father had accepted her decision to apply for medical school without comment. His only advice was she'd better get good scores on her A-level exams.

Her parents had always supported her decisions, but perhaps this one was a bit risky. After all, as a woman alone, she could find herself in all kinds of precarious situations. How could she subject them to worrying about her for months with no easy way of contacting her? She would be four thousand miles away in a third-world country. However, since her early years, she had tried to face her fears and usually succeeded. After some soul-searching, she firmly decided to put her concerns behind her and focus on her immediate tasks.

———

The weeks passed quickly. Penny delivered her quotient of twenty uncomplicated births as well as a set of twins and two breech deliveries, despite intense competition from other medical students and student midwives. She reveled in the work and soon became convinced she wanted to specialize in obstetrics. At the very least, she figured it would be useful in a bush hospital.

Early one cloudy morning in October, she was standing at the departure gate at Heathrow and waiting to board. Liz had insisted on coming with her to the airport.

Worry clouded her large blue eyes, and Liz said, "Now *please* be careful. If you need me for anything, call my mum if you can. She'll know how to get hold of me."

The women hugged fiercely. Penny said, "OK. Even though you'll be in Canada in a couple of days! I'm not sure what you'd be able to do. Anyway, you and Diane enjoy yourselves over there. I'll see you in a few months. At least this no-name charter service is using a VC-10 plane. I'll be fine. This is 1970 after all. What could go wrong?"

Liz handed her a small paper bag.

"What's this?" asked Penny.

"Two packs of English cigarettes. On me. Travel safely."

————

Penny settled back in the roomy seat and accepted the offer of coffee from a dark-skinned flight attendant wearing a smart red suit sporting the emblem of the company, gold hoop earrings, and a gorgeous red and orange cap fashioned from silk and arranged in intricate folds. Penny had been apprehensive about booking with a charter company, but it had been the cheapest flight she could find. *Well, so far, so good.* She had been suffering some anxiety for the past few days but now tried to relax and enjoy the flight. Other than a quick trip to Spain the previous year, she had never traveled outside of England. The seat next to her was unoccupied, and she soon slept. She was worn-out from the preparations for her trip and her early morning start.

A melodious chime sounded followed by someone with an accented voice announcing dinner would soon be served, and that they would be arriving at Entebbe, Uganda, in about ninety minutes. Penny looked out the window next to her but couldn't see anything except clouds. She made her way to the tiny bathroom and washed her hands and face. She was surprised the woman she saw in the small mirror appeared calm, collected, and utterly normal, despite wearing a dress patterned with large green palm fronds. Presumably this was her mother's take on an African theme. Her blue-gray eyes were clear, and her long, curly hair was under control. Back in her seat she lit one of her precious smokes and waited for dinner to arrive.

The meal proved surprisingly tasty—a small piece of chicken, a few little red potatoes and carrots, a bread roll, salad, and a large chocolate-covered biscuit. She splurged by ordering a glass of white wine. She thought it might calm her nerves. When the lady in red brought it to her, Penny gave in to her curiosity. "Thank you. May I ask if you live in Kampala?"

The attendant smiled sweetly and replied, "Yes. I have lived most of my life there. My family came originally from India."

Ah. That explains it. She certainly didn't look African.

"Are there many people from your country living in Uganda?" Penny asked politely.

"Not as many as there used to be. Many have had to leave for… political reasons."

She didn't elaborate but nodded pleasantly and moved up the aisle of the cabin, leaving Penny musing on her answer. Soon the announcement came of their impending descent into Entebbe International Airport with the usual instructions on extinguishing smoking materials and fastening seat belts. The local time was 7:30 p.m., and the temperature in Entebbe was ninety-two degrees. After a smooth landing, the cabin door opened, and the hot, humid air rushed in.

Penny took a deep breath and gathered her few belongings. She had arrived.

3

THE PASSENGERS CLIMBED down the metal stairway that had been pushed up to the cabin door and straggled toward the low white-painted building some hundred yards away. Penny just followed the crowd and found herself in a bleak room lined with tables upon which people piled luggage. Under the glare of stark white lights, everyone looked drawn and tired. She turned to a heavily tanned middle-aged man standing next to her. "Excuse me, sir, do we just pick up our suitcases here?"

"First time, eh, love? Follow me. I'll see you through the nonsense. Get your passport out." He had a thick North Country English accent that reminded her of her dad's.

With their luggage in hand, they fell in behind a line forming at the far side of the room where two official-looking men in dark suits were checking papers and belongings. They were flanked by other men in green uniforms carrying rather large guns.

Her new companion went through the inspection quickly and stopped to wait for her. She stood in front of the table and held out her passport. The first person barely glanced at it but asked why she had come to Uganda.

"I'm going to the mission hospital in Kisimba," Penny replied, and she fished in her purse for the letter from Dr. Hope.

"Why? You sick?" he asked.

The men around him laughed, and she flushed. "I'm going there to observe," she said quietly.

— 13 —

"Open your suitcase, miss."

They rooted through the sparse contents and fingered her clothes. To her intense mortification, one held up a pair of her plain white cotton panties for everyone to see, and the men sniggered. Then the first inspector motioned for her to close her bag again and challenged her with an intimidating stare. Penny stood silently. There was nothing much she could say.

The man lost interest and said, "Fifty shillings airport tax."

She hadn't seen anyone else handing over money but opened her purse and counted out five ten-shilling pieces from her small stash of Ugandan money. Beyond the barricade she saw the man who had led her so far. He was shaking his head in disgust. She was waved through and walked with her guide into the chaotic crowd in the main terminal building.

"Look, love, I know you're new here, but don't just hand over money like that!" he said in an exasperated tone.

"What on earth was I supposed to do? They had guns!"

He sighed. "OK. There is that. But a word of advice: don't trust anybody—especially if that person is wearing a uniform. Look, where are you headed? Is anyone meeting you? By the way, the name's Geoff, and I assure you I'm not a creep."

"Pleased to meet you. My name's Penny. I thought I was being met, but I don't spot anyone. I'll just wait and see if they appear."

"No you won't, lass! Do you at least have a phone number to call?"

She retrieved her folder of papers and found it. Her new friend led her to a phone on the wall, inserted money in the slot, and stood by while she spoke to the operator. Then she was connected.

"Hello? Is this Dr. Campbell's number? This is Penny Drayton. I have arrived in Entebbe." She paused to hear the response. "Oh. What do you suggest I do? Take the bus? OK. I have your address. I hope I'll be there soon. Thank you."

"I heard that," Geoff said. "What's going on?"

"They were expecting me tomorrow," she replied glumly.

"Well then, let's find you a bus."

They soon found out no more buses were running that night to Kampala. Geoff shook his head worriedly. "Look, Penny, I'd get you there meself, but I have a business meeting tonight, and then I'm headed out again. I'll put you in a taxi."

"You've been so kind. I don't know what I'd have done without you," she said.

"Hey, I've got a daughter not much younger than you. I'd hope someone would help her out if she was in a jam."

As they walked outside to find a cab, Penny asked, "Does your family live nearby?"

"No," he answered shortly. "The missus doesn't care for it here. But I get back to England when I can."

He quickly found a Peugeot station wagon with four young African girls already sitting in it, and he asked the driver the cost to take Penny to Kampala. He dismissed the first response with a laugh and a wave of the hand, and a few minutes later they had agreed on a reasonable price.

"Take care, Penny. This is a great country, but you have to watch out for yourself."

On impulse she gave him a quick hug. "Thank you so much. Your daughter is lucky to have you for a dad."

She climbed into the car next to the young girls and waved to Geoff through the window, and then off they sped over the unevenly paved road to Kampala. The car radio was blaring pop music, and Penny could hardly hear the driver's questions.

"Are you a *sista*?" he asked.

Sista? Oh! Sister. Does he mean a nun?

"No. I'm just visiting," she said.

The girls in their bright dresses began giggling and touching her arm and clothes.

She asked the driver, "What are they saying?"

"They say you dress funny and speak funny. And you smell funny."

Crikey! Do I smell that bad? She was beginning to feel a little conspicuous. However, a short time later, the car was climbing a short hill, and up ahead she could see a large white house surrounded by wide verandas.

"Here we are, *Sista*," the cabbie said.

Geoff had picked the right one. As she slipped out of the station wagon, she saw a woman come out of a door onto the front porch. The driver took her suitcase out of the trunk and set it on the ground. Penny paid him the agreed amount and waved to the girls as they drove off into the night.

The woman ran lightly down the steps to greet her. Her short brown hair bounced as she did. She was in her thirties, slender, and attractive in a quiet way. She had lovely hazel eyes and was dressed in a cotton dress that fell below her knees.

"Penny, welcome! I'm so sorry I wasn't there to meet you, but my husband was called into the hospital, and we only have one car. And Dr. Hope told us you were coming tomorrow. Typical."

"It's OK, Mrs. Campbell. I met a very kind man at the airport who saw me through the difficulties."

"Call me Sue, won't you? And please don't make a habit of talking to strangers over here."

Penny felt like responding, "Yes, Mother," but she refrained. The last thing she wanted to do was upset her hostess.

"Come in. Come in! I'll show you your room, and then we'll get you something to eat!"

Sue was clearly a woman who spoke in exclamation points. She grabbed the suitcase before Penny had a chance to pick it up, led the way into the house, and chattered all the way.

"Here's your room. The bathroom's next door. These are the other bedrooms." She gave an expansive wave. "And these are the kitchen, dining room, and sitting room. You can't see the garden right now; it's too dark. What would you like to eat? How about a sandwich? You must be starving! How was your flight? What's going on in jolly old England? Well, never mind that now. We'll talk later. Thomas?" She ended the verbal stream with a polite call. "What do we have for Miss Penny to eat?"

A tall, very black man in a crisp white shirt and dark trousers appeared. He inclined his head toward Penny and said, "If the miss would care for a ham sandwich, it would be my pleasure to make it. And perhaps a glass of lemonade?"

"Thank you. That would be lovely," Penny replied.

Her head was spinning. She had taken to Sue immediately, but it was hard to keep up. As Penny ate she was surprised at how hungry she was.

Sue continued to chat. "You must be exhausted! Try to stay awake to meet Jim—my husband. He should be back soon. Anyway, you have a couple of days to rest. They're not expecting you in Kisimba until Thursday. I called them while you were on your way here. Fortunately the phones are working. I'll show you around Kampala. We'll have a lunch tomorrow at the club, and there are all sorts of interesting things to see. Oh, it's so nice to have a visitor again!"

Sue sat with Penny in the dining room as she ate. Sue talked about Kampala, her life there, and her husband's work at Mulago Hospital in the city. Penny asked her about her family.

"They're all over there in Luton. Hoping we'll go back to see them soon."

"Do you have any kids?"

A brief shadow passed over Sue's face. "No. Not so far. Maybe it's for the best. Ever since my husband…we got the call from God, what we do here is the most important thing in our lives."

Just then the front door opened, and a man wearing a long white coat walked in.

"Jim!" Sue jumped up. "Look who's here. This is Penny. She's going to the mission in Kisimba. Penny, this is Dr. Campbell."

He strode into the room with his hand extended. Despite the heat in the house, his fingers were cold.

— 17 —

"Welcome to Uganda. I apologize for not meeting you at the airport. God's work does take precedence over visitors."

OK. I get that.

He turned his attention to his wife. "Is my dinner ready, dear?"

"Of course. I'll call Thomas," she said quietly.

The bubbly, gregarious woman had disappeared. They all sat at the dinner table until Thomas had brought out a plate of food and placed it before the man of the house.

"Let us pray," the worthy doctor intoned. "Bless us, Father, for this food that will sustain us as we fulfill our mission here. Keep watch over your daughter Penelope Drayton as she goes forth to continue your work of healing. Keep her safe. Amen."

Sue chimed in with a hearty "amen" as did Thomas, who was hovering beside the door. Penny wondered for a second if this was like a toast where the toasted one sat and just smiled graciously. Then she realized Sue was glancing at her from under her eyelids, and Penny responded with a murmured "amen."

When Dr. Campbell had finished his meal, he rose and announced it was time to retire. Then he said, "Penny, I think it would be very instructive for you to accompany me to the hospital tomorrow morning for rounds. We will leave at seven."

"Certainly, Doctor," Penny responded dutifully.

Then Sue hustled her off to her room.

"Don't worry. I'll get you up in time," Sue said. "Then I'll pick you up at noon, and we'll go sightseeing." Her pretty eyes sparkled with glee. "It'll be fun. Just wait and see."

"I'm really looking forward to it," Penny said. Then she paused and listened. "Sue, is that the sound of drums?"

"What? Oh, yes. I hardly notice it anymore. It's like a bush telegraph around here. People exchanging news and so forth. It's quite soothing, isn't it?"

Then she showed Penny how to tuck in the mosquito netting around her bed, bid her a pleasant night, and departed with a warm smile.

4

PENNY AWOKE TO a gentle hand shaking her shoulder. Sue stood by the bed, holding a steaming cup.

Could it be? Yes! Coffee!

"Good morning. Rise and shine!"

Sue looked fresh and alert. Penny felt sleepy and grubby.

"Oh, thank you for the coffee. Do I have enough time to get ready?"

"Certainly. It's only six. When you're done, come to the kitchen, and we'll have breakfast. Is cereal all right?"

"That would be fine. Thanks. I'll be there in a bit."

She had had a relatively peaceful night other than an unexpected encounter with a bat that had gotten into her room when she left the door open while in the bathroom. It had zoomed around at ceiling level as she watched it apprehensively and thought of all she had learned about rabies. Finally it had escaped through the same door, which she closed thankfully behind it. She had settled into bed, covered herself with a sheet—it was still quite warm in the room—and fallen into a dreamless sleep.

Dr. Campbell was already seated at the kitchen table when Penny arrived. They exchanged greetings, and then she wandered over to where Sue was preparing breakfast.

Sue said, "Help yourself to more coffee, unless you'd rather have tea."

"Coffee please. What are you doing, Sue?"

Sue had opened a big plastic container of cornflakes onto the kitchen counter and was thumping the surrounding surface with her closed fist. "Just driving out the beasties," she replied airily. "The wretched things get in no matter how tightly I close this thing!"

Penny watched as a few small bugs of some sort exited the pile of flakes and headed off the counter. Sue swept up the now bug-free cereal into three dishes and added milk. She handed one to Penny.

"Sit. Eat. Would you like some toast?"

"This is enough. Thank you again."

She was about to dig in when Dr. Campbell carefully folded his newspaper, placed it on the table, and clasped his hands. "Thank you, dear Lord, for these thy blessings. We venture forth this day to do thy work. Amen." As they chewed their way through the rather stale cornflakes, the doctor said, "Penny, my wife tells me you intend to finish early and take an expedition to see the city."

"Yes, sir. If that's all right with you. I'd really like to look around."

He sighed. "Well, I suppose there will be time soon enough for you to do some real work. I'll meet you by the car in ten minutes."

When he had left the room, Sue said, "Don't worry about Jim. He's a good man and a very skilled doctor. I should know. I worked with him as a nurse back home. He's just a little…intense. Go get ready. I'll see you at noon."

Penny combed her hair and pulled it back in a tight ponytail, visited the bathroom (who knew when she'd have a chance later), did a quick bat check of her bedroom, and paused to examine herself in the mirror. Today's dress was a demure white with tiny yellow daisies. *Not bad. It could have been tiger stripes or something!*

Dr. James Campbell waited outside his house and drummed his fingers impatiently on the steering wheel. He was exhausted. He had been working at least fourteen hours a day at the hospital, and now he had to deal with this green medical student as well. To cap it all, last night Sue had again brought up the subject of her working as a nurse at Mulago Hospital. He had replied with his usual response. She had been sick, and she had enough to do running the house and looking after him. To his surprise she had answered him more vehemently than usual.

"For God's sake, Jim!" When he raised his eyebrows at her, she continued. "I mean that literally. You're so short of staff at the hospital, and I could really help continue the Lord's work here. Look, Penny came here, and she's just a medical student. She'll really be useful at Kisimba. Why can't I be useful here?"

He told her he would think about it and rolled over to sleep.

The subject of their discussion came flying through the front door and slid into the seat beside him. He looked her over dispassionately. "Very appropriate attire, Penny. I'm glad to see it." He gave her a small smile.

She grinned back at him and was pleased to see the first sign of a thaw in his expression. "So, Dr. Campbell, are we doing rounds first?"

"Yes. We'll begin with the medical wards and move on to the maternity ward. I'll be in clinic this afternoon while you and Sue are touring the city."

She deliberately addressed the first part of his answer. "Great! You specialize in both?"

She glimpsed a smile again as he concentrated on the road down the hill. "And surgery and accident and emergency when I'm on call, which is every fourth day."

"Good heavens!" Penny exclaimed, and she looked at him with increasing respect. "That's amazing!"

"That's Africa, my dear."

As he drove he pointed out the hills surrounding Kampala and named them along with some of the large buildings they passed in the city. The streets were teeming with people on foot or riding bicycles. Small rickety buses were packed to the gills. Most of the women were wearing brightly colored long dresses or skirts. The men and boys were more plainly dressed in Western-style shirts and trousers or shorts. Jim drove slowly and carefully as he continued the brief trip. It was a soft, clear October morning. Penny sat forward avidly, taking it all in and enjoying the feel of the cool breeze from the open windows on her face. From all directions came the sounds of innumerable noisy conversations and laughter, and many people waved to her as they passed by. Before long they were climbing up another hill toward a large, sprawling white building of several stories. She had been enjoying herself so much she was almost disappointed when they drove up to what turned out to be the hospital.

As they stood in front of it, Penny admired the peaceful park-like area surrounding the hospital complex. She was very impressed. The doctor pointed out another building nearby and informed her it was the medical school. Then he showed her the bus stop where she would be meeting Sue.

Inside the main building, bedlam reigned. People lined the hallways. Some sat or lay on the floor, and African women in nurses' uniforms and young men in white coats moved among them. Dr. Campbell seemed oblivious to the chaos as he strode toward a flight of stairs. Penny struggled to keep up. He turned abruptly into a small, windowless room. It was sparsely furnished with an overflowing bookcase, a battered old desk, and one hard wooden chair.

"This is my palatial office." He chuckled.

"Doctor," Penny said, "the place is packed downstairs. How many beds do you have?"

"Oh, about fifteen hundred, but there are usually two thousand or more inpatients on any given day."

"Where do you put the extras?"

"On the floor. Where else?" he responded wryly. He looked at her seriously. "Penny, we do valuable work here. This is the most advanced hospital in Uganda. We have quite a few Ugandan medical graduates and a handful of British and American doctors. It's very different from what you'll see in Kisimba. Let's get to work."

He handed her a white jacket that was rather large on her smaller frame, and then they were off on ward rounds. The next few hours passed in a blur. As Dr. Campbell questioned her relentlessly, she palpated enlarged livers and spleens, peered into eyes, listened to wheezing lungs, inspected recent amputations, and examined pregnant women. She was pleased when she diagnosed a breech baby and could intelligently discuss treatment options. She saw malaria, measles, tetanus, and tuberculosis. All the while she carefully stepped around patients lying on the floor between beds. When they came to a young boy with a large swelling of his jaw, she was stumped.

"I really have no idea, Doctor. Is it some sort of cancer?" she asked quietly.

"Fair enough. It's a lymphoma. Mr. Denis Burkitt worked here until recently. Did you know that?"

Penny's eyes widened. "*The* Burkitt? He's famous for his work in childhood cancers!"

"Yes. Well, there's not too much we can do about this yet. Although, methotrexate treatment has been successful in inducing remissions of the tumor. You know what methotrexate is?"

She nodded. "Yes, sir."

"Unfortunately the drug isn't always available, and most children with the disease never have access to it. Mr. Burkitt still visits occasionally. Maybe you'll get to meet him."

The last patients they saw were in a small room off the men's ward. The two men lay listlessly on their beds, and they barely lifted their heads when she and Dr. Campbell entered. They were emaciated and looked like people she'd seen in pictures of prisoners in Hitler's concentration camps.

Jim Campbell spoke gently to them as he examined them. He waved her back as she approached, and then they left the room.

He said sadly, "We don't have any idea what's causing this. We call it 'slim disease' or 'wasting disease.' My guess is it's probably due to a virus, but who knows? All I know for certain is these men will die. Soon."

"Doctor Campbell, I noticed most of the patients we saw today were young. What is the life expectancy here?"

"Good question. I'm sorry to say it's only about forty-five years. There is definitely a huge problem with access to medical care, and infections are the most common cause of death. Many of them are preventable or treatable with modern medicine." Then he looked at his watch. "Oh dear. It's nearly twelve thirty. Sue will be very cross with me. Do you think you can find your way back to the entrance?"

"Yes. I'm sure I can. Doctor, thank you for this. It's been an incredible experience. May I come back tomorrow?"

Jim smiled at her with approval. "Absolutely. I'm very pleased with your enthusiasm. And, Penny, you may call me Jim when we are not in the hospital. Off you go!"

She left on winged feet.

5

Sue was standing at the bus stop and chatting to a woman with a baby on her hip. Penny ran over to them. She was breathless. "I'm so sorry I'm late. I do hope you haven't been waiting long."

"No, no. I was a little late myself. Penny, this is Mirembe and her baby, Akia. Mirembe worked at the hospital until Akia arrived."

Penny held out her hand a little tentatively. She was unsure of the local customs. "I'm pleased to meet you, Mirembe. My name is Penny. You have a beautiful baby."

The infant reached for her with a chubby little hand, and Penny let him grasp her finger. *He has a strong grip!*

The woman responded in perfect English, much to Penny's relief.

"I thank you, miss. His name means 'firstborn.' When he is older, he will be given a Christian name."

Penny noticed the small cross shining against Mirembe's chocolate-colored skin. "If I may say so, I love your dress," Penny continued bravely.

A striking array of purple flowers against a pale green background adorned the material. Mirembe also wore a contrasting green head scarf. The plump young woman smiled and ducked her head. "It is a *kitenge*, miss. The flowers are those of the bougainvillea tree. You can find many *kitenges* in our markets."

Sue interrupted politely. "Well, it was good to see you, Mirembe. I will make sure Miss Penny visits the big market before she leaves. She's traveling to Kisimba in two days."

"Kisimba?" The woman looked surprised. "Miss Penny, it has been a pleasure to meet you. Take care."

She walked toward the hospital entrance, and the baby waved erratically to Sue and Penny over his mother's shoulder.

Penny looked after them and said, "What an interesting woman. Do most people here speak English?"

"Here in Kampala lots of them do. Many of them went to mission schools. Mirembe did. She's a wonderful nurse." Sue looked thoughtful for a second and then continued. "I'm starving! How about you? I thought we'd splurge and take a taxi to the club. Then we'll see some sights. Do you want to go shopping in the market or see some historic places? And you must see the cathedral!"

Penny laughed and wondered how Sue could talk like that without taking a breath. "Anything, anywhere, Sue. I'm in your hands."

"Excellent. Come on."

They piled into a car, and Sue gave the driver directions to their lunch destination and then interrogated Penny about her morning experiences. Apparently satisfied she leaned back and said, "Now you can relax. Time to enjoy yourself."

"Sounds good," Penny said and discreetly slipped the sandals off her aching feet. "By the way, why did Mirembe look so dubious about my going to Kisimba?"

Sue paused before replying. "Well...it's rather, shall we say, basic medicine they practice out there in the bush. They see so many patients and have so few resources. The last time we were there, they didn't even have any oxygen. They had ordered it, but someone had stolen it in transit. Anyway, the people there are very... dedicated, and I know you'll learn a lot and be a great asset. *And...* here we are! This is the club. Very expat but splendid food and clean bathrooms."

Easing her sandals back on, Penny said, "Expat? Oh! Expatriate!"

"Yes. Lots of English, Australians, and Americans. You name it."

The place looked like a mansion from *Gone with the Wind*. An elegantly dressed black man greeted them and asked them if they would care to dine inside or out on the patio by the pool. They chose the latter. The day was still cool, and the water looked inviting. Penny wished she had thought to bring a swimsuit. They sat back under the large umbrella and surveyed the scene. The only Africans in view were the servers.

"I very rarely come here, so this is a real treat for me too," Sue murmured confidentially. "Their catch of the day is usually excellent. Would you like a glass of wine?"

Horrors! Penny stared at Sue and wondered if this was a test.

"Relax, girl! I'm Anglican. But let's just keep this to ourselves. OK? We don't have alcohol in the house. Why don't you have a smoke? I see you eyeing that ashtray."

"Would you like a cigarette?" Penny asked.

"No. Thanks. I gave it up years ago. Well, maybe a puff or two!"

They sat in silent camaraderie, sipped chilled white wine, and smoked while waiting for their lunch. Finally Penny took the bull by the horns. "Sue, do you like it here? Don't you miss your family?"

The older woman eyed her pensively. "Of course I do. I miss my parents, my sisters, and my nephews and nieces. And life here isn't always easy. It gets lonely sometimes when Jim is away working day and night. But I know what we...he is doing is important. I just wish..." She trailed off. "And trouble is coming. We all know it. They are deporting or imprisoning so many Indians and Pakistanis. The economy is really suffering."

"I spoke to an Indian stewardess on the plane who told me that a lot of them had left. I didn't know it was so bad."

"Yes, it is. Anyway, here comes our lunch!"

After a meal of superbly cooked unnamed fish and rice, they both popped into the gleaming, white-tiled ladies' room and then took off on their sightseeing trip. Penny could have wandered around for hours in the bustling market and would have spent far too much money if Sue hadn't intervened in the bargaining process. She bought an intricately carved black soapstone vase for her mother and brightly colored *kitenge* scarves for Liz and Diane. Mindful of her dad's instructions, she took photos of everything.

Later they arrived at the Narimembe Cathedral, which stood on yet another of Kampala's hills. It was a surprisingly modern-looking red brick building graced with tall arches and a large dome. They stepped into the cool interior, and Sue immediately sat in a back pew and bowed her head. Penny followed respectfully and waited for a clue as to what to do next.

Sue leaped up and said, "Gracious me. It's five o'clock. You must be exhausted. Shall we go home so you can rest before dinner? We can see the King's tomb tomorrow if Jim lets you loose in the afternoon."

Penny was actually beginning to feel tired. It had been quite a day. So they picked up another taxi and headed back to the Campbell house. They pulled up, and Sue let out a delighted squeal when she saw a dilapidated jeep in the driveway.

"My goodness! Nick's here!"

"Who's Nick?" Penny managed to say, and she scrambled behind her hostess with her packages in hand.

"Nick Sottile. He's an American doctor from Atlanta, Georgia. We haven't seen him in months. Nick! Where are you?"

"In the kitchen. Where else?" came a baritone response from within the house.

Nick Sottile was leaning against the kitchen counter and looking very much at home with a bottle of beer in his hand. Thomas stood at the stove, cooking something. Penny caught her breath. The man was drop-dead gorgeous. His black hair curled above rich brown eyes, a deep dimple was in his firm chin, and his muscular arms outlined a T-shirt emblazoned with a large cursive "P." He wore rumpled khaki pants.

"Sue, honey! It's been far too long. I'm just in from Kenya and was hoping you guys could put me up for the night before I head up-country."

"Of course. Thomas, did Dr. Campbell call?"

"Yes, Mrs. Susan. He will be late and said you should not wait dinner for him."

Sue collected herself and turned to Penny. "Penny, dear, this is Dr. Sottile. Nick, this is Penny Drayton, a medical student from London." She made a grand flourish as though she had pulled Penny out of a magician's top hat like a rabbit.

"Delighted," Nick said.

He took her hand and smiled broadly. She found herself wishing she were wearing something more pleasing.

He continued. "So, are you a junior missionary? Would you like a beer?"

She couldn't help laughing. "Actually no to both. Thank you. I'm just here to learn. I'll be on my way to Kisimba soon."

"Kisimba, huh? Last time I was there, they were struggling a bit."

Sue interrupted. "Nick, you bad man, you know we don't have alcohol in the house."

She wagged her finger at him reprovingly. Nick draped his arm casually over her shoulder, and Sue looked up at him with her eyes twinkling.

"It's only a six-pack. Safer than water, and it has lots of vitamins in it!" He grinned. "What's for dinner, Thomas? I could eat a horse!"

Thomas replied with mock solemnity, "I have made a shepherd's pie, Doctor. And it is made from a cow. Not a horse."

"Ah. British soul food," said Nick happily. "Just like me poor old mum used to make!" His mock English accent was terrible.

Penny was entranced. The kitchen seemed larger and brighter with this tall, cheerful man in it. She murmured, "Excuse me. I'll just go and tidy myself up."

"Me too," chirped Sue. "We're both rather grubby after all our sightseeing."

Sue followed Penny to her room and sat on the bed. "So, what do you think of Nick?" she asked.

Penny hesitated as she pulled her hair from its ponytail. "He seems very pleasant."

"I feel I must tell you: he's married. Don't look at me like that. I thought you should know."

Oh shit! Was I that obvious?

"Doesn't his wife travel with him?"

"No. We've seen neither hide nor hair of her for over a year. I think she's living with her parents somewhere in Florida. Anyway, watch yourself. He's a very...appealing man. Now comb your hair and come eat your dinner."

She hugged Penny briefly and left the room. Penny washed her face thoroughly and brushed out her hair, which was curling wildly in the humidity. On impulse she changed into another dress. This one was swirling blue cotton and not made by her mother but bought from a London store. She told herself it was more suitable for a dinner with guests, and she knew she probably wouldn't have a chance to wear it out in the wilds.

The dinner passed with light conversation and lots of laughter. Penny discovered Nick was an epidemiologist working out of the Centers for Disease Control in the United States.

"It was called the Communicable Disease Center until a few months ago," Nick said, suddenly serious. "I'm primarily involved in surveillance studies. Not only of TB and so on but also malnutrition, which is becoming a real problem—especially in the outlying areas."

Penny asked him if he still practiced medicine.

"When I'm needed. You never know what might come up."

"Are you part of a missionary group?"

"Lord, no! I visit and work with all the hospitals: Catholic, Methodist, Anglican. It's all the same to me."

Sue shot him a reproachful look.

"Come on, Sue. I'm only teasing. So when's that man of yours coming home anyway?"

"It looks as if he's going to be later than we thought. Nick, I've put you in the usual guest room. You must be tired. Don't feel you have to wait up for him."

"Hey, I'm just getting my second wind. Why don't you girls come out with me for a drink at the American Bar down the road?"

"Nick, you're incorrigible! You know I can't do that! Anyway, your jeep's a two-seater," Sue said.

"Well, will you let Cinderella here out for an hour?"

Penny held her breath. Sue looked at them both steadily and finally said, "If Penny would like to go, I see no harm in it. Bring her back before midnight, Nick. She's off to Mulago again with Jim in the morning."

"Yes, ma'am." Nick saluted. "You game, Penny?"

"If it's all right with Sue…"

"Go, go!" Sue said, and she flapped her hands at them. "You watch out for her, Nick. All right?"

6

THEY SPENT ALMOST two hours at a bar that looked as if it had been transported from Middle America. There was even a mirror behind the bartender. All the patrons were white. Nick sprawled at the table and sipped a beer while Penny nursed a glass of wine. She relaxed as they talked of medicine, England, America, and life in general. Nick asked her about herself.

Still rather shy, she said, "Not much to tell really. I grew up in Yorkshire in the north of England, and then I went to London for medical school. I'm nearly finished. This is a final year elective for me, and I'm in Africa for only a few months."

In turn he told her about growing up in Philadelphia with his parents and two older sisters. When he was sixteen, the family had moved to Seattle, Washington, where his father had landed a job with Boeing. At eighteen he joined the navy and spent two years in Vietnam as a medic with a marine outfit. She had never met anyone who had fought in that war and told him so.

"Well, trust me. It was nasty. But being a medic made me realize I wanted to become a doctor, so when I got out, I went to NYU on the GI Bill. That was when the government gave veterans the money to go to college. I stayed on in New York to get my medical training. I'll be paying off *that* loan for a while! It's been a long road. My dad's an airplane mechanic, and my mother's a teacher. What do your folks do?"

"They're both in the civil service now. My mother was a nurse for a while. Dad was an army officer in World War II, and that qualified me for a scholarship toward medical school. The government kicked in most of the rest. My parents are very socially minded people. They live in a tiny house in a village near Leeds."

"Ah, I like that. So neither of us comes from the aristocracy. Good to know."

He smiled and then continued his story. After medical school he had done a residency in infectious diseases at Emory University in Atlanta and then accepted a fellowship at the CDC.

Penny tried to remember where Seattle was. "So, being in Atlanta, at least you're close enough to visit your family."

Nick looked at her blankly and then laughed. "I think you're confusing Washington State with Washington, DC. Unfortunately Seattle's about three thousand miles from Atlanta, so no, I don't get to see the parents very often."

After a pause Penny pointed at his T-shirt. "What does *p* stand for?"

"You're kidding, right?"

She shook her head.

Nick heaved a sigh. "That stands for the Philadelphia Phillies. Only the greatest baseball team ever seen on the face of the Earth!"

"Oh. I'm a soccer fan myself. I presume you've heard of the Leeds United team. By the way, where does your accent come from?"

"I don't have an accent. *You* do."

She chuckled. "Is it Philadelphia, Seattle, Atlanta, or what? I can't tell."

"Dunno. A mix I guess. Yours is terrific. Very *proper*. Like one of those British radio announcers."

The time flew by with light chatter, and then too soon Nick glanced at his watch and said, "I'd better get you back before you turn into a pumpkin."

As they left the bar, Nick caught her hand casually as he led her to the jeep. They walked to the front door of the house, and Nick's warm fingers rested lightly on her back to guide her. Jim Campbell was in the kitchen eating his dinner with Sue at his side. His face lit up when he saw them, and he stood.

"Nick! You scoundrel! What've you been up to?"

Nick strode across the room to him, and they clasped hands. Everyone seemed to like Nick. The two men chatted for a while, and then Jim looked over at Penny. "You'd better get to bed, my dear. We have another early start in the morning."

Penny bid everyone good night and thanked Nick for the outing. He said, "Any time, Penny. See ya!"

She lay awake for a while and listened to the muted voices from the kitchen and the sound of the drums in the distance. When she awoke in the morning, Nick was gone.

Breakfast was a quiet affair. Nobody spoke of Penny's night out— much to her relief.

Then Sue said, "Jim, Penny will have to get ready for her trip, and I want to show her the tombs, so please let her go at noon. Penny, I know you'll need to get some laundry done before you leave. Pop it in the hamper in your room, and Thomas will take care of it."

"Are you sure?" Penny was a bit uncomfortable with the thought of having a man do her washing.

"Absolutely. Thomas is indispensable. I hope he doesn't leave us."

"Well, if he does, he does," said Jim. "Penny, I think it's time for you to get ready."

She dutifully left the room and wondered about the general unease she sensed in everyone.

She spent another challenging morning at Mulago Hospital with Jim Campbell. This time they went by one of the operating rooms and peered through the porthole window in the swinging door. An African surgeon looked up briefly and waved to them.

As they moved on, Penny asked, "Doctor Campbell, what did you mean yesterday when you said things would be different at Kisimba?"

Jim stopped, leaned against a wall, and folded his arms. "How much did Dr. Hope tell you?"

"He said it has a nice chapel."

Jim gave a short bark of laughter. "That it has. What about the hospital?"

"Well, Sue said it's a bit basic there."

"As usual she is correct. Look, Penny, they have one doctor on-site to care for several hundred people every day. The hospital has about a hundred beds and one operating room. There are…" He paused and thought. "Four English nurses, two of whom are currently incapacitated, and a fair number of African girls they have trained in the basics of nursing. They have very little in the way of a diagnostic laboratory. No X-ray equipment, no autoclave, and no modern anesthesia capabilities. They try to send complicated cases to the hospital in Jinja or here at Mulago, but most patients refuse to leave, so they do the best they can. It's more like a first-aid station in some ways than a hospital. Having said that they accomplish a great deal with very little. You'll be a useful asset to them during your stay, and I guarantee you'll learn a lot of medicine." His gaze was level. "So, are you still in?"

"I'm in, Jim…er, Doctor. But could you tell me a bit more about the anesthesia part? What do they use?"

He looked at his watch and said, "We have a little time. I'll show you."

She followed him and was surprised when they descended the stairs into what appeared to be a large storage area stuffed with rusty bed frames, unopened boxes of supplies, a broken table, and what looked like an old dental chair. Jim headed for a stack of shelves leaning precariously against a wall, and after rooting around for a bit, he found an old, oddly shaped metal appliance, which he held out to her.

"That's a Schimmelbusch mask. It was used for administering ether. And still is in places like Kisimba."

Penny turned the piece over and examined it closely. It did look a bit like a mask or perhaps a medieval instrument of torture. When it came apart in her hands, she was horrified. "Oh no! Did I break it?"

Jim chuckled and took it from her. "Don't worry. It's meant to do that. See this groove here around the edge?"

He took a handkerchief from his pocket, carefully folded it, and laid it on one half of the mask. Then he placed the second half on top, pressed it into the groove, and trapped the cloth snugly.

"Of course you would use layers of gauze. Not a piece of cloth. The patient has to be able to breath easily through it. You drip liquid ether onto the mask, it vaporizes, and the patient breathes it in along with air. That's why it's called the 'open ether' method. You start off slowly for the induction phase and speed it up to go deeper." He looked at her sharply. "Do you know what the induction phase is?"

"Yes, Doctor. The first phase that lasts until the patient loses consciousness. So the mask isn't hooked up to anything?"

"No. It's held firmly over the patient's mouth and nose. If you're the one doing it, don't get too close. You don't want to be breathing in the ether vapor!"

She eyed the contraption rather dubiously. "Is it safe?"

"Actually it's very safe. Just keep a close eye out for cyanosis, and monitor the pulse and blood pressure. And I wouldn't recommend having any open flames around. Once you've done it a few times, you'll get the hang of it."

I hope he's right!

"Cheer up! The doctor at Kisimba is very competent. And don't forget you can always call me if you have questions about anything. That is, if the phones are working. Now off you go to meet Sue and make all your preparations for the trip. I advise you to go to the bank and get some more shillings if you need them. But don't carry them in your handbag."

Not daring to ask where she should carry her cash, Penny thanked him and made her way upstairs to meet Sue.

7

"PENNY, HURRY UP! Our bus is coming!"

Sue was at the bus stop and waving frantically. They clambered aboard the small, dusty bus and took seats at the rear. Penny thought fleetingly of photographs she'd seen of the not-so-distant past in America when the black people had been forced to sit at the back of the bus.

Sue was already in full flow. "I hope you don't mind traveling this way. It's not far, and you'll get to see more of Kampala. I made us a picnic. It's such a perfect day!"

Pausing to take a breath, she opened her large straw bag and pulled out a wide-brimmed hat decorated with a large green ribbon. Sue was wearing an almost identical one.

"Here. Put it on. You don't want to get sunburned. And take it with you to Kisimba. I'm surprised they didn't tell you to bring one."

"Thank you. I really appreciate it," Penny said. It was charming.

"My pleasure. I've got tons of them. I keep forgetting to wear one and have to buy another. I get them at the market. Anyway, I thought we'd go see the Kasubi Tombs where three of the kabaka, the kings of Buganda, are buried. The last one died only last year. It's a very special place for the Baganda people. A bunch of the rest of their royal families are buried there too."

"Is there a king now?" Penny asked.

"No. The British governor exiled the last king, Mutesa the Second, to England for a while. But he came back as president when Uganda became independent. Then Obote overthrew him, exiled him to England again, and did away with the constitution." Sue pulled a face. "I'm afraid things have gone downhill ever since. Mutesa died recently in London, but there's talk he'll be brought back here for burial eventually."

"Didn't I hear Obote got shot recently?"

"Yes. In the face. He was treated at Mulago actually and survived. Jim met him. Anyway, this is our stop."

Penny had a million more questions but got up and followed Sue off the bus. The story had so enthralled her she hadn't even noticed they'd been driving up another of the Kampala hills. A short distance farther up the road was a large, circular dome-shaped building with a grass-thatch roof that came down to the ground.

"That's the main tomb." Sue pointed. "Let's eat."

Only a few other people were near the tomb. They wandered around or sat in the shade of the sparsely scattered trees.

"It's OK to have a picnic here in a graveyard?" Penny asked.

"We'll sit outside the gatehouse."

Sue plopped herself down on the dry grass and delved into her bag. She handed Penny a bottle of warm, fizzy orange drink and a paper-wrapped sandwich.

"It's just cheese and tomato," Sue said. "I didn't want to risk anything going off in the heat."

The women tucked in and soon finished their sandwiches and apples. Sue picked up the remains and tucked them back in her bag.

"Let's go. There's a lot to see," said Sue.

They toured the almost-deserted site for about an hour. Sue drew Penny's attention to the stunning workmanship of the thatch roof as seen from the inside, and Penny particularly liked the drum house. Ceremonial drums of all sizes and shapes filled it. They didn't get to see any coffins since they were hidden behind screens made of bark cloth. Fanning herself vigorously with her sun hat, Sue decreed they'd had enough. "Anyway, I need to get you to a bank," she said.

"And to a bathroom please."

Sue pondered briefly. "I think there's a small hotel a little way down the hill. Are you up for walking a bit more?"

As they strolled away from the Kasubi Tombs, Penny said, "That was really interesting, Sue. Thanks for the tour. I'm beginning to wish I had more time here."

"Well, when it's time for you to go back to England, you must stay with us for a couple of days. We'd love to have you."

After a brief stop at the hotel, they hopped on a passing bus down into the city. Penny exchanged a traveler's check for more shillings—this time in large bank notes. She told Sue what Jim had said about not carrying too much in her handbag.

"No problem. I've got a small pouch you can wear under your dress. It won't show, and unless you're searched, no one will know it's there."

Searched?

Sue read her mind and said hurriedly, "Not that it's likely to happen."

They went to the market, and Sue selected oranges and papayas from colorful mounds of gleaming, fresh fruits, peas, and beans. Penny bought herself a simply carved wooden figurine of a kneeling African woman and another *kitenge* scarf for Sue as a thank-you gift.

As they were leaving to catch a bus, sudden loud shouts and screams behind Penny startled her. When a gunshot sounded, Sue grabbed her arm and pulled her close to a stall away from the open area. Penny watched aghast as a middle-aged African man dressed in a white shirt and dark pants ran by with two men in army fatigues gaining rapidly on him. One fired his pistol into the air. The other caught their prey and used the butt of his gun on the man's face. Penny heard the distinctive crack of bone, and the man fell awkwardly. In the sudden silence, she realized Sue was whispering urgently to her. "Penny, turn away. Don't look at them. Take this." She handed her a small straw basket. "Admire it, girl. That's it."

All around them people were silently engrossed in the merchants' wares. Out of the corner of her eye, Penny saw the two men dragging the bleeding victim by his feet toward an army jeep that had driven close. Then they were gone.

Penny carefully replaced the basket on the stall table. Sounds of excited chatter filled the air. Shakily she said, "What just happened, Sue? Who was that man? Why did the soldiers run him down like that?"

"I've no idea. Probably a political undesirable. It's been happening quite a lot recently." Sue's voice wobbled a bit. "It's usually the Indians they go after," she added bitterly. "Penny, there was nothing we could have done. If we'd intervened, the same thing would have happened to us. Come on. Let's go home and have a cup of tea or something."

On the bus Sue patted her hand. "Penny, it's really important you don't go out anywhere by yourself."

"What about in Kisimba?"

"There've been no stories of anything happening up there. It's a bit off the beaten track. Just stay alert and use your common sense."

Back at the house, Sue made her a cup of instant coffee and brewed a cup of tea for herself while they talked about nothing in particular. Their thoughts were elsewhere. Then Penny went to her room to pack the neatly folded clothes Thomas had washed and ironed. She lay on the bed to rest her feet and calm her nerves for a while. The next thing Penny knew, Sue was calling her to eat. Penny was amazed to find she had slept for a couple hours.

"We're having dinner in the kitchen," Sue said. "Jim will be late again."

"He works really long hours, doesn't he? He's an excellent teacher. Sue, do you think you'll go back to nursing one day? I hope you don't mind my asking."

"No. That's OK. I'd love to. I miss it so much, and I really don't have anything important to do here," she said wistfully, and her shoulders drooped. "I want to be useful, but I haven't been able to persuade Jim to let me. Not yet anyway."

Penny wondered why, but seeing the look on Sue's face, Penny didn't say any more about it and changed the subject. "I was thinking about the plans for tomorrow. Will I be going to Kisimba by bus?"

As they sat at the table, Thomas brought plates of salad and chicken to them and a freshly baked loaf of bread still warm from the oven.

Sue took a bite of lettuce. "Yes. I'll drive Jim to the hospital and then come back and pick you up at about eight o'clock. We have to get to the depot fairly early. The buses don't run on a fixed time-table, and I want to make sure you get on the right one. Then I'll call Kisimba and let them know you're on your way so they can meet you. "

"I'm sorry to put you to so much trouble," Penny said diffidently.

"Heavens, it's no trouble! We don't want you ending up in Mbale or somewhere. Anyway, I don't have any other plans for tomorrow."

"How long is the trip?"

"Not too long. It really depends on how many stops and detours the bus takes. Probably about four hours. The road to Jinja is decently paved, and then it's a dirt road to Kisimba. It's about fifty miles to Jinja and another twenty to where you're going."

Four hours to travel seventy miles?

Just then Jim came in, kissed Sue on the cheek, and smiled benevolently at Penny. Thomas brought him his plate, and he bowed his head in silent prayer. "Penny, how was your excursion?"

"It was very interesting. Thank you. Sue is a fantastic tour guide."

Neither of them mentioned the horrific incident earlier in the day.

"Good. By the way, one of those patients with wasting disease died today."

"Oh, that's so sad! How is the amputee doing?"

"He's stable." Then he looked over at Sue and said, "My dear, I'll be sorry to lose Penny. I wish the mission could have sent her here to Mulago."

"So do I," Sue replied. "Shall we have some papaya?"

"I've never tried it, but I'd like to," Penny said.

The doctor looked at her, frowned slightly, and said, "Well, don't eat too much of it. It...um...excites the digestive tract."

When she finally got to bed and climbed under her mosquito net, Penny realized the friendly neighborhood bat had returned. She sighed, got up, opened her door again, and hoped for the best. She dreamed—not of bats or guns but of tombs, friendly black faces, picnics, and Nick Sottile.

8

SUE HUSTLED PENNY onto the right bus about nine thirty the next morning. The driver threw her suitcase up on the roof of the vehicle, and she found a window seat. Penny rested her arm on the window frame next to her and noted that none of the windows were glassed in. Sue stood outside and shouted last-minute instructions Penny could barely hear over the hubbub. When the driver finally started the engine after a couple tries, Sue yelled one last time, "Be careful! Call me when you arrive!"

Penny waved to her as the bus pulled away onto the road, and she sat back to examine her surroundings. The bus was larger than the small ones they had ridden in the previous day. There were about twenty hard wooden seats. Women of all ages, a few men, and a gaggle of small children took most seats. All talked excitedly. Two women had boarded with large woven baskets balanced effortlessly on their heads. Those baskets were now deposited in the aisle and almost blocked it. She could see one was full of what appeared to be potatoes. It must have been heavy, and she wondered if carrying such a load caused any long-term damage to the neck and spine.

They made their first stop about ten minutes into the journey. They were near the big market, and two more women got on. Everyone seemed to know each other and craned their necks to stare curiously at Penny. Most returned her smile. The bus set off again, and this time it got onto what looked like a main road. Penny spotted

— 44 —

a sign to Jinja, which she took to be an auspicious omen. They were well out of Kampala before one of the men climbed over the assorted bundles, baskets, and bags and spoke to the driver. They stopped again, and the man descended and walked slowly off. Penny looked out at the bare countryside sparsely decorated with a few gnarled trees and no sign of human habitation. She wondered where the man was going. The driver turned to his passengers and called out what seemed to be a question, and an enormously fat woman struggled out of her seat and also got off. Penny had no idea what was going on until she saw the woman hike up her long skirt and squat by the road. The driver waved her back on the bus, and they took off once more.

More than two hours passed, and they still hadn't arrived at Jinja. The cast of characters kept changing as the bus stopped innumerable times to pick up and disgorge passengers. Once they drove off the road toward a small bunch of thatch-roofed huts with naked children running around and shouting and women sitting in the shade and stirring pots of something over wood fires. As she looked on, an African man in a dark suit, white shirt, and red tie came out of one of the huts with a young, very pregnant woman in a loose *kitenge* dress. The contrast between the scene and the man's appearance bewildered Penny. He helped the girl aboard the bus and shooed her to the back while he sat behind Penny.

The bus driver increased speed as traffic on the road became almost nonexistent. With each dip and bump in the road, her bottom came off her seat and then thudded down again. The passengers began to shout out angry comments to the driver. He had taken out a large bag of peanuts and was cracking the shells between his teeth and flinging them out his window. All the while he kept only one hand on the wheel. He completely ignored them all.

A while later Penny's behind was aching, and she was acutely aware her bladder was sending her insistent messages. *Well, I'm not going to relieve myself by the road. Local custom or not!*

She was distracted when the suited gentleman behind her leaned forward and asked if he might sit next to her. She noted he was quite young and had a polite smile, so she agreed.

"Hello, miss. How are you?"

"I am well. Thank you."

"Do you mind if I speak? I would like to practice my English."

Penny could tell the entire company was listening avidly, even if not comprehending. "No. Not at all."

"So, you are going to Jinja? I am going to Jinja. That is where I work. In an office," he said with some pride.

"I'm going on to Kisimba to work in the hospital," Penny replied.

"But that is wonderful! My name is Irumba. What is yours? Are you a *sista*?"

She had heard this question enough times that she knew how to answer. "Yes. Sort of. Sister Penny."

He looked momentarily crestfallen but then perked up again. "Your parents must be very rich. What work does your father perform?"

"He is in the civil service in England. And no, they're not rich." *Although I suppose they're fabulously wealthy by Ugandan standards!*

Irumba thumped his chest dramatically. "I too am in the civil service. In Jinja. I am only twenty-four, and I have an important position and two wives."

Penny thought she must have misunderstood. "I'm sorry. How many wives?"

"Two. One is sitting back there." He pointed to the rear of the bus. "And one is in Jinja." He eyed her speculatively and continued. "A white woman such as yourself would make a beautiful wife also."

She had the presence of mind to answer. "Thank you. What you say honors me. But I am a sister. Remember?"

He sighed regretfully. "That is indeed a great pity. Well, we are nearly arrived in Jinja. I am very sad, but I must leave you. I wish for you a happy time in my country."

He stood, smiled cheerfully, and went to the front of the bus. It stopped a short time thereafter in a large depot next to a railway station in what was clearly a thriving town. She waved to him as he, his wife, and others got off the bus. She found his open demeanor and cheerful nature charming.

By this time there were only four passengers remaining. The bus turned around and got back on the road, which soon turned into a red earthen track. As they careened around a bend, Penny was enthralled to see a glittering, blue expanse of water and a magnificent waterfall. She leaned precariously out of the window. The driver increased his speed, and the bus swayed dangerously. She took in the glorious view. *Why didn't anyone tell me about this?* She sat back and pulled her small map of Uganda from her handbag. *This must be Lake Victoria, the origin of the Nile!*

She bent over to fish her camera from her bag. She'd already used up one roll of film taking snaps of the cathedral, the market, the tombs, and some of Sue in the garden at the house. She had a new roll in and ready to go. Just as she focused on the lake, five or six large, colorful birds strutted into the shot and posed. They stretched their long, white, elegant necks, and ruffs of golden feathers above scarlet throats crowned their black heads. Penny clicked away enthusiastically and finally paused. She hoped she'd captured the scene adequately. Her father would be thrilled.

They bounced along the ocher road. The driver managed to avoid large potholes filled with muddy water despite clear skies. They began to pass people along the way. Some were on bicycles, and others were on foot. All scurried to get off the road as the bus hurtled past them. Many of the women were carrying large bundles or the ubiquitous baskets on their heads, and some had babies strapped to their backs in folds of their *kitenges*. The countryside was becoming lush, and small groups of huts surrounded by fairly extensive cultivated areas dotted the landscape.

— 47 —

The very large lady struggled to her feet and grabbed her belongings. When the driver jammed on the brakes to let her off the bus, she almost hurtled through the windshield. She yelled at him, "*Basha!*"

Then she slapped him hard on the back of his head. Penny had no idea what that meant, but she could guess. He waved cheerily and took off again. He left the woman in a cloud of dust as he gunned the engine.

When they screeched to a halt outside a small wooden shack with a beer bottle roughly painted on the side wall, Penny thought it was just another break in the journey. However, the driver stood, opened the door, and beckoned to her. He leaped out and offered her his hand. As she looked around and wondered what to do next, he scrambled on the roof and dropped her suitcase in the road. Just then an old but fairly clean car pulled up. A white girl wearing Bermuda shorts and a T-shirt hopped out. An imposing black man followed.

"Penny! Welcome!" the young woman greeted her excitedly. A riot of red curls framed her plump face, and her green eyes shone. "I'm Chrissie, and this is Joseph, our general factotum. He runs everything."

The man bowed slightly, silently picked up her suitcase as though it were a feather, and put it in the back of the car.

"Hi, Chrissie. I'm really pleased to be here," Penny said, and she stretched her back.

She turned to the bus driver and thanked him insincerely for a safe journey. At least she was in one piece. He grinned broadly and said, "*Kwaheri, Sista!*"

Then he climbed back into the bus and drove away.

"Wow!" Chrissie blew out a breath and checked her watch. "Not bad. You made it in three and a half hours. Of course it takes longer in the rainy season." She looped her arm in Penny's and walked her to the car. She was still chattering. "I know what you need most! A loo. Yes? We'll be back in Kisimba soon. Then if you're not too tired,

I'll show you around and introduce you to everyone. And you could probably use a snack. We had lunch earlier. In you get!"

Joseph drove the car down a rutted track that Penny hadn't even noticed. It abruptly became a roughly paved road. Ahead lay a large compound of several buildings surrounded by a low, crumbling earthen wall. There were bougainvillea trees everywhere dripping with pink and red blossoms.

Penny said, "This is Kisimba? It's charming!"

"Yes. It's pretty, isn't it? Joseph, please drop us at the main house." She turned to Penny and said, "That's where you'll be living with me and a couple of others. By the way, I see you got the memo on appropriate attire. I hope you brought some shorts. If not I'll lend you a pair. Might be a bit big, though. Maybe we can buy you some next time we go to Jinja. Anyway, you'll be wearing scrubs most of the time. They're very comfy. Remind me to find you some."

Penny was beginning to wonder if Chrissie was related to Sue.

"How are Sue and Jim?" Chrissie asked, neatly catching her thought. "Who else did you meet there—other than the handsome Nick?"

Penny's head was whirling. "They're doing well and send their best wishes. So, you know Dr. Sottile?"

"Oh, yes. He visits occasionally. I heard you went out with him."

She sighed. Did everyone in Uganda know her business? She imagined the drums sending out snippets of gossip—new white *sista* arrived in Kampala, visited Mulago Hospital, and met sexy American doctor!

They got out of the car in front of a white-painted house with a tin roof on the edge of the compound. Chrissie said, "Thank you, Joseph. I'll see you later."

He nodded, turned to Penny, and said in a deep voice, "Welcome to Kisimba, *Sista*. Please let me know if I can do anything for you."

"Thank you."

Chrissie was laughing as she picked up Penny's bag and ushered her through the front door. "You're blushing! Don't be embarrassed. If I weren't engaged, I'd go after Nick like a shot."

Penny opened her mouth and closed it again. She finally settled on saying, "You're engaged?"

Chrissie gave her a quizzical look. "Why do you sound so surprised? Stranger things have happened!"

"But...aren't you a nun?"

That set Chrissie off again into another fit of giggles. She finally caught her breath. "No! Well, sort of. I'm a nurse and a lay sister. We've got only two real nuns here. You'll be meeting them soon along with everyone else."

Sort of! It must be catching.

"Where is your fiancé? Does he work here?"

"No. He's back in London right now," she replied rather sadly. "I haven't seen him for about six months." Then she brightened and said, "But he'll be coming back soon to work in Kenya, so he won't be far away. He's a teacher." They were still standing in the spacious front entryway of the house. Chrissie seemed to shake herself out of a reverie, and her gaze focused on Penny again. "Oh, I'm sorry! I'll show you to your room, and you can freshen up."

Her room turned out to be at the end of a long hallway and past the kitchen. It was tiny with a narrow bed neatly made up and a mosquito net in place. A small chest of drawers was wedged under a high window that had neither curtains nor glass in it. A wooden cross hung on the wall over the bed, and a chair was placed rather haphazardly in the remaining space.

Chrissie pulled a face. "It's a bit spartan. I know. But it's quiet at this end of the house, and you have a bathroom next door. This used to be Sister Clare's room."

The bathroom was almost as big as the bedroom. It had an old white claw-footed tub, a sink, and a toilet.

"Wow!" Penny said. "There's even a shower fixture."

KISIMBA

"Yeah. I found a bunch of them in Kampala." It was a rubber hose that attached to the taps with a spray nozzle on the other end. "It makes it much easier to wash your hair. Here're some towels. Now do whatever. I'll wait in your room."

Penny was soon cleaner and much more comfortable. She found Chrissie had put her suitcase on top of the little chest and two pairs of green cotton pants and shirts on top of that. She said, "I wouldn't put clothes in the drawers. They tend to get eaten. And keep the net tucked in all the time so the nasties don't get in. There are a lot of mosquitoes around here. Hope you've been taking your malaria pills! Now, would you like to meet everyone or eat first?"

"Eat, I think. I'm rather hungry after the trip."

"Follow me then."

Chrissie stuck her head around the kitchen door and called, "Zach? Is there anything left from lunch? Come in, Penny, and meet Zach. He's one of our houseboys."

He was a young man with a wide face and a jolly smile. "Welcome, *Sista*! And this is my brother, David."

David hung back shyly behind his brother. He was about eight or nine years old. Penny smiled at him, and he ducked his head.

"Hello, David. Do you go to school around here?"

The boy shook his head and said nothing.

Zach replied for him. "No, *Sista*, except for Sunday school. David helps me in the kitchen and the garden, and he looks after the goats and chickens. *Sista*, if you are hungry, I can boil eggs, and we have fruit."

"That sounds delicious. Thank you."

"While you're doing that, I'll show Sister Penny the rest of the house," Chrissie said. As they walked down the hall again, Chrissie opened a door on the right. "This is my room." She closed it and pointed to the next door along. "That's Sister Clare's room. She's one of the nuns and the nurse in charge. She's sleeping right now. She's been unwell."

— 51 —

Moving along without further elaboration, they came to a dining room and then a sitting room that looked out onto a veranda. A small, scruffy dog was snoozing under one of the chairs.

"That's Buddy," Chrissie whispered.

Buddy opened one eye and wagged his tail indolently.

"Why are we whispering?" Penny asked.

"I don't want to get him going. He'll wake Sister Clare." She then indicated the next room and completed the circuit of the house. "This is Kathy's room. She's an obstetric nurse and a great one. I think she's sleeping too. She was up most of the night with a problem delivery. Now let's get you fed."

The dining room table was laid with one place setting, a glass of tepid water, and a plate with two hard-boiled eggs, two slices of bread, a raw carrot, and a slice of pineapple. Penny sat and took an eager drink.

"It's boiled. Don't worry. And take a jug of it with you later for brushing your teeth," Chrissie said as she absentmindedly nibbled on one of the pieces of bread.

Penny tucked in to the simple meal and asked, "What's wrong with Sister Clare? Is she very ill?"

"She fractured her right tibia and fibula about ten days ago. There's no way of telling how bad it is without X-rays, but at least it's not compound. She was in too much pain to be moved at first, poor thing. We were nursing her around the clock, but we got a cast on her, and now she's able to sit up. She's finally agreed to go to Kampala and get it fixed, stubborn old gal! Joseph will drive her there next Monday. She's been running Zach and David ragged. She's a bit of a martinet."

Penny absorbed this information. "So who'll be head nurse while she's away?"

"You're looking at her," Chrissie grinned. She filched another piece of bread and spread jam on it. "So you'd better behave yourself!"

"I have so many questions," Penny said. "Do all the African staff members here speak such good English? Sue Campbell told me many of the people at Mulago went to mission schools."

"Yes. Except David. He's still learning. There isn't a school near here, and he doesn't want to leave Zach. The rest of his family is dead. Anyway, we do the best we can. We try to teach him to read and write when we have spare time. Mother Mary Agnes reads with him most days. Maybe you could help with that. He's coming along well."

"I'd love to," Penny replied truthfully.

On cue David slipped quietly into the room and said softly, "Please, *Sista* Clare ask to see you and the new *sista*." Then he disappeared again.

Penny wiped her mouth and stood. Chrissie looked at the few remaining crumbs on the plate and said, "Oh dear! I seem to have eaten the rest of your bread. Would you like some more?"

"No. Thanks. I'm done."

"Are you going to eat that carrot?" When Penny shook her head, Chrissie picked it off the plate and crunched a large bite out of it. "Come on then. Let's introduce you to Sister Clare."

Chrissie knocked on the door with the carrot in her other hand, and someone with a strong alto voice shouted, "Come in!"

Sister Clare was tall—even sitting down. Her short, iron-gray hair was combed behind her ears, and she was wearing a pink bathrobe and clear plastic-framed glasses. Penny had somehow been expecting her to be dressed in a habit and wimple. Penny stepped forward and offered her hand, which Sister Clare took in a firm grasp. The elderly nun looked her up and down with a rather stern expression and then smiled at her. The skin around her faded blue eyes crinkled.

"I am very glad to see you, Penelope. And that is a suitable dress. At least you don't look like a boy, unlike dear Christine here!" There was a faint but distinct Irish lilt to her voice. "I'm sorry I have to

— 53 —

leave next week to get this wretched leg fixed, but I'm sure I'll be back soon."

"I do hope so, Sister Clare. Have you been in Africa for a long time?"

"Years, my dear. More years than you've been alive I'd venture to say. I've got some stories to tell, believe me! Come back and chat later. Now I need Christine's help getting on that horrible thing."

She waved over to a chair with a bedpan perilously balanced on it. There was a screen leaning handily against the wall. The room was much larger than the one assigned to Penny and seemed to function as an office as well as a bedroom. A desk and three battered metal file cabinets took up most space. The bed was tucked away in a corner.

"By the way, Penelope, your arm is quite badly sunburned. I would guess you sat with it resting on the window ledge of the bus on the way here. Get Christine to put something on it."

Penny bade farewell to Sister Clare and discreetly left the room. As she waited for Chrissie, she examined her arm. It was turning a deep lobster color, and blisters were beginning to form. *How could I have been such an idiot?* Belatedly she realized it was beginning to hurt. When Chrissie came out, she immediately looked at the burn.

"Trust her to notice," Chrissie said. "She gave me an earful about it. Go to your room. I'll get some salve to put on it and a light bandage so it doesn't get infected."

Once Chrissie had dealt efficiently with Penny's arm, she said, "Right. Onward and upward! Let's see. Where next? Yes. The hospital."

The hospital was another low, long, white-painted building with a sign above the main door that announced "Hope Hospital, Kisimba." At least thirty people were seated on the red earth in front. They were chatting and eating, and some of the women were breast-feeding babies.

Penny asked, "Are these people patients?"

"Most of them are family members who came with them. Sometimes from miles away. They stay around and help look after them. We have cooking pits out back away from the buildings. That's where they make meals for their relatives. Of course, if a patient doesn't have anyone, we feed them, and a lot of times we give their families food too. It can get kind of pricey, but we obviously can't let them go hungry."

The hospital was agreeably cool inside. From the entrance two corridors split off in opposite directions. A third led to the back of the building. As in Mulago people crowded the hallways. Here in Kisimba, though, they were laughing and entertaining each other.

"The women's ward is on the left. The men are on the right." She opened a door next to the women's ward. "This is one of the bathrooms."

"Wow! It's spotless!" The row of gleaming toilets and sinks impressed Penny.

"That's because they hate to use it. They usually go outside." She grimaced ruefully.

"How on earth does the plumbing work here miles from anywhere?"

"Everything goes into some sort of pit." She waved vaguely. "Thank the Lord we don't have to deal with it."

They moved down the corridor. "And back there..." Chrissie pointed. "Those are the delivery rooms and the operating theater. C'mon. Let's see if the doc is available."

An African girl in a blue dress and white apron informed them the "doc" was in surgery and couldn't come out. Chrissie introduced her as Margaret, one of the surgical nurses.

Chrissie said, "I was hoping he'd be free. Most surgeries are performed very early in the day before it gets too hot. But there are always emergencies. Never mind. You'll see the operating room tomorrow. You'll probably be working there at dawn. Let's move on."

— 55 —

Penny suddenly stopped dead in her tracks. Chrissie turned to her and saw her stricken expression. "What? What's wrong?"

"I completely forgot to call Sue Campbell."

"Calm down. I already told Joseph to call her when we got in and tell her you'd be in touch tomorrow. Never fear. Chrissie's here! Do you want to see the chapel?"

Breathing a huge sigh of relief but still feeling guilty, Penny walked with Chrissie around the back of the hospital building. Before them was a small, plain A-frame building. A neat brass plate on the wall next to the door read "Hope Chapel." Somehow the name fit.

When they entered the single room that comprised the chapel, Chrissie sat down in a rear pew and bent her head. Penny stood at the back and admired the plain lines of the walls and ceiling, which seemed to shimmer slightly in the dim light from the single side window. A table covered with a white cloth served as the altar. She felt herself relaxing for the first time that day. She was about to sit and rest when Chrissie rose and said, "What do you think? We have service every Sunday, and sometimes we even get a visiting priest or minister to officiate. Most of the time, though, either Mother Mary Agnes or Sister Clare runs the show. I hope you'll join us now and then."

"I'd like that," Penny replied and surprised herself. She hadn't been to church in years.

Chrissie checked her watch and said, "Oh goody. Time to go visit Mother."

"Is she the…er…Mother Superior?"

"Gracious, no. She's a regular nun, but she's old—nearly eighty by now. She rather likes being called 'Mother.' She's quite a character! Come on. We'll spend some time with her, and then you should get some rest. You look wiped out, and tonight we'll be having everyone over at the main house after dinner."

9

CLOSE BY THE chapel were two tiny wood-sided cottages. They were painted the usual white with neat little flower gardens in front. Penny was entranced. They looked like dollhouses. Buddy, the scruffy mutt, was sitting outside the nearest one.

"These are the guesthouses," Chrissie said. "Mother Mary Agnes lives in this one. She moved here last year. It's hard for her to walk far, and she likes to be near the chapel."

The door to the cottage was ajar. Chrissie knocked lightly and called out, "Mother? Jamal? May we come in?"

Someone with a clear voice called, "Yes, dear girl. You're right on time."

The little room contained only a bed, a small, round table, and four chairs. A gallery of black-and-white photographs and colorful religious paintings decorated the walls. A small, insubstantial old woman was sitting hunched over in one of the chairs. *Osteoporosis*, Penny immediately thought. There was no doubting this was a nun. A long, black habit enveloped her, and a simple crucifix hung around her neck.

"Chrissie, good afternoon. And this must be Penny. Come sit close to me, dear. These old eyes are finally failing me."

Penny sat obediently, and the two women, young and old, appraised each other. Mother Mary Agnes had pale, almost translucent, papery skin and piercing gray eyes. A few wisps of white hair had escaped from her elaborate wimple. Penny wondered what the

— 57 —

nun saw when she looked at her, but she apparently passed muster. The dog sat at the feet of the old lady and gazed up at her adoringly.

"May I offer you a sherry?" Mother said. "Jamal, where did you get to?" She delivered this at higher volume. "Drat that man! Maybe he had to go to the lab. Chrissie, would you do the honors?"

"It would be my pleasure, Mother," replied Chrissie with a big smile.

She poured amber liquid from a bottle of amontillado sherry into three small glasses and handed them around. Mother Mary Agnes raised her glass to Penny and said, "To you, Penny. May you learn of many mysteries."

Penny felt as though she was receiving communion. She took a small sip and responded, "Thank you, Mother."

A slender, light-skinned man with finely chiseled features silently entered the room. *Indian*, Penny thought. *Or Pakistani*. He was wearing a white tunic that fell almost to his knees and white cotton pants.

"Did you call for me, Mother?"

"Oh, there you are. Pour yourself a drink, Jamal," Mother said. Then she addressed Penny. "Jamal is our laboratory technician. In his spare time, he comes by for a chat. Jamal, this is Miss Penny. She's a medical student from London. Do we have any of those yummy water biscuits you found in the market?"

He placed his hands together and bowed. Penny responded in the same manner. She had met many Indians in London. "Greetings, Miss Penny. Yes, Mother. I will bring them to you."

"Ah, nothing like a glass of sherry for easing the bones. Jamal doesn't drink, of course, but I always offer. So, Penny, how is my dear Nicholas? He brought me that radio last time he was here." She indicated a transistor radio set on her bedside table. "He's such a darling boy."

Penny stifled a groan and took a larger sip of sherry. "I believe he's somewhere up-country, Mother."

"Oh well. I'm sure he'll get back here sooner or later. Have you met everyone yet? What do you think of Sister Clare?" Without waiting for an answer, she continued. "She and I were together in the Congo. Terrible time. Terrible. We barely escaped with our wimples intact!" She chuckled. It was obviously an old joke. "Thanks be to God and the Blessed Virgin," she added as an afterthought.

Mother eyed her glass. "Chrissie, where are your manners, my dear? Please pour another glass for everyone. It's a grand tonic, you know," she added to Penny.

They sat, sipped sherry, and nibbled on water biscuits for twenty minutes. Finally Mother Mary Agnes announced she needed a nap before she went over to the main house that evening. As Penny and Chrissie rose to leave, Mother was already nodding off in her chair.

On the way back to the house, Penny asked, "Is Jamal from India?"

"His family came from there. He was born in Uganda. He's a really nice man…and supersmart. He wanted to go to medical school in Kampala but couldn't get in." Chrissie pulled a face.

"Why?"

"Because he's Indian. The Obote regime frowns on them and the Pakistanis because they're the money class. Anyway, Jamal went to Mulago and trained to be a lab technician. He first came here over a year ago when he visited with Jim Campbell. That was when he met Theresa."

"Theresa?" Penny was having a hard time keeping up.

"You met Margaret earlier. One of our surgical nurses. Theresa's her younger sister. She's a nurse here too. Very pretty and vivacious. Anyway, it was obviously love at first sight for both of them. Jamal asked if he could stay here at Kisimba and offered to set up a diagnostic lab for us. He's been indispensable. Not only does he run the lab, but he also gives injections and so on in our outpatient clinics. And he keeps an eye on Mother Mary Agnes."

"Are he and Theresa married?"

— 59 —

"Yes. They were married here, even though he's Hindu and she's Christian. They're very happy together. Although, Jamal doesn't see his family anymore. They were none too thrilled about it. Of course, neither was Theresa's family. That included Margaret." She sighed. "Apparently Theresa was always a bit of a handful, always getting into trouble, but when she insisted she was going to marry Jamal… well, Margaret stood by her. She's been more of a mother to Theresa than an older sister. But now she's been alienated from her father and brothers as well. What a mess."

"How sad to lose your family because of prejudice," Penny said. "I'm looking forward to meeting Theresa."

Chrissie yawned and said, "You will. Now you need to rest. I'll wake you when it's time for dinner. I have to go check the wards. See you later."

———

Penny stripped her dress off, slid under the mosquito netting, and fell into a deep sleep. A repeated soft tapping on her door roused her.

"*Sista! Sista* Penny! Please awake for to be eating!"

She recognized the small voice and called back, "Thank you, David. I'll be there in a jiffy."

Chrissie and another woman were seated at the table in the dining room. Sister Clare had her leg propped up on a stool. Chrissie shot up from her chair and said, "Penny! Are you rested? You must see the sunset after we eat. It's always spectacular. Are you hungry? Oh, I'm sorry. This is Kathy Edwards, our obstetric nurse. Sit. Sit."

Penny offered her hand to Kathy. She hesitated and then shook it limply. She was quite a bit older than Chrissie—maybe in her late thirties. She was wearing heavy black-framed glasses and a rather disgruntled expression. She looked worn-out. She didn't speak but sat back in her seat as Zach served dinner.

The meal was rather insubstantial. It consisted of a little piece of anonymous meat, a small pile of mashed yellow vegetables (she was informed they were yams), and a heap of green beans. Sister Clare said a brief prayer, and they tucked in.

"So, Kathy," Chrissie said, "I haven't seen you in two days. What've you been up to? Do you have a boyfriend?"

"Try not to be ridiculous, Christine. I have been working and sleeping."

Uh-oh. Trouble in paradise!

In the ensuing silence, Kathy sped through her dinner and rose. "Excuse me, Sister Clare. I have a twin delivery that's imminent. I need to check on the mother."

"Can I help?" Penny asked hopefully.

"No. What could *you* do?"

The sister smiled mildly. "Certainly you are excused, Kathy. I hope we'll see you later at the meeting."

"If it's possible I'll be there."

When Kathy had left the room, Sister Clare said gently, "She is an accomplished nurse. The patients love her. And she is very skilled, but she does feel obstetrics is her domain. We all have our little vanities. Don't we? By the way, Christine, I think someone needs to do some grocery shopping. You should send Joseph to the market to stock up on provisions."

Sister Clare is clearly still in charge.

Chrissie said imperturbably, "No problem. I'll take care of it."

The sister shot Chrissie a look. "Very well. Everyone will be here soon. Christine, why don't you take Penelope out to see the sunset? I'll wait right here."

Once outside in the gathering dusk, Penny became acutely aware of a cacophony of croaks, hums, and clicks growing louder by the minute.

"What on earth is that noise?"

Chrissie waved a hand casually to the bushland beyond the grounds. "Mostly cicadas and bullfrogs. Cicadas are like crickets. They're said to be quite tasty when fried, but I've never tried them."

Spectacular streaks and swirls of red, orange, and violet painted the sky. Penny caught her breath. She'd never seen anything like it. She raised her camera and clicked off shot after shot. (These later proved indistinguishable.) Then the sun disappeared suddenly and without warning. She took a deep breath.

"Chrissie, this is fantastic. The air is so fresh and clear. No smog or diesel fumes. I love it. And it's cooler here than in Kampala."

Chrissie smiled. "That's because we're a bit closer to Lake Victoria."

Then she led Penny back into the house. Mother Mary Agnes and Sister Clare sat talking quietly in the sitting room as Buddy zoomed around in fine fettle and snapped at large bugs crawling on the screen door to the veranda. A tiny kitten crouched behind Mother's chair, ventured out to swipe at Buddy as he passed, and hissed like a beast five times her size.

Penny laughed. "Who's the fearsome cat?"

"She's a feral kitten. Jamal found her in one of the storage sheds that soldier ants had totally skeletonized. They arrive in a legion and absolutely straight columns, and they devour all the wood in their path. They leave the remains of the original structure intact. When it's disturbed, it collapses in a heap of wood dust. The kitten was trapped in it. We were lucky to rescue her." Mother Mary Agnes said fondly, "She'll leave soon and join her own kind."

As the assembled company contemplated the metaphor, the front door banged open. A slight man of medium height with a rapidly receding hairline and pleasant but ordinary features burst into the room.

"Evening, all!" he said as he made a beeline for Penny. "Hello there. I'm Daniel Greenleaf. So glad you're here!" He shook her hand vigorously as he surveyed the room. "Sorry. Can't stay. The baby's got colic again, and Emily's a bit frantic. Penny, we start at five thirty tomorrow morning. Two hernias and an appendix abscess. OK? See you in the operating room at five."

"Yes, Doctor. I'll be there," Penny said without hesitation. She was caught up in the whirlwind.

"Excellent! Well, I must be off."

And off he went without another word. As the doctor departed, Jamal entered with a tray on which was balanced a bottle of sherry and a few glasses. He set it carefully on the table in front of Mother Mary Agnes.

"Your tonic, Mother," he murmured and retreated.

"Thank you, Jamal. Who needs a little boost?" Mother asked the assembled company.

Everyone politely declined. That included Penny, who was feeling a bit light-headed. Mother sipped her sherry, and Sister Clare ignored the interplay completely. "Let us pray," she said.

The prayers continued for some time, and Buddy continued to hunt bugs. Penny suddenly flinched as she noticed a huge praying mantis on the wall behind her. Kathy never materialized. Then it was time for bed. Penny couldn't believe she had only arrived that morning.

Finally in her room after brushing her teeth with the boiled water, Penny got into bed. She looked around and was horrified to see a host of insects surrounded her. That included a few mosquitoes that had sneakily invaded her space under the net. Beetles crawled and buzzed around the room, and various species of spiders were on the walls and hung down from silken threads. She loathed spiders. The bedside lamp was still on. She either had to stick her hand out to turn it off or sleep with it on.

After several sweaty minutes, she came to a resolution. Either she would die of a heart attack brought on by panic, or she would face her phobia. Deciding eventually the latter was preferable, she focused her attention on a midsize bright green spider hopping about on the outside of the net with great agility.

"OK, spider. You stay out there, and I'll stay in here. Just don't make too much noise. I have to get up really early." Resolutely she reached one arm outside the net and turned off the light. Finally able to relax, she fell asleep to the sound of distant drums and smiled. "White *sista* arrived safely at Kisimba!" she imagined them saying. "Enough news for today!"

10

SHE AWOKE TO the sound of a high voice calling her. "*Sista! Sista!* It is time for your breakfast." The sky outside was turning a pale gray shot with soft pink light. A small black head was barely discernible bopping up and down outside the window. "*Sista!* You must up get! Doctor Dan will be angry with me!"

"David? OK, OK. I'm getting up." It was so dark in her room she couldn't read her wristwatch.

"I have heated water for your bathing, *Sista.*"

"Thanks," she said and yawned.

She reached out and turned on her lamp. It was four thirty in the morning. *Well, it was worse when I was on call for deliveries.* She crawled out of bed and noted most wildlife had vanished—apart from the green spider, which was stuck outside the mosquito net and apparently in an advanced stage of rigor mortis. *Ha. I won that round!*

She showered quickly, pulled her hair into its ponytail, considered briefly cutting it into a short bob that would be much easier to deal with, donned a pair of scrubs, and headed for the dining room. To her surprise Sister Clare was already there and drinking coffee.

"Good morning, Penelope. It's going to be a glorious day. God be praised. Have some coffee," she said and indicated the pot. "Zach has made you eggs and toast."

To her delight Zach presented her with a plate of creamy, perfectly cooked scrambled eggs. She thanked Zach profusely and realized she was very hungry.

"A useful rule to follow in the mission life, Penelope: eat when you can!"

Penny wolfed down her food and then said, "Well, I'd better be off, Sister Clare. I hope I'll see you later."

The nun looked decidedly wistful as she replied. "I wish I were coming too. God be with you."

Penny ducked her head in response and took off into the brightening dawn toward the hospital. Scores of African people were already outside the building and waiting patiently. She noticed a few kids who looked decidedly sick and wondered when they would be seen. She assumed she would be participating in that.

The door to the operating theater bore a large, obviously temporary sign that hadn't been there the day before. It had a colorful picture of a huge red flame. The words underneath read "ETHER in use! No smoking!!!"

She cautiously pushed the door open and stopped just inside. Dr. Greenleaf and Nurse Margaret were already preparing for the first patient. She scanned the small room and noted the concrete floor and absence of windows. She saw no equipment other than an instrument tray next to the operating table and a small cart against one wall.

"Morning, Penny. Have you met Nurse Margaret?"

Penny said, "Yes, Doctor."

Margaret gave Penny a big smile.

"OK," Dan said. "This is how it's going to happen. In the hospital you will be referred to as Doctor Penny. I am Doctor Dan. The nurses will be addressed as 'nurse.' Understood?"

"Yes, Doctor."

"Right. Today's schedule." The mild-mannered man from the previous night had vanished. In his place was a focused, organized person. "Fortunately we only have three cases this morning. I put the complicated one last. The first is a relatively healthy man of thirty-nine years with an inguinal hernia that is beginning to cause symptoms. Nurse, has the patient been prepped?"

"Yes, Doctor Dan."

"We will bring him in but will not start the disinfection or draping process. The people here have dreadful fears they will still be awake when surgery begins. Nurse will talk to him calmly and explain what is going to happen. We don't ask questions that require a response. It changes a person's breathing pattern, which alters the reaction to ether. You will administer the anesthetic. Have you ever used ether?"

"No, Doctor, but Dr. Jim Campbell showed me the equipment and explained the process."

He eyed her dubiously. "Do you think you can do it?"

"Yes," she replied firmly.

"OK then. Familiarize yourself with the anesthesia tray on the cart over there, and then we'll scrub up."

The tray held a brown bottle of liquid ether, a glass syringe, a neat pile of gauze squares, a sphygmomanometer for taking blood pressure, and one endotracheal tube. She was a little startled when a small cockroach exited the tube and disappeared off the side of the cart and onto the floor. She decided to ignore it.

"Will I be starting an IV? I don't see any tubing."

"Not unless it's necessary. We don't have enough IV sets to go around as it is. I was hoping you'd bring some with you. The mission usually suggests it. Let's go. You'll do the usual washing, gowning, and masking but no gloves. They don't do well with ether. By the way, take your watch and sandals off. We go barefoot here. We don't have booties, and bare feet are more sanitary."

Stunned by the last instruction, Penny offered no reply but silently followed him to a small side room. Dan, Margaret, and she then stood at three large sinks and started to wash and scour their hands for about ten minutes. Another young nurse had appeared and held out worn white cotton gowns for them to slip their arms into and then thin rubber gloves. Finally she put cloth masks on their faces. Penny was immediately uncomfortably warm and realized why they had started so early. They returned to the operating room. A young black man in white scrubs accompanied the nurse. She wheeled the patient in and they transferred the unfortunate man to the table where he lay rigidly. He was obviously terrified.

Nurse Margaret immediately began speaking to him softly in her native tongue, and the man smiled a little and began to relax. Penny slipped the blood pressure cuff on his arm, and then Margaret signaled that Penny should begin. She assembled the ether mask with four layers of gauze and hoped it would be enough. Daniel Greenleaf watched her closely. Then she gently placed the mask over the patient's face and filled the syringe with ether. The doctor nodded to her, and she began to drop the ether slowly onto the mask. The patient quickly fell asleep, and Daniel quietly told her to speed up the timing of the drops of ether. Then the second nurse exposed the area of interest. Penny saw his groin area had been closely shaved, and a large arrow had been inked on the patient's right side. She was impressed. There was no chance of cutting into the wrong side here.

Margaret swabbed the skin thoroughly with iodine. Dan looked over at Penny and asked, "Blood pressure?"

Shit! She checked it. "Pulse and blood pressure holding, Doctor. Sixty-eight per minute and one twenty-five over seventy," she announced crisply.

"OK. Keep him at this level and monitor the vitals. Nurse Margaret, let's go."

The operation was over quickly. Penny was so consumed with watching her patient that she didn't ask any questions, which was unusual for her. Then it was finished, and Dan was suturing the incision.

"Bring him out slowly, Penny. Watch him for gagging. Some patients react to ether with vomiting. Vitals?"

"I think we're good," she said with relief.

The patient began to rouse, and then he opened his eyes. Margaret called for the other nurse and the orderly, who carefully transferred the groggy man back onto the gurney and wheeled him into a side room.

Daniel stripped off his gown and gloves and wiped his face with a swab. "Getting hot in here already! All right, Penny. You did OK. You'll get used to judging how fast to get them under. Questions?"

"Yes. I noticed you didn't use a mesh in the repair."

"We don't have any. Just have to sew them up and hope for the best. Anything else?"

"What about postoperative pain and the risk of infection?"

He grimaced. "We don't have any analgesics other than aspirin. As for postop infection, it's actually quite rare here, despite the rather primitive conditions. We use routine penicillin prophylaxis for the more invasive procedures. You ready for the next one? Let's go! Time to clean up again."

The second hernia repair also went smoothly, despite this patient having a very large bulge in the groin area containing a mass of coiled intestines. Carefully cutting the tissue around it, Daniel thoroughly inspected the gut. Then he asked Penny, "Can you see this from there? Does it look necrotic to you?"

Unaccountably pleased to be asked her opinion, Penny leaned forward and replied, "Can you free a little more so we can see what's trapped inside?"

He gingerly eased more of the loop of intestine out. "Looks healthy to me."

"Yes, Doctor. Nice and pink."

She couldn't read his reaction because the mask mostly covered his face. He nodded and said, "OK, Nurse, let's close him up. Start bringing him around, Doctor Penny."

Grinning at their success, Penny said eagerly, "Now the appendix abscess?"

Daniel looked at the big clock on the wall. "It's seven fifteen. We're ahead of schedule. What do you say to a ten-minute break for a cup of coffee?"

"There's a pot ready in the sterilization room, Doctor," Margaret said. "Shall I call Nurse Chrissie?"

"Yes. Please. Tell her we'll be ready in a few minutes."

He turned to Penny as they removed their gowns. "Nurse Chrissie will administer the anesthetic for the next surgery since we will be going into the abdominal cavity. You will assist me please."

She was thrilled. "Thank you. I've assisted in plenty of appendectomies but never in removal of an appendix abscess. What's the history with this case?"

As they drank their coffee in the tiny sterilization room, which turned out to consist of a long bench holding four large metal trays of boiling water filled with the instruments used in the previous surgeries, he explained the next patient had been carried for two days through the bush to the hospital. By that time her acutely inflamed appendix had abscessed. She had been given penicillin to settle the inflammation, and now they would remove the sealed-off pocket containing the diseased tissue and pus.

Penny went wide-eyed. "Isn't that dangerous?"

"Actually it's safer right now to excise the abscess. The body has done a pretty decent job of walling it off for us. Are you ready to begin?"

Wild horses couldn't have dragged her away. Chrissie was already scrubbed and talking quietly to the young girl lying on the operating table. She glanced up and said, "Well, hello, you two. I thought I was going to have to do this all by myself! How're you holding up, Penny?"

"OK. Thanks. I guess we'll be there in a few minutes."

She looked over at Dan, who was already heading for the sinks.

"About flipping time," grumbled Chrissie. "Hurry up. I'm starting."

The third surgery was successfully completed sometime later. Chrissie said, "OK. How about a break? We can start the outpatients in a half hour. The assistants have already whittled the crowd down to a relatively few really sick patients."

What assistants? Penny decided she would find out soon enough.

11

WHEN THE WOMEN walked together back to the hospital, Penny noticed what she had missed earlier. In the open area in front of the building, several tables had been set up. Behind the first sat a native man in a white cotton shirt and pants with an African nurse by his side. Chrissie led Penny to the next two tables. They were unoccupied. The last one on the far right had a makeshift screen behind it. Jamal sat there with a large container beside him. More than a hundred patients, most barefoot in the dirt, were still lined up in relative harmony in front of the first table. Some lay on the ground. Others balanced on primitive crutches. Fretful children with skinny limbs and distended abdomens due to malnutrition clung to their mothers' skirts. The noise level was incredible. The moans, children's cries, and loud, unintelligible conversations reminded her of a typical Saturday night in a London accident and emergency room.

Belatedly Penny realized the outpatient clinics were held outside. Chrissie said, "I'll help you for a bit until you get the hang of it. That guy is one of our assistants. All assistants have been trained in what is essentially triage. They take care of the simple stuff and pass the rest on to us."

They sat down and Penny asked, "How many patients usually show up? I thought you said most of them had been seen already."

"Anywhere between two and five hundred or so."

Penny's eyes glazed in disbelief. "And who sits at that table?"

"Doctor Dan. He'll probably be here in a minute. Have you met his wife, Emily, yet?"

"No. I should probably pay her a visit."

"I think she'd like that. She gets quite fed up being alone with two kids all day."

Just then the male assistant approached their table. A woman in a simple *kitenge* dress carrying a small child wearing nothing but wet shorts followed closely.

"Hello, *Sista* Chrissie. Doctor Penny. I am called Luke. I am most happy to meet you. This child is of three years. His mother say he is very sick and not eating or drinking. I believe he has the measles, and he has a fever of one hundred four degrees. I think we cool him and watch him in case he seize."

"Thank you, Luke," Chrissie said. "Doctor Penny, what is your opinion?"

Penny rose from her seat and stood before the patient. She said, "Luke, please could you ask the mother if I may examine the boy?"

Luke rattled off a few words, and the mother nodded but looked scared. The child was lethargic and burning to the touch. A rash covered him, and his eyes were crusty. She got him to mimic her opening her mouth, and with her penlight she saw the telltale white spots on the inside of his cheeks. When she put her stethoscope on his little chest, the breath sounds were normal. She straightened up and said, "Luke is correct. He definitely has measles but no pneumonia. He should be admitted for observation, as Luke suggested."

Luke gave her a short bow, looked pleased, gestured for his nurse to take the boy inside, and then returned to see his next patient. Dan appeared and sat at the next table. "Did I miss anything?"

"No, Doctor. Everything's under control so far," Chrissie answered.

The next patient was quickly brought over to Dan's table. Luke said, "Doctor Dan, this child has meningitis."

"You're right as usual," Dan said after a quick examination. "Let's get her inside so I can do a spinal tap."

They left in a hurry.

"Your assistant seems very skilled," remarked Penny. "Who trained him?"

"We did," Chrissie grinned. "Uh-oh. We're up again."

Luke was back and leading a young man who was trying his best to look unconcerned. "Mister Ubulo here has gonorrhea. *Again!*"

"OK. I believe you." Chrissie sighed before Penny could even get up. "Take him over to Jamal for a shot of penicillin. And you!" She pointed at the now-cowering young man. "Don't you ever learn? How many wives do you have? Two? Bring them in here so we can treat them."

"Yes, *Sista*," he muttered, and he headed for Jamal's table.

The next hour passed quickly in similar fashion. At one point Dan returned to his table and asked Penny if she'd ever done a spinal tap on a small child. When she answered in the negative, he said, "OK. You can do the next one. I'll help you."

"Next one? Do you see a lot of meningitis?"

"Oh yes," he replied grimly. "If we can catch it in time, we have a fighting chance of saving them with penicillin."

"Do we have any other antibiotics?"

"I think we might have some sulfa drugs left. We go through a ton of penicillin. Fortunately antibiotic resistance isn't common here yet. Although, that'll probably change."

The line of patients gradually dwindled to a straggling few. Dan rose and stretched. Fatigue was etched on his angular face. "Chrissie, thanks for watching Penny. Do you think she'll be OK on her own?"

"From what I've seen, yes. Anyway, I have other stuff to do." She grinned at Penny.

"Splendid. You ready for rounds, Penny?"

She looked at her watch. She'd been up since four thirty, and it was well after three. They'd missed lunch. *Oh well.*

"Is that a problem?" Dan asked her.

"No, Doctor. It's just that I really need to go to the bathroom."

"Me too," Chrissie said brightly. "Shall we meet you on the women's ward?"

"Fine, fine," Dan replied. "Don't take too long!"

"Slave driver," Chrissie muttered as they walked away. "Come with me. We'll use the one off the operating room."

Penny hadn't even noticed the tiny room with a toilet and small sink. They physically relieved themselves and then met Dan on the ward. He was examining the child with meningitis.

"How is she?" asked Penny.

"See for yourself. What do you think?"

First she looked at the chart hanging on the end of the bed and noted the fever had subsided. The little girl was, however, lying unmoving and didn't stir when Penny touched her little body lightly. She gently lifted the child's head and couldn't detect any stiffness. Then she opened the girl's mouth and peered inside.

"She's stable. Meningismus is subsiding, but there are signs of dehydration. Her mouth is very dry."

Dan raised his brows at Chrissie, who hurried away.

"Good," he said. "Very good. Let's move on."

Most of the patients were doing reasonably well, and they moved to the men's ward. The little boy with measles was sitting up in bed and playing with some old wooden blocks. His temperature was only slightly up, and Dan instructed the nurse who had taken Chrissie's place to watch him overnight and tell his mother he could most likely be released the next morning.

As they left the hospital, Penny asked, "Do we do rounds on the maternity ward?"

Dan smiled at her and said, "Kathy will let me know if I'm needed. By the way, she delivered those twins successfully. Although, the mother lost a fair bit of blood. Kathy managed to get the family to agree to hold off on the twin ceremony until tomorrow. You should come to it. It's quite...interesting. Now go home, Penny. Eat and rest. I'll see you in the morning. You can sleep in. We don't schedule surgeries or hold clinic on Sundays. Even so, a few dozen usually show up. We'll begin rounds at seven. That way we'll be finished in time for chapel."

"Thank you, Doctor. What happens if an emergency comes in overnight?"

"Don't worry. You'll know when it happens! See you tomorrow."

Back in the house, Penny took off her sandals and slumped on the sofa. When Chrissie came in and called to her cheerfully, she didn't move. Penny peered at her new friend and said, "How on earth do you do this day after day?"

"Clean living, I guess! Don't forget you should call Sue Campbell."

Penny had completely forgotten again. She struggled to her feet and asked, "Where's the phone?"

"It's in my room. We moved it in there when we knew Sister Clare would be going off to Kampala on Monday. Come on, girl. Shift your behind!"

It was the first time Penny had been invited into Chrissie's room. She looked around in surprise. "My word! This is wonderful!"

It was a fairly small space but richly decorated. Someone, presumably Chrissie, had hung colorful *kitenge* cloth curtains at the window, and there were matching cushions on the bed and chair. Little flowers cut from the same material decorated the mosquito netting, and it hung in graceful folds. A gramophone sat on a table by the wall next to a pile of seventy-eight records, and a guitar leaned against one wall. In pride of place next to the bed was a framed photograph of an attractive blond man with a rather serious expression.

"That's my fiancé, Alan," Chrissie said. "Isn't he handsome?" Without waiting for an answer, she pointed to the phone. "Sue's number is on that pad. You might have to wait for a while to get connected. Make yourself at home. I have to see what Zach is planning for dinner," she said as she left the room. Then her head popped

— 75 —

around the door. "By the way, did you let your parents know you'd arrived safely?"

Penny shook her head in dismay.

"That's OK. I've got some airmail paper you can use. I'll give it to you tomorrow. Sunday's the best day for writing letters."

Sunday? Tomorrow is Sunday? Oh, right. No surgeries. Attend chapel, try to talk to Sister Clare before she leaves, visit Emily Greenleaf, attend twin ceremony...

———

The women shared an early dinner with Sister Clare, who seemed pleased when Penny asked her if she could spend some time with her the next day. "Absolutely, Penelope. You can help me pack."

When they had all bid each other good night, Penny decided to take a quick shower before bed. On the way back to her room, she heard a soft melody coming from down the hallway and wondered if it was a record or if Chrissie was playing her guitar.

She crawled thankfully into bed and didn't even bother to challenge her roommates, which that night included not only the usual spiders but also a small scorpion. She reminded herself to shake out her sandals before she put them on in the morning, and she drifted off into an exhausted slumber.

Sometime in the middle of the night, a loud clattering from the metal roof over her head woke her. Whatever it was causing the noise seemed to be running up and down at some speed. She listened for a while. No one else seemed awake, so she determinedly closed her eyes and went back to sleep.

12

"WHAT ON EARTH was that horrendous noise on the roof last night?" asked Penny as she and Chrissie sat down for breakfast.

"Oh, that!" Chrissie chuckled. "That was Muriel, our very own monitor lizard. She helps keep us free from snakes and other tasty treats."

Penny decided Muriel was her friend. They met Dan outside the hospital. He was deep in conversation with an assistant whom Penny hadn't yet met.

"Morning," Chrissie said. "What's up?"

The problem case was a baby whose mother had brought him in earlier. He had the classic signs of tetanus—the arched back and the grimace on his tiny face. Penny thought her heart would break.

"What can we do?" she whispered.

"Nothing. Nothing, dammit! We have no antitoxin, no sedatives, and no ventilator. He's going to die. Jesus, why can't we get these people to stop smearing dung on their babies' umbilical stumps?"

"Dan," Chrissie said, "I'll deal with it. Do your rounds."

As they walked away, Penny asked, "What's she going to do?"

"Keep him in a dark room with as little stimulation as possible. No light, no loud noises, no touching. We keep hoping one of them will survive."

They finished rounds having said little more than the essentials. Dan was brooding, and she didn't feel like chatting. However, as they left the hospital, she noted no patients were waiting outside. She ventured diffidently, "Excuse me, Doctor. I would really like to visit Mrs. Greenleaf and the children. Do you think this afternoon would be convenient for her?"

His expression lightened, and he gave her a small smile. "That would be great, Penny. Emily's been wanting to meet you. Hey, sorry I got a bit distracted back there. You planning on attending chapel? The service starts at nine. Em and the kids will be there. You can get together and make plans."

"Super. I'm looking forward to it." She checked her watch. She had almost forty minutes to get washed up and changed. "I'll see you there."

———

Penny walked over to the chapel with Sister Clare. She was ensconced in an ancient wooden wheelchair with Zach at the helm. Even at the necessarily slow pace, they arrived with ten minutes to spare. She was surprised to see a sizable crowd outside the small building and waved to those few she recognized: Joseph, the driver; Zach's little brother, David; Jamal, who was holding hands with a petite black girl in a pink dress; and Nurse Margaret. She asked Sister Clare who everyone else was.

"Well, let's see. All the nurses. They're the ones in pink or blue. Most of the ambulatory patients. And the rest are their families. Big turnout today," she said approvingly. "Zach, let's go in out of the sun please."

Inside the cool building, Penny followed Sister Clare like a lady-in-waiting to the front row. Dan and his family were already seated, and he waved her over to come and sit with them. Mother Mary Agnes was perched on a pew on the other side of the aisle and called to her at top volume, "Penny! Penny! So happy to see you here! Isn't this a lovely chapel? Bless you, child!"

Sister Clare was neatly positioned next to Mother. She solemnly bowed her head for a few moments and then turned, took the old lady's hand, and murmured to her. On Mother's other side sat Kathy Edwards. She was plainly dressed in dark blue and studiously reading her hymnal.

Where's Chrissie? Oh, there she is.

Chrissie was seated to one side of the small pulpit. She was wearing a crisp white dress that almost resembled a nun's habit and quietly tuning her guitar. She looked up at Penny and grinned.

Penny made her way toward Dan and his family. "You must be Emily," she said, and she offered her hand to the tired-looking woman holding a baby.

Dan's wife was obviously a few years younger than he was. She had dishwater-blond hair and flat eyes so pale they appeared colorless. She flushed slightly as she shook hands with Penny and murmured, "How do you do."

"I'm sorry it took me so long to get to meet you. It's been a bit hectic since I arrived," Penny said. She felt too large and colorful in Emily's presence.

"Yes. It usually is," replied Emily with a wry twist to her thin lips. "This is Jonathon." She indicated the little boy, who was busily scribbling in a coloring book. "And the baby is named Winifred."

Winifred? Poor kid!

Quiet descended on the full room. "Hi, Jonathon," Penny whispered. "What are you coloring?"

He ignored her and snuggled closer to his mother. Then a few clear guitar chords sounded around the chapel, and the congregation rose with some commotion while Chrissie played the rousing opening stanzas of "Onward Christian Soldiers."

After two more cheerful hymns, Chrissie sat down, and Joseph escorted Mother Mary Agnes to the front. She was so tiny that only her head and shoulders appeared above the pulpit. She smiled benignly at the assorted crowd and said, "God bless you all!"

"Amen!" everyone shouted enthusiastically.

"God loves you and wants you to care for each other as he loves and cares for you!"

"Amen!"

"There are many temptations in this world." She paused, seemed to drift off for a while, and then resumed. "We are all his children, and while we all sin occasionally, he forgives all who repent."

This was beginning to sound a bit like a revival service, but obviously the congregation loved it.

"And the Blessed Virgin Mary watches over us all to help us do the right thing."

"Amen!"

"This includes helping your brother when he is sick and has no food to feed his family. And it means respecting the sanctity of marriage—no matter how many wives you have!" This time the response was a lot less fervent. She sighed. "Do the best you can. And before I forget, I want you to meet Doctor Penny. She is visiting us from England. Stand up please, Penny dear."

"Amen! Amen!"

Penny raised her hand awkwardly and sat again.

"And remember, God loves you. Bless you all!" Mother finished with a wave of her hand that could have been a sign of the cross and walked slowly back to her seat.

Nice brief sermon. What's next?

Chrissie rose again and said, "Thank you Mother. Now, everyone, the twin ceremony will be held later this afternoon."

As cheers broke out in anticipation of the upcoming party, she broke into a rollicking version of "Jesus Loves You," and everyone sang along. Then it was over.

"What did you think, Penelope?" asked Sister Clare on the way out as Zach manfully pushed her chair.

"It was such fun. I mean, so inspiring!" Penny answered, and she earned herself a sharp look from the nun.

"And what about you, Zach?"

"You know I love to sing," he answered ambiguously. "Shall I make your tea, *Sista*?"

"Thank you. Yes. Penelope, would you care to join me?"

She really didn't like tea but graciously accepted. Just then Jamal approached with the young African girl he'd been holding hands with earlier in the service. Penny guessed she was Theresa, Margaret's sister. He bowed formally to them all and then addressed Penny. "Doctor Penny, this is my wife, Theresa. She has been looking forward to meeting you."

"It's my pleasure, Theresa," Penny said, and she offered her hand to the young girl.

"Oh, thank you. It is so wonderful that a woman can become a doctor. I hope we will work together. I am learning to be a surgical nurse like Margaret," she said enthusiastically and without a trace of shyness. Jamal looked at her proudly.

"Good for you," Penny answered warmly. "I hope so too."

Then she followed Sister Clare back to the house. The sister's room was in disarray. An open suitcase was on the bed, and books were littered around.

"Please excuse the mess, dear. Come and sit by me. We'll have a chat."

Zach brought in a teapot, a little milk jug, and two china cups without saucers. Sister Clare poured for them both, settled back, and said, "Now, what shall we talk about?"

Penny said hesitantly, "Mother Mary Agnes told me you were in the Congo together."

"We were. It's not a happy story, Penny, but it's not an uncommon one." She paused and collected her thoughts. "It was 1960, I think, just after the Congo gained independence from Belgium. Mary Agnes and I had been serving for about eight years in a Catholic mission just outside a place called Thysville in the far west of the country. It was fairly close to Léopoldville. It was a splendid place." She smiled sadly. "It had a school as well as a hospital. We even had our own priest, Father Emile. He was a gentle soul, God rest him. Soon after the independence celebrations, people started to run amok. The black troops were still under the command of the Belgians, and that didn't sit well with the troops. They wanted to be in charge of the army. So mutiny broke out and spread around the whole country. There was a garrison stationed a few miles from us, and we found ourselves caught in the uproar with no real warning."

Sister Clare fell silent. She was lost in her memories. Penny reached out and touched her arm gently. "Sister, I didn't want to upset you. Let's have some more tea, and you can tell me some of your other stories."

"No, child. I think it's important you hear this. I don't believe you know very much of the world. Surprisingly few young people do. When the riot broke out at the garrison, it spread through the local area. That included the mission. Father Emile was the first to be taken. He suffered terribly but tried so hard to be brave." She swallowed painfully. "All the white nurses were raped and killed, and then they came for the nuns. We were praying in our chapel. After they were done with the young nuns and postulants, they killed them too. In a way Mary Agnes and I were fortunate. They weren't too interested in us because we were older—particularly Mary Agnes. It didn't last too long. As Mary Agnes likes to say, 'At least we left with our wimples intact!'"

Penny was so horrified she could hardly breathe.

"My dear," Sister Clare said softly, "they can violate your body, but they can't touch your soul." After a pause she continued. "A few days later, those brave Belgian sailors found us in rags and tatters. We were very hungry, and they got us out of the Congo and into Tanzania. We arrived here a year after that. We had lost everything we had, but that was very little because of our vows of poverty. I managed to save a little book of the Holy Gospels I had been given as a young girl. That was it. What a dreadful time. But those poor people who were massacred later at Stanleyville had a far worse time of it than we did."

"I had no idea it was so bad. Sister Clare, may I ask you something?" The nun nodded. "I keep feeling there's something worrying people around here that they're not talking about. Am I imagining it?"

"You have sound instincts, Penelope. I too feel there's trouble brewing. The political situation in Uganda is a little...unstable. Many people are very unhappy with President Obote. The cost of living has skyrocketed, and the average income is still pathetically low. People are having a hard time affording food—never mind everything else they need. We've felt it here. And we certainly can't get the supplies we need desperately. The fabric of this society is shredding. There's no doubt.

"Listen, Penelope, I think it only prudent you should know a few things Chrissie might not have told you. That girl!" She laughed suddenly. "She's an incurable optimist. Anyway, don't go wandering off too far into the bush on your own, and run back if you see anyone in uniform."

Penny nodded solemnly.

"We also have an evacuation plan if worst comes to worst. We leave, take the bare minimum, and get across the border to Kenya at the nearest point. It doesn't take too long from here by car."

Penny stared at Sister Clare. She was aghast at the information she had imparted in such a calm tone. "Who leaves? What about the patients?"

The nun reached out and took Penny's hand. "They stay or go back to their homes. Some of the nurses and assistants would most likely stay with them—at least for a while. There really is no alternative, my dear. We can either go, or stay and most likely face death if another Stanleyville happens here. The patients would be left in the same situation either way. Now we will pray hard this will not occur."

— 83 —

She dropped Penny's hand and folded her own in silent prayer. After some minutes Penny rose to go. Sister Clare said sharply, "Penelope, I thought you were going to help me pack for Kampala. Come on, girl. Let's get to it before lunch!"

13

The packing took less than ten minutes. Sister Clare instructed Penny to pack her habit first. Unlike Mother's traditional, heavy black attire, this garment was a lightweight, loose white gown that probably fell to the middle of the calf on Sister Clare's tall frame. Penny folded it carefully and put it in the small cardboard suitcase, which it nearly filled.

"I like this habit. It looks really cool and comfortable," Penny remarked.

The sister muttered, "Hmph. Those old black ones are unbearable in this heat. God forgive me for my weakness." She pointed to the chest where the rest of her clothes were. "All that better go. I don't know when I'll get back here."

"All that" consisted of five pairs of voluminous knickers, two sleeveless liberty bodices, and two long night shifts.

"I don't think your dressing gown will fit in here," Penny said.

"Never mind. I'll borrow one from Sue Campbell. Just lay the veil on the back of that chair with that blue dress. I'll wear those while traveling. Books can go in my cotton shopping bag. Well, that's done. If you push me into the dining room, we can have some lunch."

A plate of ham sandwiches and a bowl of tomatoes sat on the dining table. Chrissie came out of the kitchen with a jug of lemonade just as Dan appeared.

"Sorry, all. Got to leave again," he said. "This time it's Jonathon who's sick. Fever. Penny, Em asked me to explain, and she hopes you'll be able to get together some other time. Enjoy the ceremony."

Penny was contemplating the possibility of a postprandial nap when Chrissie said, "Now you'll have time to write to your family. I put the airmail paper in your room."

———

The twin ceremony was held in front of the hospital. The area was obviously used for large gatherings such as the outpatient clinic and dances.

It was a glorious sight. A group of men were playing drums of different sizes and shapes. Intricately painted patterns decorated some. Two small boys were playing flutes fashioned from short tubes of wood. Another hit a small hammer on what looked like a wooden xylophone. A strange instrument held by one of the musicians fascinated Penny. It consisted of metal rods of different lengths attached to a crude wooden plate. He was using his thumbs to pluck on the spokes. Penny snagged David, who was running around with some kids his age.

"David, what is that instrument called?"

He screwed up his face in concentration. "Name is piano with…" He wiggled his thumb at her.

"Thumb piano?"

"Yes, *Sista*. Made from bicycle."

As David took off again, Penny wondered if she'd heard that part right. She was distracted when a long line of women and girls arrived. Each moved gracefully to the music. They wore colorful skirts and white short-sleeved blouses. One wore a frilly red top. They formed a circle with the woman in red at the center. Penny guessed she was the new mother. Soon everyone was dancing to the hypnotic beat. The men leaped and stamped outside the protective circle of women.

Penny noticed Kathy Edwards, the obstetric nurse, standing alone. She was watching the scene with an almost maternal smile of pride on her usually expressionless face. Penny walked over to join her and swayed to the irresistible rhythm of the drums.

"Hi, Kathy. This is fascinating. I've never seen anything like it."

"Uh-huh," said Kathy without looking at her.

The drumbeats accelerated to a frenzy. The mother of the new twins was still dancing within the circle, and she twirled around a few more times before sinking fairly gracefully to the ground and lying on her back with her knees bent. Amid much hooting and hollering, a young man clad in what looked like a knee-length white skirt edged with a gold-colored ribbon appeared. As far as Penny could tell, he wasn't wearing anything else. He pushed his way aggressively through the protective ring of women and knelt between the woman's legs. He placed his hands flat to either side of her shoulders and began jerking his body over hers in time to the drums to the obvious approval of his male friends. Penny was mystified and asked Kathy what was happening.

The nurse midwife looked at her as though she was the village idiot. "Isn't it obvious—even to you? Simulated copulation. Intercourse. Supposed to guarantee future fertility in the woman. Believe me. It's not necessary. She'll be delivering another baby within the year. Men! The number of kids they can claim is a sign of their power and prestige. They don't care a whit about the fact the woman...or women are worn-out from childbearing by the time they are twenty-five! Or that every pregnancy carries increasingly higher risks."

The tirade ended as quickly as it had started, and Kathy turned away to leave. By this time Penny was seriously irritated, and she caught the woman's arm to stop her. "Look, Kathy, it's obvious you aren't a happy person, but you've only just met me. Why are you being so nasty? I've never done anything to you."

Kathy shot her a venomous look. "Right. You have wealthy parents who no doubt got you into medical school through their connections, and now you're here like a little white princess with everyone fawning over you while the rest of us do the work. It makes me sick!"

Penny stared at her. "What the hell are you suggesting? You know nothing about me. I'm not going to stand here and refute all your ridiculous accusations. If you want to get to know me, go about it the way normal people do—in the course of civilized conversation. I really wanted to talk to you about things I'm interested in such as the neonatal mortality rate here and how you deal with the complicated deliveries. I'm thinking about specializing in obstetrics one day. But if you can't be bothered, forget it. By the way, aren't you supposed to be a lay sister like Chrissie? What happened to love thy neighbor and all that crap?"

Disgusted with Kathy and her own outburst, Penny turned away. When she turned back again, Kathy was frowning at her.

"OK. Since you're so interested, the infant mortality rate here is a little more than one in ten," Kathy said with a tinge of sarcasm. "Not acceptable but probably better than what you expected."

"Thank you. I apologize," Penny said. "That was rather rude of me."

Penny was still fuming when she left and headed for the house. After dinner she found Chrissie in her room. She was lying on her bed, reading, and listening to a classical guitar record.

"Hi there, Penny. 'Scuse my not getting up. My dogs are killing me. Not you, Buddy," she hastily said to the mutt sitting beside her. "What's up?"

"You probably heard about my little run-in with Kathy this afternoon."

"I also heard you apologized to her. So what's the problem?"

"I wanted you to know it won't happen again."

"Blimey. I'm not your mother! Look, Kathy's being a real pain in the neck. Her best gal pal was transferred out a few weeks back, and she's been miserable ever since."

"Gal pal?"

"You know…special friend. Figure it out for yourself. Anyway, she's a terrific nurse. She wanted to be a doctor but couldn't get into medical school. It was really hard for a woman back then. Still is I imagine. Bet you have a lot of men to pick from."

"Not hard when you're one of twelve women in a class of over a hundred."

"Now go on to bed. We've got another early start tomorrow, and we have to see Sister Clare off on her trip. Good night."

Penny felt much better and turned in.

14

VERY EARLY THE next morning, the household was abuzz as the women prepared Sister Clare for her drive to Kampala. The nun had eaten her breakfast and was now seated in her old wheelchair and irritably ordering everyone around. She was wearing a plain blue dress and her veil, which she fiddled with until Chrissie said, "May I, Sister?"

She straightened it to her satisfaction. Joseph pulled up in the car, loaded the sister's suitcase and small bag, wheeled her outside, and helped her into the front seat. Chrissie and Penny climbed in the back for the short ride to the hospital.

When they arrived a large contingent of nurses was standing on the front steps with Dan, Kathy, and Mother Mary Agnes. Scores of patients milled around in the outpatient clinic area. Chrissie leaned in through the open car window and gave Sister Clare a brief hug. Penny joined the others. Then Joseph slowly pulled away. Everyone waved, and the nun sniffled a bit. "God be with you all! Christine, did I tell you to—"

"I'm sure you did, Sister. Have a safe trip."

As the crowd dispersed, Dan called out, "Penny, let's go. Lot to catch up on today."

Penny quickly fell into a routine of rising at dawn, working through myriads of patients, wolfing down skimpy meals, attending sporadic prayer meetings (now held at Mother's house over glasses of sherry), and retiring early. She was seeing outpatients by herself and gaining confidence while knowing Dan was nearby. She became proficient with using the ether, and glowed with satisfaction when the doctor announced he was pleased with her progress.

On Thursday morning, she was awoken not by young David but by the sounds of rain battering the tin roof. She leaped out of bed and moved the chest away from the window. She had just finished breakfast when there was a loud knock on the front door. Seconds later Zach came in and told her, "Dr. Dan needs you right away, *Sista.*"

As Penny stepped out into the downpour, Chrissie passed her coming in and warned her. "The water's deep in places. Watch out for snakes."

"Yikes! What do I do if I see one?"

"Best to leave it alone. If it bites you, bite it back!"

Penny waded over to the hospital as fast as she could and poked her head into the operating room. Dan was already working on a patient as Margaret administered the ether.

"Sorry I'm late, Doctor."

"You're not. We're early. Two emergencies. This is one, and you get the other. Need another nurse in here!" he yelled.

A young girl flew in. It was Theresa.

"Nurse Theresa, please take Doctor Penny to the suture room and make sure she has what she needs. OK, Penny?"

She followed the girl to a small three-sided room that was open to the elements on the fourth. A man sat mournfully on a stool. He was clutching his right hand, which was swathed in cloth. "*Jambo,*" she said. "I'm Doctor Penny. Let's have a look at that."

She carefully peeled away the blood-soaked material to reveal a large but clean cut across the man's palm. She flexed her fingers and pointed to his hand. The man dutifully mimicked her actions. All the tendons and muscles seemed to be working. *Good.* She stuffed a big wad of gauze into his hand and turned to the sink to wash up. She asked Theresa if she knew what had happened.

"He say accident. His name is Kikongo. Your suture tray is ready."

She scrubbed her hands and nails, and the nurse held out her gloves. "No gowns for this?"

"No, Doctor Penny."

"Where is the local anesthetic?"

"We ran out, Doctor."

Damn. "OK. Let's go."

"I have to leave, Doctor. I am very sorry, but I'm needed in the surgery."

Penny watched and smiled as Theresa ran lightly through the rain and leaped effortlessly over the puddles like a little kid.

She gently bared the man's hand again and started talking calmly. She did not know if the patient had any idea what she was saying. She cleaned his hand thoroughly with antiseptic and mopped blood as she went. The flow had subsided. She paused and scrutinized the wound carefully. There were no obvious bleeding points. She recalled a lecture on forensic medicine from way back. *Yes. That was it.* She was certain this was no accident but most likely a defensive knife wound.

"Been in a fight have you, Kikongo? I'm going to stitch you up now, OK? It's going to hurt."

He looked at her and nodded slightly.

Thirty minutes later the wound was neatly sutured. Kikongo had sat through it stoically and never moved. She applied a dressing, gave him a penicillin injection, and told him to come back the next day. Again he nodded. Then he walked out into the rain wordlessly. She sat for a minute and wiped sweat from her brow. The humidity was almost unbearable. She walked slowly back to the operating room. Dan looked up. "Everything OK?"

"Yes, Doctor. He'll be back tomorrow for a wound check."

"Good. Scrub up. This is an easy one."

It was another hernia. She stood opposite Dan and assisted.

"OK, Penny," Dan said suddenly. "Step away from the table please."

Uncomprehending, she didn't move.

"Penny, get away from the table! Oh, for God's sake. Margaret, Theresa, move her away!"

Margaret pulled her back. *What on earth is going on?* Then oblivion took her.

———

Chaotic visions were still swirling through her mind as she slowly became aware of a soft light beyond her closed eyelids. She recalled standing in the operating room and assisting Dan, but then everything had dissolved into a hazy dream in which she was being made to drink copious amounts of water—more and more water. She vaguely remembered the pleasurable sensations of a cool, wet cloth on her skin. Her body had felt as if it was on fire. Then she remembered being wrapped in a blanket like a baby as she shook with cold. Stirring under the light sheet, she realized someone was holding her hand and squeezing it gently. She wanted to go back to sleep, but the pressure on her fingers grew more insistent. Reluctantly she opened her eyes a little and squinted against the light. Then they flew open of their own accord.

"What are *you* doing here?" Her voice sounded strange to her, and her mouth was suddenly parched.

"And *buongiorno* to you too," Nick Sottile said. "Is that any way to address your personal physician?"

"What happened to me?"

She surreptitiously checked what she had on in the way of clothing and was relieved to find she was wearing one of her cotton nighties.

"You've been off in malaria land for three days, honey. Your fever broke only a few hours ago."

— 93 —

"How on earth did I get malaria?"

He smiled at her. "Well, this little mosquito comes along and bites you. In the process he injects the parasite into you. Are you sure you're a medical student?"

"But I've been taking those wretched pills every Sunday."

"They do help but clearly don't work all the time."

She processed the information. "OK, but why are you here? I thought you were somewhere up-country."

He released her hand, and his long, tanned fingers found the pulse at her wrist as he said nonchalantly, "Oh, I was just passing by a few days back."

Really?

"And I thought I'd drop in. Good thing I did. You were in a bad way. Though I must say, you fought like a tiger while I was trying to stuff the quinine into you. You used certain words that surprised even me! Hmm. Your pulse rate's still a bit rapid. Maybe it's me. Try to imagine I'm Dan."

She gave him what she hoped was a chilly stare, and his hand moved to her forehead and then smoothed back her hair.

"OK. Cool and dry. Your hair's a bit nasty, though, from all the sweating. I certainly don't mind giving bed baths, but I do draw the line at washing hair."

"What?" Penny shrieked. She was horrified and suddenly more awake. "You didn't."

He winked at her. "Don't worry. I'll never tell. And I'll have you know I led the prayers for your recovery."

She finally realized he was pulling her leg and chuckled weakly. "You're impossible, Nick."

"Well, I threw in the odd 'amen' here and there, and it clearly worked. By the way, who's the current US president?"

"Why? Have you forgotten?"

"It's just something doctors always seem to say in movies to their patients."

"But you are a doctor. Aren't you?" He just grinned at her while she thought hard. "Johnson," she finally said.

"No, but close enough. Now let's have a look at you. Keep quiet."

He shone a penlight in her eyes, peered in her mouth, and listened to her breathing through the nightgown. Then he stood and called for Chrissie. As it turned out, she was in the hall outside her open door.

"Yes, Your Highness?" Chrissie said demurely. "Your wish is my command."

"I don't need a genie. I need a nurse to chaperone me while I examine the patient's liver. You know how I can be."

"Thankfully I don't, Doctor," Chrissie said. She straightened Penny in the bed, eased her nightgown up to her rib cage, and arranged the sheet below her navel. "OK. Get on with it. I've got work to do."

Nick viewed the exposed area critically. "Looks as if you've lost some weight here, girl."

"Good," Penny muttered.

Chrissie asked sweetly, "And just how would you know that, Doctor?"

He ignored them both and kept his eyes on Penny's face while he palpated her abdomen lightly and then more deeply. She knew he was observing her for any pain reaction to pressure. She'd done it herself enough times. However, she was nonetheless strangely moved as his expression became serious and his warm eyes became slightly unfocused as he concentrated on his examination of her. Then he pulled down her nightie and gave her a purely masculine smile that made her catch her breath. "All's well in there. Where else would you like me to look?"

"OK. That's enough shenanigans," Chrissie said briskly. "Didn't you say you had to leave this morning? Say good-bye to your patient while I go get her something to eat."

"Where are you off to this time?" Penny said rather shakily. She felt suddenly bereft.

He sat down on the bed again. "Kenya. I'll call in a few days and check up on you. Behave, take your pills, and do what Chrissie tells you."

He leaned forward and planted a soft kiss on the tip of her nose. Then the room was suddenly and totally quiet. A few minutes later, she heard the sound of his jeep revving up and taking off toward the road.

15

PENNY LAY IN bed and was feeling better until she checked her watch and realized it was after eight o'clock. She got out of bed, picked out a dress, and checked the kitchen.

Zach cried, "*Sista* Penny, you need to rest!"

"What I really need, Zach, is a cup of coffee. Where is everyone?"

"At the hospital. *Sista* Chrissie said you not to go. Rest for two days."

We'll see about that!

She drank her coffee and ate an apple. Mindful of Nick's remark, she got in the shower and washed her hair. It was bliss. As she toweled off, the thought of Nick got her smiling. She imagined what the drums might have been relaying the previous night: "White *sista* alive! Saved from fever by American doctor! She likes him very much!"

Too much.

She wandered over to the hospital and met Chrissie outside. She was seeing outpatients.

"Why are you here? You're supposed to be resting."

"I don't have anything to do. Can't I help?"

"You have plenty to occupy you. Write to your mum. Read a book. Go visit Emily. Use your wits, girl, and make the most of the vacation."

Dan was no help. She poked her head into the operating room. When he saw her, he said, "Glad you're up and about. Go away."

Restlessly she walked the compound and ended up at the Greenleafs' house. Emily was thrilled to see her and dragged her inside. "Sit down. You're supposed to be resting."

"If one more person says that to me, I'll scream."

"Thank you for coming by. For once the children are well, so we have a chance to talk. I've got coffee on. Would you like a cup?"

They sat comfortably sipping coffee and nibbling on cookies as the baby snoozed on her back on the floor. Jonathon played with a red plastic truck. Penny asked her how she had been coping in Africa with two young children. Emily sighed.

"It's been much harder than I anticipated—especially when Winifred was born. She wasn't exactly planned, bless her. I'm constantly worried when they get sick that I won't be able to get them the best treatment."

"Your husband is a great doctor," Penny murmured.

"He is. Isn't he?" The light faded from her eyes as she continued. "But he's away from the house so much. One of the local girls comes in to help, but I'm still exhausted all the time."

"Do you think you might be anemic?"

"Dan checked my blood and says I'm not. Don't say anything to anyone else, but I really want to go back to England. Dan doesn't want me to go, but he'll be done here in a few months. Then we can get on with our regular lives."

"May I ask...what will Dan do then?"

"He wants to do a fellowship in surgery."

"That's a hectic life too."

"Yes, but at least I'll be at home with my family and friends around."

Penny felt sorry for the unhappy woman and searched for a more cheerful topic. It turned out Emily was an accomplished cook, which Penny definitely wasn't, and they spent an hour talking about recipes. It bored her to tears, but she was pleased to see her hostess cheerful again—if only for a while.

OK. What next?

She decided to take a short walk. She needed to get some exercise and build her strength again. It was a lovely day, and the air was still pleasantly cool. Mindful of Sister Clare's warnings, she carefully noted her position as she set off into the bush. It was mostly red dirt and trees—certainly not a dense rain forest. She was delighted when she spotted two small monkeys of some species chattering high up in a tree. With the compound still in sight, she confidently headed for a small house in the middle distance she had never noticed before. As she drew nearer, a man suddenly appeared from behind a grove of brilliantly flowering bougainvillea trees. She squealed in surprise, and the man held both hands up reassuringly. "It's OK. You're safe. Who are you?"

"Who are *you*? You startled me."

He had a boyish face and untidy, straight, fair hair that fell over his big, round glasses. He was wearing a wide-brimmed hat and knee-length shorts with multiple pockets. He had two cameras slung around his neck. Without advancing he said politely, "Please excuse me. My name is Peter Nygaard. I am a freelance photographer from Norway. My colleague and I are compiling a portfolio of Ugandan flora and fauna."

He pointed to the house. She could see a dark-haired, stocky man sitting on the veranda. He was puffing on a cigarette. He stared their way but didn't acknowledge them. For some reason she suddenly wanted a smoke, which hadn't happened since she had arrived.

"And your name, miss?" he asked.

He seemed safe enough. However, she answered cautiously. "Penny. I'm staying at the Hope Hospital back there. And if you'll excuse me, I must be getting back. They're expecting me."

He bowed slightly. "I'm very happy to have made your acquaintance. I have only just arrived, and I know no one here. May I call on you at the hospital sometime?"

"I'm sure everyone will be pleased to meet you. Good-bye."

She was still uneasy and walked briskly back to the compound. She turned once. He was standing where she had left him and watching her with a slight smile.

That evening after prayers Penny told the assembled company about her meeting with Peter Nygaard. Chrissie immediately said, "Joseph told me there were two strangers living in the old house. You know, I never heard who owns that place."

Dan frowned. "I've no idea either. But you women should be more careful where you walk alone."

"He seemed harmless," Penny said. "I was just surprised when he suddenly appeared from nowhere. I wanted you all to know about him in case he comes around here."

"Who are we talking about?" Mother Mary Agnes asked querulously. "Is Nick coming back again?"

Chrissie patted her hand gently. "No, Mother. It's just a photographer."

———

By noon the next day, Penny was bored silly. She tried reading a book on the lives of the saints, but it didn't help. She was happier to find an old dog-eared copy of a P. G. Wodehouse book in the sitting room. That kept her entertained for a while. When Chrissie asked her if she wanted to go to the market just outside Jinja, she leaped at the chance.

The offerings in the small open stalls were meager compared to the variety of food, household items, and other goodies she had seen in Kampala. They carried with them a basket of carrots and another of yams from the hospital garden and a dozen eggs carefully wrapped in a kitchen towel. Penny watched admiringly as Chrissie traded the vegetables for a scrawny chicken. She asked why they didn't eat one of their own.

"Ours are decent layers. We always have lots of eggs. The meat is a treat. Now let's see what we can get in exchange for the eggs. Do you like oranges? Haven't had them for a while."

"I hope you don't mind my asking, but is the mission so short of money?"

"Don't worry. We'll be OK. We've had to spend a lot on hospital supplies lately, so we're a bit low on funds. And the price of food keeps going up."

"I have some money with me if that helps."

"Keep it for something else. Like a pair of shorts. I think I know where we can get you some."

They toted the chicken carcass and the oranges around while they hunted for a clothing stall. It was worth the search. Penny found a pair of sky-blue knee-length shorts that Chrissie deemed suitable, and Penny happily paid a few shillings for them. On the way back to the car, they passed a coffee seller and stopped to take in the fragrance of the brew. Penny stepped over without hesitation and picked up a large brown bag of coffee beans. Since her arrival the brew at Kisimba had become noticeably weaker by the day.

"Chrissie, do we have a grinder for beans?"

"Yeah. An old metal one. Still works well. But you can't buy that! It costs an arm and a leg. Most of the coffee grown here is exported, and what's left for the locals is exorbitantly expensive."

"Too bad. I'm getting it."

"At least let me bargain for it. You didn't even try for the shorts."

Five minutes later Chrissie had negotiated a significant price reduction, despite the wails of protest from the vendor, and they carried off the prized beans in triumph.

They dropped their packages off in the kitchen, and Penny changed into her new shorts. They just skimmed her knees. They were perfect. Chrissie's energy was undimmed. She checked the time and asked if Penny was up to a visit with Mother. The thought of sherry was enticing, but then Chrissie informed her alcohol was forbidden for at least a week. They walked into Mother's little house after a warning knock and stopped short when they saw she wasn't alone.

"Girls! Come in. Come in. Penny, are you feeling better, my dear? That malaria can be very nasty. No sherry for you. Oh! Have you met this gentleman? His name is Peter. He brought me this interesting book of photographs."

Penny glanced at Chrissie, who suddenly appeared older, serious, and rather stern despite her casual attire. She extended her hand to Peter Nygaard. "Good afternoon. I'm Sister Christine. I'm the nurse in charge here. What can I do for you?"

Nygaard wiped the surprised expression from his face and bowed as he took her hand. "Sister, I am very pleased to meet you. I believed mistakenly Mother Mary Agnes was responsible for the mission."

"Oh. No, dear," Mother chimed in. She added slyly with a twinkle, "I appreciate the gift, but was it perhaps intended for Sister Christine?"

He flushed slightly and said hurriedly, "No, no, Mother. Please keep it."

Chrissie said, "Mr. Nygaard, I believe you have already met Doctor Penny. May I ask the purpose of your visit to the hospital? Do you need medical attention?"

He looked with new interest at Penny but answered Chrissie. "Thank you, but no, Sister. I am in excellent health. I wished to introduce myself as your new neighbor and was hoping I might take some photographs around your hospital while I am here."

Penny noted his English was impeccable but stilted. She waited for Chrissie's reply with curiosity.

"You are welcome to take pictures of the compound, but I can't permit you to go into the wards or the operating room. Or the grounds while we are holding outpatient clinic. That would be an inexcusable violation of patient privacy."

He blandly ignored the firm response. "I'm sure I can get the patients' permission. I always do."

"Not in my hospital, Mr. Nygaard. Now, if there's nothing else..."

He paused, bowed again, and bestowed a charming smile on them all. "Please forgive me, ladies. I fear I have overstepped my bounds. I am overeager for company it seems."

He left the house.

After Dan pronounced her fit, Penny was finally permitted to begin work again. The memory of Nick came surging back as Dan gave her a thorough examination. She suppressed it with difficulty. She resumed the familiar hospital routine but still chafed against her imposed afternoon rests. She felt strong and back to normal.

One evening after dinner, Chrissie said, "Guess who paid us a flying visit today. Nick, of all people. He left something for you, Penny. Come with me, and I'll get it for you."

She kept up her chatter when they got to her room. Finally Penny interrupted her. "So, about Nick. I'm sorry I missed him."

"Yeah. He's fun company. And smashing to look at."

Penny agreed—perhaps a little too fervently. Chrissie looked at her sharply and said, "Pity he's married. Isn't that always the way? All the good ones seem to be taken. Anyway," she said as she got up and fetched a paper bag from her dresser, "here's your present."

Inside was a large plastic bottle of skin softener. Without thinking she rubbed her hands together. The skin felt normal to her. "I don't get it. Why would he give me this?"

Chrissie laughed at her consternation. "It's not an insult, girl. It actually helps protect you from mosquito bites. It doesn't smell too bad either. I took a whiff."

Penny smoothed some of the lotion on her hands and arms and had to concur. She offered some to the other woman. She declined. "The bugs don't bother me anymore. I guess I'm not tasty enough for them. Anyway, time for bed. Sweet dreams."

———

Chrissie mentioned a few days later that Peter Nygaard had visited the hospital on a few occasions while Penny was working. It seemed he too had come bearing gifts: fruit, cookies imported from Europe, and even a jazz guitar record for Chrissie.

"What's he up to?" Penny wondered aloud one day at lunch.

"Who knows? But I'll take the food any day." Chrissie grinned at her. "Maybe it would be polite to ask him to dinner."

"What about his mysterious colleague? Have you met him?"

"No. Must be some sort of hermit. Anyway, what do you think about a dinner?"

Mother stayed silent and continued to eat. Kathy was absent as usual. Penny looked curiously at her friend. "What's going on? I thought you didn't like him."

"He's not so bad. Quite amusing actually. I appreciate his taste in music."

Is Chrissie interested in Peter for more than she lets on?

"I thought this Saturday would be OK for dinner. What do you think, Mother?"

The old nun waved her hand dismissively. "I try to be accepting of all people. We are all made in God's image. But…" Her gaze fell on Penny. "He doesn't hold a candle to Nick. Him I trust. Now I should retire. Penny, could you walk back with me?"

"Certainly, Mother."

On their way out, Penny mouthed to Chrissie, "Let's talk."

16

"I DON'T UNDERSTAND, Chrissie. What do you really think of Peter Nygaard?"

"What's to understand? I think he's probably OK." She paused and glared. "I have no personal interest in him. Every time he's been here, he's been nothing but polite, and every time he has asked about you. I don't think it would hurt if you got to know him. He's a neighbor after all and someone you could become friendly with."

"Are you trying to set me up with him?" Penny was stunned.

"No. But there are people in Uganda other than us old fogies here."

Penny started laughing. "I'd hardly call you an old fogy, Chrissie!"

She smiled reluctantly. "Well, I still have my moments." She glanced at the photograph of her fiancé by her bed and sighed. "It's just that they seem to be getting fewer and farther between. Anyway, if Peter is interested in you, why not give him a chance? Talk to him on Saturday. See how you feel. I might be all wet anyway. Maybe he's after Mother."

"Just don't try any matchmaking. Please. I'm far too busy for anything like that. And anyway I'll be gone in January." When she heard her own words, she felt a pang of regret. "Chrissie, I wish I could stay longer. That's only a few weeks away."

"So make the most of it, girl. Go to bed now. Time for your nap."

Peter accepted the dinner invitation with alacrity and showed up half an hour early on Saturday. Penny was still showering and didn't rush to join the others. As they ate she was surprised to find she was enjoying the evening. He talked about the countries he had visited in the course of his work and had some interesting stories to tell about people he'd met in India, Iceland of all places, and England. He and Penny compared notes on their favorite spots in London. Dan sat and watched everyone else. He said little. Emily had begged off the dinner party and stayed with her children.

When the evening ended, Peter said, "Sister Christine, Doctor Penny, I would be honored if you would join me for dinner next weekend. I have heard of a highly recommended restaurant on the outskirts of Jinja and would be delighted if you could try it with me. And Doctor Dan also, of course."

Dan declined politely, and after a brief hesitation, Chrissie said, "No. Thank you, Peter. But you and Penny could go, if she would like. How about it, Penny?" When Penny nodded in agreement, Chrissie continued. "Joseph will drive her there. I don't want her out in the bush at night alone."

Peter's expression was hard to read behind his large glasses. He said shortly, "So be it. Good night. I look forward to seeing you next week, Doctor Penny." He took his leave.

Penny chuckled. "I'll be twenty-five soon, Chrissie. Do you really think I need a chaperone?"

Before she could answer, Dan said, "Yes. This is Africa, Penny. I suggest you do as Chrissie says. And don't forget we're visiting the leprosy hospital after chapel tomorrow. Rest up. It's a couple hours away by car. Night, all."

———

When they drove into the compound of the leprosy hospital, Penny gasped in amazement and struggled to retrieve her camera from her bag. The place was ablaze with color. There were so many flowering trees and bushes set between the small dirt paths that the few buildings were barely visible. Children were racing madly around. They chased each other and a dog, and hoots of laughter sounded from the house nearest to them. Their arrival was soon noted, and scores of men, women, and children ran out to assemble in a parklike area shaded by two giant mango trees laden with fruit. They separated into two groups. Men were in the shade of one tree, and women and kids were under the other.

A burly black man walked over to them. A huge grin split his face. "Doctors! Welcome. It is good to see you again, Doctor Dan. We have missed you."

The men shook hands. "Isaac, this is Doctor Penny. She is working with us at Kisimba for a while. Penny, Isaac is our nurse in charge here. Actually he is the only nurse."

The man let out a rich laugh as he shook Penny's hand. "There's not much to do here. The doctors come once a week. I take care of the rest. Anyway, I live here. I am a patient also!" He held out his arms, and Penny saw the large depigmented areas of his skin.

"Where do the doctors come from?" she asked curiously. Dan had not been very forthcoming on the drive.

"We are blessed to have the help of those from many missions: Catholic, Protestant, English, and French. I'm happy to say at least here the differences do not matter."

"We rotate on a schedule set up by Sister Clare," Dan said. "It's been working really well. Isaac, shall we begin clinic?"

"Certainly, Doctor. We are ready for you."

Two tables were brought out and set under the huge trees. Penny sat at one on the women's side, and Dan sat at the other. He called over, "Give me a shout if you need help."

No one who came up to Penny's station appeared to have any new serious medical issues, and the patients seemed more interested in meeting her than in receiving any kind of treatment. She saw classic examples of the chronic disease that was familiar to her only from her textbooks. Most of the children were uninfected but had to live with their mothers in the compound. She examined a young girl with large skin lesions on her back. The little boy in her arms shyly watched her, and on impulse Penny asked the mother (through Isaac) if she could take a photograph if she didn't show her face. The girl happily nodded. Penny thought of all the pictures she had taken, this one would be the epitome of Africa for her—the girl in her *kitenge* skirt and the toddler grinning at the camera as they sat under the mango tree in the hot sun.

Finally they toured the almost-empty wards. Some men were practicing various exercises. A teenager was walking on one leg with the aid of crutches. His other leg was a bandaged stump. Another amputee was trying to ride a bicycle around the large room and kept falling off. They were all laughing so hard that at one point she snapped a picture of them as they all rolled helplessly to the floor, overcome with hilarity.

"Is it always like this, Dan?"

"Every time I've been here. They have a home. No one bothers them. They grow their own vegetables and have their hens. I think there are even some cows. And all the missions chip in for medical costs. They lead far better lives than they would outside. People don't understand leprosy. Even their families shun them. They don't realize it's just not very infectious."

They bade their farewells and set off back to Kisimba.

17

At four o'clock on Saturday afternoon, Penny was sitting on her bed and grumbling. Chrissie rummaged through her clothes to choose a dress for Penny to wear on her "big night out" with Peter.

"I'm exhausted. I really don't want to go out."

Chrissie had been bugging her unmercifully until that point, but she suddenly became solicitous. "You poor thing. It's been a tough week. Maybe you should just stay home and rest."

This had the effect of rousing Penny from her funk, and an hour later she was in the sitting room dressed in her green frond-patterned dress, which she really didn't care for. When Joseph appeared she heaved a sigh and walked out to the car. Chrissie stood in the doorway with a satisfied grin on her face. Joseph was wearing a black jacket over his white pants and a faded black cap reminiscent of the chauffeurs' hats she had seen in old movies. He opened the rear door of the car for her with a bow. He looked quite impressive and very solid under his uniform.

"Do you know where this restaurant is, Joseph?"

"Yes, Doctor. We will be there in time. Then I will wait for you outside and bring you back."

She relaxed on the bumpy drive, looked out at the stars, and listened to the evening drums. She was startled when Joseph announced, "We are arrived, Doctor. Please stay here while I find the gentleman."

She thought he sounded disapproving, but maybe that was her imagination. He was back in a couple minutes with Peter, and Joseph opened her door. Peter was wearing a crisp khaki shirt and matching pants. "Good evening, Doctor Penny. Thank you, Joseph. You may leave now. I will drive the doctor back to the hospital."

"No, sir. *Sista* Chrissie told me to wait." He spoke firmly, and his expression was implacable.

Peter shrugged. "We'll see."

He led her into the restaurant. Although large, it looked like an ordinary house. Porches and twinkling lights strung on the trees surrounded it. They were immediately seated in a spacious dining room, which was softly lit and cooled by large ceiling fans.

"I hear they have local delicacies here, but if you would prefer European food, that is also available. Would you like a drink?"

"Yes. I think I would. A glass of white wine please," Penny said.

They studied the menu. She decided to play it safe and ordered a chicken dish with pasta in a white sauce. Peter was more adventurous and decided on goat meat with cassava and peanut sauce. They sipped wine and sat back to wait.

"Penny—may I call you that? Tell me all about yourself. I know you live in London, but where have you visited since you have been here in Africa?"

Her story of arriving at Entebbe, staying in Kampala for a few days, and then coming to Kisimba sounded boring even to her. However, he persisted with his questions. He asked whom she had met, where she had stayed in Kampala, and where she had visited there. Eventually she found she was having a hard time maintaining her end of the conversation. She began to look around the room at the other guests, and he suddenly grabbed her hand. "Penny, you are not listening to me."

"Please forgive me. I'm a little tired. It's been a hard week."

He was immediately apologetic. "No. Forgive *me*. I am too eager to get to know you. You are a fascinating, alluring woman after all. We will just sit comfortably and enjoy the peaceful evening."

"No, no. I'd really like to hear about what you've been doing here in Uganda."

Their dinner was served. Hers was delicious. To her eye his looked rather unappetizing—especially the cassava, which resembled tapioca—but he tucked into it with gusto. As they ate he talked incessantly about himself, and her mind wandered again. The sight of a couple seated at a corner table suddenly caught her eye. The woman was slender, African, and stunning in a simple ivory-colored dress. *The man. Oh, God. Is that Nick?* He looked quite different from their last encounter during her bout with malaria. His hair was long and curling over the collar of his crisp white shirt, and he sported a short, smooth beard and mustache. *Mmm. Very dashing!* She smiled to herself. Just then he looked straight at her across the room. His left eyebrow lifted, and he raised his hand slightly off the table. Then he resumed his conversation with his companion.

She realized Peter had once more taken hold of her hand. She gently pulled away. She excused herself to go to wash her hands. When she returned Nick and his friend were nowhere to be seen. Her spirits fell.

"Peter, that was an excellent meal. A real treat. And I had a very pleasant evening. Thank you so much. Now I think I should go home. I'm still not totally recovered from the fever, and I'm supposed to take it easy."

"You're a bit hard to get, aren't you? I don't like playing games."

His suddenly hostile tone took her aback. "I do not play games, Mr. Nygaard. I'll be leaving now. Joseph will be waiting for me."

She turned and fought the urge to run from the dining room. She forced herself erect and walked out sedately. Joseph was nowhere to be seen. She cursed under her breath and lingered by the door under a light to wait. There was no one around, and she began to feel uneasy. Then Peter burst through the door. He grabbed her arm hard. His fingers dug into her flesh. "How dare you walk out on me like that? What is the matter with you? *Suka!*"

He pushed her roughly against the wall and tried to kiss her. She twisted her head from side to side and willed herself not to panic. *Joseph must be around somewhere.*

The deep voice was familiar, but the distinctly Oxford accent was not. "My word. Penny? Penny, is that you? I almost didn't recognize you."

Peter let her go, and Nick strolled over to them. A raffish smile gleamed under his mustache. He swept Penny into his arms and gave her a sedate kiss on the cheek. His mouth close to her ear, he murmured, "Play along. OK?"

Peter asked angrily, "Who the hell are you?"

"Oh, Penny and I have known each other since she was in her playpen. Haven't we, poppet? I was forced to babysit her when our families got together. She was a real little hellion growing up. How's your dear mama, treasure? What on earth are you doing here?"

"I'm…uh…visiting Kisimba. You do know I'm in medical school. Right?"

He smacked his brow. "I heard there was a young English girl working at the hospital there. Who knew it was you? Small world, isn't it?"

"Well, I hate to break up this touching reunion, but Penny is my date tonight," Peter interrupted.

"Is that so? Good for you, my dear. I always thought you should get out more. Of course, you're older now. Your clock's ticking." He looked Peter over. "So you are…"

"Peter Nygaard, photographer. Now I must take Penny back home."

"Hold on, old chap. Nobody here has a train to catch. So you're a photographer? Jolly good. Where're you from? Interesting accent."

"I am from Norway. Where are *you* from?"

"Here and there. Originally Derbyshire. Most recently over here in the colonies, don't you know. Hmm. I've spent quite a bit of time in Norway. Whereabouts?"

"Oslo." He was beginning to steam.

"Great place. I stayed there for one memorable weekend." He winked. "At a hotel called…wait. It'll come to me. The Hotel Falk? Do you know it? Right there on Maridalsveien."

"Yes. Of course I do. Now, if you will excuse us, we are leaving."

"Relax, dear boy. I've got my jeep right here, and now I'm thinking of dropping by the hospital. I'll drive the young lady back. Hey, Penny, is Mother Mary Agnes still there? Wonderful old gal. I'd love to visit with her and pay my respects. D'you think those lady nuns would put me up for the night?"

She nodded and didn't know whether to laugh at his outrageous performance or cry. The two men stared at each other. Nick towered over the younger man. Peter finally dropped his gaze and walked to his car. With no further acknowledgment of either of them, he drove away on squealing tires.

"Are you all right, girl? Did that bastard hurt you? I had a powerful need to kill the little shit. But that would have dented my image a tad."

"Just some bruising. Nick, I can't believe it's you. What was all that nonsense about? And who was your friend in there? And where's Joseph?"

"Hold up. I can't remember more than a couple questions at one time. I sent Joseph home when I knew it was you. I got suspicious when I saw you with that little creep and decided to stick around just in case there was any trouble. Besides, I wanted to be the one to take you home. What were the other ones?"

"Who was the young lady?"

He smiled teasingly, touched her hair, and tucked an errant curl behind her ear. "She's a very agreeable woman with a very large husband. She's a colleague. She left in her own car to go back to Jinja."

"Oh. OK. What was your nutty performance about? It was like something out of a bad movie."

— 113 —

"I'm hurt. I thought it was worthy of an Academy Award. Didn't you like the accent? I'm a big David Niven fan." He looked rather pleased with himself.

"Hmm. I do like the mustache, though."

"Don't get used to it. It's coming off. It itches like crazy."

He took her hand and led her to his jeep, which was parked around the corner. "By the way, I want you to steer clear of Safari Man. I take it he's the guy living in that house not too far from the hospital."

How does he know that?

"Don't worry. I will." She shuddered. "Safari Man?"

"Uh-huh. Who the heck dresses like that anyway?" He paused and then said seriously, "I wouldn't trust that guy farther than I could throw a buffalo. He's not from Oslo. That's for sure."

"Really? He did call me what was probably a rather rude name."

"What was it?"

"It sounded like '*suka.*' Is that Norwegian?"

"No. It's Russian," he said grimly, "and I'm not going to tell you what it means. Whatever. I bet you dollars to doughnuts he'll be gone by the end of the week."

"I hope you're right. And I hope he takes his creepy friend with him."

His gaze sharpened. "Who are you talking about?"

"The other man in that house. Short, dark, ugly. Never speaks."

"I might just have to check him out too."

"What are you up to? What's going on?"

"Probably nothing. I'm just being overprotective. I've never lost a patient, and I don't intend to start now."

"I'm all better now, thank you. So I'm not your patient anymore."

She was aware her heart was beating rather fast, and she felt a flush rising in her cheeks.

He smiled down at her. "OK, lady. Let's get you back to Kisimba. You've had enough excitement for one night."

"Nick?"

"Yeah, honey?"

"Thank you for intervening with Peter. I was a little scared back there. This is the second time you've shown up when I needed you."

"You are most welcome. Maybe I'm your guardian angel."

"Did you mean it about staying over?"

"Absolutely. I really would like to see Mother, and anyway I need to go to chapel. I haven't been for far too long."

"Are you a religious person?"

"Lapsed Catholic. But I do love singing hymns. C'mon. Let's go."

18

S HE FELT A jolt of sheer happiness when she found him clean-shaven at the breakfast table the next day. He and Chrissie were chatting quietly.

Chrissie looked up at Penny. "Glad to see you in one piece. Sorry you had such a rotten evening. I'll pay attention to your instincts in the future. I hope you had a decent meal at least."

"I suppose so. Let's forget about it. Good morning, Nick."

"Hi there. Chrissie tells me your birthday's coming up in a couple weeks. Any celebrations planned?"

The women answered at the same time.

"No. I don't believe so."

"Of course we are. We'll have a party. You are welcome to come if you're in the area, Nick. Isn't he, Penny?"

She nodded mutely.

"Thank you. I'm sure I'll be able to make it."

Nick stood next to Penny in chapel. He sang the hymns loudly and off-key and was clearly enjoying himself. Then he accompanied Dan and Penny during rounds and clinic. He asked questions and made comments about the patients they saw.

After lunch he said, "Sorry, everyone. I gotta go. Off to Kampala this time."

He bent to give Mother a peck on the cheek, and she reached up to pat his hand.

"Penny," he said, "could I speak with you before I leave?"

Assuming she was in for a lecture of some sort, she was surprised when he walked her outside and said, "Your birthday's a week from Saturday. Right?" She nodded. "How about I pick you up on Friday afternoon and take you to see the Owen Falls? And then we'll have dinner in Jinja." Her expression must have changed because he leaned closer and touched her cheek reassuringly. "No. Not the place where Nygaard took you. The Majestic Hotel in Jinja has a much better restaurant."

Without hesitation she replied, "Thank you. I'd like that very much. Don't you think you should check with my chaperones? They'll probably want Joseph to drive me again."

"I already did. Everything's set. I'll get word to you if anything changes. Bye, honey."

She waved as he drove away.

On the eve of her birthday, Penny was excitedly preparing for the outing. Chrissie watched her with amusement. "Are you going to wear any makeup? Pretty up a bit?"

"No! Apart from the fact I didn't bring any, Nick looked after me for three days while I was out with malaria. I think he knows what I look like by now. Actually, maybe a just a little eyeshadow would be nice. No lipstick. Anyway, if you were a man, would you want to kiss someone with gunk on her lips?"

"Kiss, huh? You have a point. So, what are your instincts telling you now, Penny?"

"I'm really looking forward to it. Oh dear. Do you think he's coming?"

"Calm down. He would have called if he couldn't be here. I think you should wear your blue dress. I hear the jeep. Coming, Nick!"

She opened the front door, and Nick strolled in. As he talked to Chrissie in the hall, she noticed he'd had a haircut. *Pity.* She had rather liked those long curls. He was wearing dark slacks and a blue shirt open at the neck.

He waved at her as he said to Chrissie, "I promise on my mom's grave I'll take care of her."

"Your mother is still alive."

"Right. Thank God. OK. I swear on Dr. Schweitzer's grave."

Chrissie sighed. "That'll do. Penny, you ready? Where's your sun hat?"

"Oops. Forgot it." She ran back to her room and returned in time to hear Nick say, "By the way, if it gets too late, we might have to stay overnight in Jinja, so don't wait up."

Chrissie hesitated as she impaled Nick with a stare, but all she said was, "Remember who Penny is. And who *you* are." Her meaning was clear to Penny, but Nick smiled gently and said, "I won't forget."

Once out of the house, Nick walked to the back of the jeep and contemplated it moodily with his hands on his hips. "Ah, *fongool*," he muttered.

"What's wrong?" asked Penny.

"Look at that! Some damn fool must have run into it."

She bent down and peered at the spot he was pointing to. "There are so many dings on it. I can't tell any difference."

"Well, I can. It's my jeep!"

"Really?" She snorted. "I thought it belonged to the CDC. Don't get your knickers in a twist."

He started to laugh despite himself. "Knickers in a twist. That's a new one to me. Nick's knickers, eh?"

"So, what does '*fongool*' mean?"

"You don't wanna know."

"C'mon. Tell me. I'd like to learn some Italian. Should be fairly easy. I did four years of Latin."

"I doubt if it's in any Latin dictionary, but who knows? You can look it up. Oh, all right. It means...er...'fuck'." When she looked startled, he hastily added, "As in, 'Oh, fuck. Someone ran into my car.' Happy now?"

"Hmm. I'll have to remember that one. Might come in handy one day."

He shook his head and opened the passenger door for her. "I haven't even said hello yet. Hi there, birthday girl. Like the hat. You look like Judy Garland in *Easter Parade*. But you're supposed to wear it so it actually shades your face." He adjusted it appropriately. "There you go."

"Thank you." She suddenly felt light-headed.

They drove at an easy pace to Jinja and then to the Owen Falls nearby. The thunder of the water was audible from a mile away. The sight of the White Nile roaring as it poured into Lake Victoria and glittering in the late afternoon sunshine took her breath away. She took a lot of photographs and then asked Nick to stand in the foreground as she snapped a few quick shots.

"Not fair. I want some of you."

He hailed a passing tourist. It seemed a popular spot. Nick asked him to take a picture of them both. They stood close together with the falls behind them as the man took their photograph. Then Nick snapped a few of her as she stood in various silly poses and a few more when she wasn't looking.

"I'll give you an address where you can send them to me," he said. "I'd like to have something to remember you by."

An unexpected wave of sadness swept over her. She reminded herself sharply there was nothing between them to be lost—no matter how much she might long for more.

"Until I meet you again," he finished his sentence. "Would you like to go to the restaurant now and check out the menu?"

"Certainly," she managed to say.

Jinja was the flourishing city she remembered from her bus trip to Kisimba. When they drove by the bustling market, she wondered aloud why Chrissie didn't shop there instead of the small one on the outskirts.

"Simple. It's much more expensive here, and they don't like to barter," Nick told her.

They made it to the Majestic Hotel in Jinja as the sun was setting, and they headed for the bar. Seated at small table by a big picture window, they were so close their knees were bumping. They sipped on the red wine Nick had ordered. He idly took her hand and started playing with her fingers. He seemed distracted and miles away.

"Nick? What are you thinking?"

He smiled and arched one dark brow at her but didn't answer.

"Gosh. I wish I could do that!"

He focused on her. "Do what?"

"Raise one eyebrow."

"Try it. Just concentrate hard."

Judging by his chuckle, she wasn't succeeding, and she started laughing too, which effectively ended the attempt.

"So, what were you thinking about?" she persisted. Then she felt a twinge of discomfort and continued hastily, "I'm sorry. That was just plain nosy."

He resumed stroking her palm with his thumb. "Actually, having determined to the best of my ability that you have a great mind, I was thinking about your body."

That body began sending urgent messages to her great mind. Penny took a deep breath and told herself to shape up. "Nick, I want to ask you something. I *need* to ask you something."

"Sure. What do you need to know?" he replied easily, but his eyes took on a guarded look.

"Well…" She hesitated and struggled with her churning thoughts.

"Come on, lady. Spit it out!"

"OK. Nick, are you still married?" *There! I said it.*

His hand stilled on hers, and he took a sip of his wine. "There is that. Isn't there? Yes, Penny. I'm still married. Legally married."

She felt as if he'd kicked her in the gut. She gently removed her hand from his and placed it trembling on her lap.

"Does it matter to you?" he asked quietly.

"Yes. Of course it does, you idiot," she whispered.

"I'm glad. I would have expected nothing less from you."

Her chin came up, and their eyes met. Nick waved away the hovering server. "Please give us a few minutes." Holding her gaze, he said, "Penny, I haven't told anyone over here about what happened to my marriage. A few people such as Sue Campbell met Vicky when we first came over from the States, and they know she went back to live with her parents fairly soon after, but that's all. Are you sure you want to know the rest? It's kind of difficult to talk about."

"If you can tell it, I can hear it," Penny said. "It's up to you. How long have you been married? You don't wear a ring."

"We met my last year in undergrad. Vicky was a student nurse. The usual cliché. She was gorgeous and a lot of fun. We were young and stupid, and within three months she was pregnant. So we got married. Don't look so shocked, Penny. You're not that naive."

Taken aback by the tinge of coolness of his tone, she said, "It's just that...I didn't know you had children."

"I don't. The baby was stillborn at thirty-two weeks."

A bleak silence blanketed them as they sat unmoving. Penny could barely take a breath. Nick's face was completely devoid of expression. Eventually Penny cleared her throat and said softly, "I am so sorry, Nick. I shouldn't have pushed. I certainly didn't mean to cause you pain. I can't imagine what you must have gone through. Now, if you don't mind, I think I'd like to go back to Kisimba. I'm not really hungry."

Nick sighed. "I'm sorry too. For my crass comment about naïveté. It was uncalled for. Now give me your damn hand back. Let's finish this thing."

"Finish what thing?" she said without moving.

"The conversation. What else?"

After hesitating briefly Penny tentatively rested both hands back on the table. Nick grabbed her left hand hard with his right and continued. He spoke rapidly in short, staccato bursts. "OK. Vicky had quit nursing school and was really looking forward to the baby coming. When he…died, she went to pieces. She was in a deep depression for months. Nothing I could say or do seemed to help, and at the same time I was trying to get through med school. It was tough. We saw a counselor for a couple sessions that Vicky wept her way through, and then she refused to go anymore. Then she started drinking and doing God only knows what else while I was at school. I came back to our apartment one Monday after a long weekend on call, and she was gone." He stopped to drain his wine and topped up both glasses. "She went to her parents' place in Florida. I was in New York and studying my ass off. Her mother called me one day to tell me Vicky was in the hospital. She had crashed her car. She was drunk at the time. I flew down there, and Vicky wouldn't see me. She sent a message through her mom. She told me that since I couldn't be there for her, she never wanted to see me again. For quite a long time, I hung in as best I could with phone calls and letters that she didn't answer. Then two years ago, she called me to tell me she'd turned her life around and wanted us to try again. I had just accepted a fellowship with the CDC, and I thought that being in a different country and living totally different lifestyles might mend whatever it was we had had together. Frankly I couldn't even remember what that was, and I was used to living a bachelor's life again. In the interest of full disclosure, I was not faithful to her during those later years."

He paused, examined her face, and gauged her reaction. She tried to look calm and supportive and took a swift gulp of wine for assistance.

"She came with me to Africa. She was clean and sober, and she stuck it out for…what? Eight or nine months. She hated it here. Hated that I was constantly traveling. She had no interest in what

I was doing. I had hoped that maybe her original desire to become a nurse might resurrect itself. Then one morning she told me she wanted a divorce and left. It should be coming through soon. That was when I gave her back my ring." He sighed ruefully and turned his head away from her. "At least we tried." He paused. "There. You have the whole story—or at least the bare bones of it. Now, do you want to eat, or would you like to go for a walk and eat later?"

Penny was silently processing what she'd just heard and didn't immediately answer. She gave herself a mental shake. "Walk I think. I need to go freshen up a bit first. I'll meet you out front."

She finished her glass of wine and set off for the powder room without looking back. *What am I doing here?* One part of her had no doubt what she was doing and wished she'd get on with it. The other part was muttering darkly about caution, broken hearts, and uncertain futures. She had never known anyone like Nick. He was so darkly handsome and compelling.

She knew she loved being with him. They had laughed together, and they both enjoyed a similar sense of humor. She had listened enthralled as he described his life and activities. He appeared equally interested in what she had to say, which she found unusual. Right this minute she could only think about his inviting eyes and beautiful hands.

They strolled through the landscaped gardens of the hotel for a while hand in hand. She gazed up at the crescent moon. She could never get used to it appearing upside down from her English perspective. The stars were amazingly bright and undimmed by the lights of the city around them. They came upon a stone bench, and Nick drew her down to sit beside him.

"Let's sit for a minute and admire the view."

She couldn't help but notice he was rubbing his left thigh. "Did you hurt your leg?" she asked. "Old sports injury or something?"

"Something like that. Nothing serious."

"How old are you anyway, Nick? Thirtysomething?"

"Old enough to know what I'm doing. OK. You've asked enough questions for one night. How old are *you*? Let me guess. Tomorrow's your twenty-fifth birthday. I must say you're aging well. Ow!" Penny had smacked him hard on the shoulder. "Started medical school a bit late, didn't you? In the English system I mean. Don't you skip college and start medicine when you're about sixteen?"

She laughed. "I finished high school when I was eighteen. Then I took a couple years to do other things and finally started med school almost four years ago. Luckily, I had the grades to get in and the scholarship money to do it. Is a list of my previous escapades a necessary part of the inquisition?"

"Not right now. Let me be specific. Are you, Penny, married, or have you ever been married?"

"No, Doctor. Nor have I ever been a member of the Communist party."

"Wiseass! I'm being serious here. Are you involved with anyone back home…romantically?"

"No. Not at the moment. I've dated of course, mostly other med students and housemen—'interns' to you—but nothing ever came of it."

"Good. Have you ever actually made love with anyone?" he asked casually. As she opened her mouth to speak, he put a finger to her lips and continued. "Before you answer 'sort of,' I mean *really* made love."

After a short pause, she said, "I'm not a virgin, if that's what you mean." She felt heat rising in her cheeks.

"No, honey. That's not what I asked." He took her hand again and looked at her steadily.

"OK. No. Not when you put it like that. Why? Does it make a difference?"

"Don't worry about it. We'll figure it out as we go. Ah, Penny, do you even realize how lovely you are?"

KISIMBA

She squirmed uncomfortably. She thought she was rather ordinary looking.

"I suspected as much." He took her face between his hands. "You have such pretty eyes. I can't tell what color they are. Sometimes blue. Sometimes gray. And a perfect English complexion with those little freckles. And your crazy hair." He ran his fingers through her curls. "And, God, that mouth."

He was so close she could feel his wine-scented breath on her cheek. She closed her eyes. She thought she was about to be kissed and leaned further in.

"Open your eyes, baby. I want to tell you something."

She was disappointed but complied. "What?" *OK. Perhaps I sounded a bit peeved.*

His lips twitched, but his tone was serious. He murmured, "I wanted you that first night we met in Kampala. The reason I was at Kisimba when you happened to come down with malaria was that I was coming to see you. Looking after you for those three days while you were so out of it was torture. Not to lay a guilt trip on you or anything."

She stifled a smile. "You never said or did anything about it."

"Hey, we hardly knew each other, and you were my patient. Still sick. What was I going to do? All I knew was I couldn't stop thinking about you, and when that Nygaard piece of shit got rough with you..."

She took a deep breath. "Nick, I've been dreaming about you too."

"Good news. Now stand."

He gently pulled her to her feet and held her close against him. She could feel his heart thudding like a beating drum in his chest.

"Why are we standing?"

"Because in my opinion there are only two ways to properly kiss a woman. Either standing up or lying down."

— 125 —

Then he kissed her. He gradually probed her mouth deeper and slid his hands over her body. He cupped her breasts and moved down to caress her bottom. Penny's legs were wobbling by the time they came up for air, and her heart was pounding.

"So what do you think?" He looked a little smug.

"Very nice. Thank you."

"Very nice? What kind of an answer is that? I thought it was outstanding!"

"I noticed. I have studied sexual physiology, you know," she said huskily and let her gaze drift down below his waist. *My God! Now that is impressive.*

"Glad to hear that. I'd hate to have to explain it," he whispered. He kissed her again and then moved his mouth close to her ear. "I think we're coming to the part where we try this lying down. Shall we go up to our room?"

Her heart was racing. "Won't the management object?"

"No one will know. Relax. We're two consenting adults. I think. Are you consenting, Penny?"

"Yes, Nick. I am."

She knew now it had been inevitable, and she had just passed the point of no return.

19

The sunlight was peeking between the curtains when Penny finally opened her eyes. She stretched and luxuriated in the comfort of a big bed without mosquito netting. An air-conditioning unit hummed quietly in the background. Dreamily she recalled the previous night and began to tingle. They had made love. Twice. Nick had been infinitely patient and gentle and had taken her to heights she could never have imagined. At around midnight they'd ordered ham sandwiches and beer from room service and devoured them like ravenous beasts before she eagerly turned to him again.

"I think you're getting the hang of this," Nick whispered.

That time he had been far less restrained as they moved together as one. Afterward she said, "Nick?"

"No, baby. I'm done. And you should be too."

She snuggled against him as he held her. "Actually I was going to ask something else. What's it like without…you know…a condom?"

He gripped her shoulder hard. "Uh-uh. Don't even think about it. We'll find out eventually but not now." He kissed the top of her head. "Go to sleep, honey."

———

"Good morning, my lady." Nick was propped up on one elbow and smiling his melting smile. "Happy birthday! *Cara mia. Come sei bella.*"

He trailed his hand slowly down her naked body until it came to rest between her thighs. "What would you like to do first?"

"Actually," she said, and she wriggled beneath his questing fingers. She reached up to twirl the soft, dark curls on his chest and tugged at them gently. "I'd like to try out that huge tub thingy in the bathroom. What's that called anyway? It looks like something out of ancient Rome!"

"I believe it's called a huge tub thingy, but I could be mistaken. Anyway, sounds like a plan. It's big enough for two. Don't you think?"

Some time later, having taken care of the tingle, they were sipping coffee by the window, enjoying the view, and trying to eat eggs one-handedly. They did not want to break the physical connection.

"Nick, do you cook?"

"Are you kidding? With a name like Sottile? I'll have you know I make the best pasta sauce in the civilized world. Apart from my mom's."

"Better than sex?"

"Hmm. Good question. Maybe we should study it."

Then the telephone rang. They both groaned, and Nick got up to answer. He was clearly not pleased at what he heard.

"That was the desk with a message for me, which is actually for you. They need you back at the hospital. A couple serious emergencies came in at the same time, and they're swamped. Shit! We'd better get going. Let's finish these eggs and get dressed."

They took off in the jeep and got on the road back to Kisimba.

"Nick, I want to ask you something."

"What a surprise!" He grinned over at her. "Let me guess the answer. Yes. It was an unforgettable, perfect night."

"It certainly was. Listen. I don't want you to get the wrong idea, but what I was going to ask was if you have to head out again today."

"What wrong idea?"

"Oh, you know. Needy, clinging women and so on."

"I see absolutely nothing wrong with that. I want you to need me and cling to me. I was thinking about tonight, but I'm not sure we'll be able to arrange it under the noses of your hawkeyed colleagues."

"Do you realize we've seen each other only a few times? It seems much longer."

"Getting tired of me already? Thought you had more stamina than that. But you're right. I feel as though I've known you for at least two weeks."

She sighed happily. Then another thought occurred. "There was something else."

"I'm getting used to it. Don't worry. It's kinda cute."

"Cute? *Cute*? How about intelligent and sexy?"

"That too. So what else is going on in that overactive mind of yours?"

"What is it you actually do? OK. I know you're a doctor with the CDC, but what else?"

"What makes you think there's anything else?"

"Well, it's the way you suddenly appear and then vanish again for days or weeks. And you don't talk much about your work here. And the way you interrogated that obnoxious Norwegian guy, and—"

"Hold up." Nick slowed the car while he pulled a wallet from his back pocket and removed an identification card, which he handed to her. "Here. That's me. Dr. Nicholas Sottile, CDC."

Penny examined the photograph. "It doesn't look like you. This guy has tidy hair, and he's wearing a shirt and tie. Is he your stand-in?"

He smiled serenely at her but didn't answer.

"Come on, Nick, I just know there's something else."

Finally he said, "OK, Penny. You probably know there are many governmental agencies in the United States. Well, we sometimes help each other out if necessary—especially abroad in places like this. Nothing more than that, and I'm *not* going to give you any details," he said firmly.

"Oh, I get it! You're in the FBI."

"And you have an excellent imagination. And now..." He smirked at her. "Now you can have an excellent fantasy life too. By the way, the FBI is a purely domestic agency. Now get your mind on emergency surgery. We're nearly there."

As Nick pulled up close to the hospital, Chrissie was heading in from the opposite direction at top speed. When Nick got out, Penny said, "So, are you staying?"

"Sure. Thought I'd help. Sounds serious."

Chrissie stood waiting impatiently for them with her hands on her plump hips. "Finally! Get in here, people. You leaving, Nick? No? OK. Both of you go wash up. Dan's nearly finished closing the last one. I've got to get some blood going into the kid."

Nick pulled a large cardboard box from the back of the jeep, and they walked quickly around to the side door and directly into the sterilization room. Penny ducked behind a screen, found a clean pair of scrubs, and began to change.

As Nick stuck his head into the main room, Dan looked up from the patient on the table and said, "Nick! Good to see you. I could use your help. The next one is a thirteen-year-old boy. Fell out of a tree, wretched kid. Ruptured spleen. Do you want to do the anesthesia or assist?"

"Anesthesia. I need a nap. You done many splenectomies?"

"Not under these conditions. It might get a bit hairy. You?"

"No. Where's the manual?"

Dan pointed at the cart bearing the ether. Penny was enjoying the easy medical jargon between the two men.

"I assume Penny's there with you?" Dan snipped the thread of the last stitch and stepped back from the table while Margaret took over. "Move this one out of here, Nurse. Vitals every five minutes. Get someone in here quickly to clean up."

Nick said, "Yeah. I found your student wandering around in the bush and thought I'd haul her back for you."

"Get out here, Penny, and get cleaned up. Nick, could you see if Chrissie needs a hand with the IV? The kid's pretty shocky. It might be hard to find a decent vein. We need to get some blood in him."

"OK. How many units do we have?"

"Only two I'm afraid. One from each of his brothers. Jamal assured me they're a decent match."

"Christ! That's pushing it a bit. Oh well. Shit happens."

On that profound note, Nick disappeared. Penny headed for the sinks while Dan stripped off his used gown and gloves. He said. "All right. You're assisting. I need a really steady pair of hands. You think you can do this?"

"Absolutely, Doctor."

She returned to the room while Dan scrubbed up again and stood out of the way as Nurse Theresa energetically cleaned off the table, the overhead lamp, and anything else she could reach. She was obviously enjoying the excitement. The floor would have to wait. The minutes passed at an alarming speed, and the tension in the room was almost palpable. Nick and Chrissie returned. They pushed a scared young boy on a gurney, and together they moved him to the table. They were careful not to disturb the needle in his arm. The blood was pouring into his vein from a bottle hung on a pole. Penny stood ready and was holding her gloved hands in the air.

"OK, Nick?" Dan called.

"Yeah. No problem. Although, his pressure's too low for my liking. I think we need to get on with it."

"Go for it. Forget scrubbing. Just put on a gown and mask. Try not to fall into the boy's abdomen. Penny, swab him down. All instruments ready, Margaret? Good. Find the section on splenectomy in the manual, and give it to Theresa to hold."

All formalities had been dispensed with. Penny swabbed the boy's abdomen with iodine and noted how distended it was. "Doctors," she said, "I think there must be quite a lot of blood in the cavity."

Dan strode over to the table. "Bloody hell. Nick? Can I start?"

"Give me another moment." He'd been murmuring to the boy in English and telling him over and over that everything was going to be OK. "All right. He's deep enough. I'll increase it if necessary. Margaret, connect the second unit of blood please."

As Dan made the first incision, Penny realized how much she really loved this. She was thrilled to be part of a team focused on saving a life. Then when he cut deeper and they were looking down into a well of blood, she knew she needed a lot more experience. Dan reacted to the situation without hesitation.

"Margaret! Find a sterile glass beaker, funnel, and a bunch of gauze. We're going to have to autotransfuse. Penny, be ready to tie off the bleeders. Nick, how's he doing?"

"OK so far."

"Coming, Doctor," Margaret said.

"Penny, retract." Dan started scooping up beakers of blood and pouring them into the gauze-packed funnel, which Nick had attached to the IV line. "Take over, Penny, while I mop up in here. I've gotta tie off these vessels."

After ten frantic minutes, they had stopped the bleeding and put a fair volume of the boy's blood back in him. Everyone heaved a sigh of relief. Dan carefully cut the damaged spleen loose and dropped it into a metal tray.

"Nick?"

"Surprisingly good. Great job, guys. And you didn't even need the instructions."

"Can you keep him under a bit longer? We need to watch for further bleeding before we close him up."

Nick nodded. "Sure thing. This calls for a beer. Don't you think?"

Everyone relaxed a bit while they were observing the condition of their patient. Dan said, "Thanks for staying, Nick. So, what've you been up to since I last saw you?"

KISIMBA

"Oh, this and that," he replied easily. His gaze met Penny's above their masks. "How are Emily and the kids doing? I have a few days off. Thought I'd stay here for a while and rest up a bit."

Penny was filled with such joy that she nearly fell to her knees.

He continued, "And I certainly don't want to miss Penny's birthday dinner tonight."

"Oh dear. I'm sorry, Penny. I forgot. Happy birthday!" Dan said.

"It's been the best one ever. By the way, while we're waiting, could I ask you something?"

"Thank God!" Nick said. "I was getting worried about her. It's been well over an hour since she asked a question. She must be all backed up."

"Excuse me, Doctor Sottile. I was talking to Doctor Greenleaf," she said frostily.

There followed a discussion on the risks of autotransfusion, clotting factors, and kidney function. Nick checked the patient and hung a bottle of dextrose saline from the IV pole.

Dan asked, "Nick, what's in the box you brought in?"

"IV kits. Thought you could probably use them."

"Thank you, my friend! Must be my lucky day. OK. Looking good here. Let's close. All right, Nick?"

"Works for me. Let's do it. What's next on the agenda?"

Just then Chrissie poked her head around the door and surveyed the scene. "All well? Splendid. Lunch is ready in the main house, so go get cleaned up. Doctor Penny, I'd like a word please."

When the women were alone, Chrissie sighed and said, "You've really got it bad, girl. Don't you?" As Penny started to protest, her friend continued, "Cut the crap. Excuse my French. I saw you both when you came in. I hope you know what you're doing. You know he's married."

"Yes and yes. He told me he and Vicky are in the process of divorce. I believe him. I trust him. It just feels right," Penny mumbled.

— 133 —

Then to her horror, tears filled her eyes. Chrissie shook her gently by the shoulders. "Shape up now. No crying in the operating room. It's not allowed. Let's walk."

As they meandered slowly around the compound, Chrissie said, "Look. I don't want details. I'm just worried about you. Why the heck are you crying? If he hurt you, I swear I'll rip his balls off!"

Penny was startled into a laugh. "Chrissie! What a thing to say. He didn't hurt me. How could you ever think that? I'm just afraid that when he leaves I might never see him again."

"That sounds familiar. You have joined a huge society of women, including me, who have said that very thing. You have to accept it or end it now. Let's eat. I'm starving. And don't forget we have your birthday party tonight!"

20

PENNY RAN TO her room and gladly removed her dirty clothes. The water from the bathroom taps was inexplicably cold, so she just indulged in a "lick and a promise," as her mum would say, and then she slipped on a clean outfit for the afternoon. She could hear Nick's deep tones coming from the dining room and hurried in. He was talking to Dan, and Chrissie chatted with Mother Mary Agnes. Both men were in fresh scrubs, and they rose when she entered the room. They remained standing until Dan pulled out her chair for her and she sat.

"Sorry," Penny said breathlessly, and she settled herself opposite Nick. "Do we have clinic after lunch?"

"Nope. It's all taken care of," Chrissie said. "And I have news! Sister Clare is coming back to us next week in plenty of time for Christmas."

That set off a wide-ranging conversation about Sister Clare, plans for chapel services during the holy days in December, and their exciting morning in surgery. Chrissie called for Zach, who came in bearing three plates of food. David followed carefully with two more. Mother looked around the table and said, "Well, isn't this lovely. Let us pray."

After the grace they all prepared to tuck in except Nick. He was looking with some dismay at his plate. "Is this it? Is this how you've been eating?"

— 135 —

Chrissie reached out and tapped him smartly on his hand. "There's not much available right now, and it's really expensive. Don't be so rude."

"Sorry. So what's on the menu for Penny's birthday dinner? Can I bring anything?"

"Certainly. If you don't mind a trip to the market this afternoon. You'll have time since we don't have clinic."

Penny interjected. "Dan, isn't Emily coming for lunch?"

"No. She and the kids have already eaten."

Nick muttered, "Good. More for us."

"Up yours," Dan replied equably and then blushed. "Sorry, Mother."

"What? What are you talking about? Speak up, young man."

Penny thought she would burst with the effort to keep from giggling. Lunch consisted of salad and a hard-boiled egg apiece. Zach brought in one of his famous bread loaves, which helped. They finished quickly. Then Chrissie laid down her napkin and said, "Penny, go lie down for a couple hours. You could pack for a week's holiday in those bags under your eyes. And you." She pointed at Nick and gave him a gimlet stare. "You're in the second guesthouse. Mother Mary Agnes will keep an eye on you."

Mother stirred when she heard her name and perked up. "Nick! You dear boy. Did you come to visit me?"

"Yes, Mother," he said, and he gently helped her to her feet. "I'll be right next door to you. Let me walk you back to your house."

He turned, sent Penny a smile, and then left with Mother Mary Agnes, who was saying, "I think I knew your father, Nick. You look a lot like him. Such a handsome man."

"Is she OK?" Penny whispered to Chrissie.

"Yes. Mostly. She's just old and tired. Her mind wanders sometimes. Bless her. She's still got an eye for the good-looking ones, though. Must have been difficult for her being a Catholic nun and all."

KISIMBA

Dan said, "Well, she's in reasonable shape physically, and she seems happy. I'm off home. We'll see you later, Penny. Hopefully nothing will come up in the meantime."

———

The house was blissfully quiet as Penny stripped off again and then slipped under the mosquito net. She had expected to fall asleep instantly, but as soon as she lay down, she started to think about Nick. She replayed every word spoken between them—not to mention every deed. Eventually she dropped off. When Chrissie banged on her door, it seemed as though she had only slept for five minutes.

"Penny! Are you there, or did you sneak out on me?"

"I'm here. What time is it?"

"Five o'clock."

Five o'clock? She shot up and called out, "Do you know if there's any hot water yet? I'd really like to shower."

"Dunno," came the response. "Anyway, a cold shower might be just what you need."

———

Penny contemplated her limited wardrobe choices. She had worn her favorite blue dress to go to dinner with Nick the previous night, and it was badly rumpled. She settled on the white one her mother had made for her and headed into the dining room.

The party was a huge success. Everyone was there at the table, even Kathy and Emily. Penny was surprised to see a small pile of prettily wrapped packages on one side. The one wrapped in newspaper looked out of place. *Newspaper?* She glanced over at Nick, who shrugged.

Dinner included a malnourished chicken and a large ham of such precise shape it had to have come out of a can. There were dishes of

— 137 —

sweet potatoes, peas, and carrots, a big bowl of fruit, and two loaves of bread with a large pot of butter and another of jam. *Maybe that's for dessert.* An unopened bottle of sherry stood next to one of red wine and another of white.

"My goodness! I should have a birthday more often."

Chrissie said, "The ham, butter, jam, and booze come courtesy of Nick. And there's a giant can of coffee in the kitchen."

"You can thank the US government for those. May I offer anyone a drink?"

Nick rose and poured. Even Kathy accepted a small glass of wine. Mother Mary Agnes struggled to her feet with her sherry in hand. She said, "Thank you, dear Lord, for this thy bounty, and for dear Nick, who was your emissary. Please bless Penny on her birthday, and may she find true happiness and love."

It was a little unclear whether that was meant to be grace or a toast. By common consent they took it for both.

"Amen! Happy birthday, Penny."

Dan cleared his throat. "Everyone, we have something to tell you, and I want to get it over with. Emily and the kids are going home to England. As you know my stint here is over in March, and Emily has decided to leave earlier to get things organized over there. I'll be driving her to Entebbe first thing Monday morning. Nick, if you can, could you cover for me until I get back? Shouldn't be too late."

Mother Mary Agnes looked unsurprised. Chrissie and Kathy took the news stoically. Nick said, "Sure, buddy. No problem."

Penny was taken aback. "I'll miss you, Emily. I hope we get to meet again in England."

Emily smiled at her.

Chrissie said pointedly, "Let's eat before this gets cold."

It was truly a feast. They all ate far too much. Then Penny opened her gifts. Mother Mary Agnes gave her a small Saint Christopher medal on a thin chain. Penny immediately put it on, rose from the table, and bent to kiss the old lady on her cheek. She unwrapped the next package. It was from Emily and Dan. She pulled out a diaphanous, aqua-colored scarf, which floated in the air currents from the open window.

"Oh, thank you. It's so silky!" She put it loosely around her neck.

Kathy handed her a book and muttered, "Thought you might like this." It was a small text on obstetric emergencies.

"I do. Oh yes. This is marvelous. Thank you, Kathy."

"Hey," Chrissie said. "Don't start reading it now! You're not done. Let's see what's inside the newspaper in that one. I'll bet that's from you, Nick."

"Just a little something I picked up in Jinja. Sorry about the paper."

Inside a small, plain cardboard box nestled a silver bracelet fashioned in filigree as light as air. Penny gazed at it and was unable to find words.

"Put it on her, Nick," ordered Chrissie. "Wow! That is exquisite."

Everyone demanded to see it, which gave her time to pull herself together. She smiled at him and murmured, "Thank you so much. I will treasure this."

They still hadn't finished. Chrissie handed her a bulky parcel that proved to contain a simple shift dress in *kitenge* material patterned with small black feathers against a white background. Penny caught her breath as she held it up, rushed over to Chrissie, and gave her a hug.

"I made it myself, so it's not perfect. I swiped one of the dresses your mum made to get the size. Hope you like it," she said in an uncharacteristically bashful tone.

"I love it! I can't wait to wear it."

At last everyone but Nick and Penny had left for his or her respective quarters.

Chrissie said, "Say good night, Nick."

"Good night, Nick," he replied obediently. Chrissie rolled her eyes, and he continued. "Actually I'd like a couple words with Penny outside, if that's OK with you."

"Uh-huh. Right. Five minutes. No longer!"

Out on the porch, Nick quickly backed Penny into a dark corner. She squealed when she nearly tripped over what turned out to be a large amphibian. "What the heck is that thing?"

"Looks like a horny toad to me. Ignore him."

"Don't you mean horned toad? OK. I get it. 'Horny' is the same as 'randy' in English, right?"

"If you say so." Nick had taken her in a firm grip and was unbuttoning her dress. "Guess that makes me a horny Yank and you a randy Brit. Nice dress. Very virginal." He began kissing her as he slipped his hand inside her bra. "Eh, *marone*, if I don't have you again soon, I'm going to get a killer migraine."

"That sounds terrible," Penny murmured. She in turn slowly unzipped his pants and gently worked her hand inside. "What does *marone* mean?"

He groaned. "It's a polite way of invoking the help of the Madonna. My mom says it all the time. For God's sake, stop right there. Unless you want to scandalize the neighbors. Oh, baby. I've got to figure something out for tomorrow."

The door opened a crack and Chrissie called, "OK, you two. Time's up. Penny, shut off the hall light when you come in please."

"Yes, Chrissie," she managed to say as Nick's hands roamed over her body. Then more firmly she said, "Good night. Thank you for the lovely bracelet."

He reluctantly pulled away, zipped his fly, gave her a last kiss, and whispered, "Button up." He turned to walk down the steps. As he walked away, his final words were, "Watch out for those horny toads!"

21

THE REST OF the weekend was over too quickly. The highlight of the chapel service was Mother's homily, which dwelled heavily on the topic of "love thy neighbor." She warbled on for several minutes and smiled fondly at Penny and Nick. Penny eventually began to feel a bit uncomfortable. The old nun was obviously more astute than she had realized. Nick leaned close, smiled broadly, and whispered, "You're blushing." This only made it worse.

Rounds were soon over once Dan and Nick had pronounced themselves satisfied with the progress of the splenectomy patient. He was in pain from the surgery but otherwise stable.

After lunch Nick asked Penny if she'd like to go for a drive to see the monkeys. Chrissie muttered, "Never heard it called that before."

Penny dashed to her room to get ready. As they set off in the jeep, Nick took her hand. "Thought we could fool around a bit."

"What? In this thing? It's uncomfortable enough to drive in. Never mind to…" Her voice trailed off.

"It does have its advantages. It's an off-road vehicle. Watch and learn." He drove into the bush. A few miles from the hospital, he pulled over into a patch of shade and looked around. "There're your monkeys." He indicated a spot in the middle distance. "And there isn't a human being in sight. Scoot down in the seat a bit." He slowly unbuttoned her dress, freed her breasts from her bra, and bent his head to her. As he moved further down with his lips, he slipped

— 141 —

his hand up her skirt and inside her panties. He chuckled. "Jesus, I haven't done this since I was a teenager."

"Lucky you."

She turned her head away from him. She was suddenly discomfited lying there half undressed out in the wide-open space of the bush.

"Honey," he said quietly, "we're totally alone. There's no one here except you, me, and the monkeys, and I'm making love to you. Look at me, Penny. Just let it happen." He stroked and teased her and then suddenly withdrew his hand. "Stay there. I'll be right back."

She wanted to scream with frustration. "What? You can't..."

He hauled a cotton bag from the back of the jeep and removed a rolled-up sleeping bag, which he laid on the ground. He opened her door and helped her out. "Lie down here. It's as soft as a feather, and there's even a pillow attached."

When he knelt before her, he gently slid her panties down and off, and then he began kissing the satiny skin of her inner thighs as his fingers explored her. When his mouth took the place of his hand, she yelped with surprise. Soon she was arching herself against him. The sensation overwhelmed her. She climaxed almost immediately and tried to push his head away when he didn't stop. "Nick, please," she whispered hoarsely. "I can't bear it. Enough."

To her relief he stopped and moved to lie with her. He had shed his pants and briefs. He was breathing hard, and his eyes were burning. He joined with her and began to move with strong, sure thrusts. "Come again, baby. Come on. Come to me."

As she did they both cried out in ecstasy. The monkeys added their own excited response from high up in the trees around them. Before they drove back to the compound, they stood and held each other tightly. Then he said, "Let me just tidy you up a bit. You look as if you've been doing what we were doing."

He ran his fingers through her curls and tucked them behind her ears. Then he wet his forefinger with spit and straightened her eyebrows. She stood obediently and reveled in the easy intimacy.

"You never wear makeup, do you?"

"No. Not often. Most of the time I'm just too lazy."

"Well, don't bother. You don't need it."

———

The next morning began peacefully enough. Dan had already left with Emily and the children when Nick and Penny got to the hospital. Surprisingly few patients were waiting outside.

"Not much to do this morning," Nick said. "We've got an amputation, clinic, and then rounds. We'll be done well before lunchtime. Hopefully we'll have time for a nap." He raised an eyebrow, and her insides clenched deep down in a now-familiar way.

"Amputation? Of what?"

"Toe. Badly mangled. Needs to come off."

They slipped into an easy routine. Margaret gave the ether, and Penny assisted. The surgery was simple. Nick quizzed her on tetanus and the risks of gangrene, and they argued amicably about suturing techniques following amputation.

They were about to close when the door banged open, and a stocky black man in a khaki police uniform burst into the room. His trousers were bloused above his boots, and he wore a beret with a black leather band at the brim. He strode over to Margaret, grabbed her arm, and yelled at her in his own language. She stared at him mutinously and didn't move.

"Sew the patient up please, Doctor," Nick said calmly to Penny.

He stripped off his gloves and walked around the table to the police officer. "May I help you? I'm Doctor Sottile. I'm in charge here. Please come with me. This is an operating room."

He spoke civilly, but there was an edge of steel in his tone. He placed his hand on the angry man's shoulder to guide him outside.

The man shrugged the hand away, and he turned to Nick. "No. I am in charge. You will do what I say." He rested his hand on the pistol holstered to his leather belt and tried to stare Nick down.

"Whatever you say. However, if you're thinking about shooting someone, I'd like to talk about it. Outside." A few tense moments followed. Nick stood with his hands hanging loosely at his side and said, "Penny? You done?"

With an effort she cleared her throat and tried to emulate his tone. "Yes, Doctor. Nurse Margaret, you can bring him round."

"OK, Inspector. Let's you and me have a chat."

Nick held the door open politely, and the man walked outside with his back ramrod stiff. Margaret trembled with fear. She was still sitting by the patient.

"Do you know that man?"

"Yes. He is my brother. I am very afraid. I have to leave and warn Theresa, my sister."

"Go then. Out the back. Send someone in to help me move the patient."

"Yes, Doctor."

The nurse was now openly crying, and she flew out of the room. Penny's mind was whirling. She had to stay and wait with the patient. She checked his pulse and blood pressure and noted his tongue and gums were both good color. She was frantic to leave and find out what was going on. Finally the assistant, Luke, appeared with a gurney, and they rolled the drowsy man onto it.

"I will take him to the ward, Doctor. Go. Please be careful."

One other assistant and Chrissie were the only ones outside taking care of the clinic patients. Chrissie was grave and businesslike. She summoned Penny.

"Over here, Doctor. Please go to Jamal's table. This young man needs a shot of penicillin."

KISIMBA

"What's happening? Where's—"

Chrissie frowned slightly at her and shook her head briefly. Penny drew the penicillin from its vial into a glass syringe and noted the steadiness of her hands with clinical detachment. She took the man behind the screen to give him the injection into the thick muscle of his butt and then rejoined Chrissie. The nurse pointed to the other doctor's table. She said tersely, "Let's move here. We're almost done."

Then we'll talk.

Fifteen minutes later the last of the patients had been seen, and there was still no sign of Nick or the police officer. Chrissie's expression was thunderous. "Walk with me."

A little way from the hospital, they stopped.

"What the heck happened in there, Penny?"

She explained briefly and felt the fear all over again.

"Dear Lord. That's why they took Jamal." Her shoulders drooped, and then she pulled herself together. "You know he's married to Margaret's sister. That's how Inspector Whatshisname knew he was here. There's been a purge of Indians and Pakistanis recently. Obote has no time for them—especially the businessmen. I never dreamed they'd go after someone like Jamal. It must be personal. Margaret's brother apparently never got over the 'shame.'" She raised her hands and mimicked quotation marks in the air. "The shame of his sister marrying one."

"But where are they? Where's Nick?" *Please, God. I'll do anything. Just let him be OK.*

"I've no idea. I'm going to find out. Stay out of this, Penny. It's not your fight."

"The hell it isn't! I'm coming with you."

Chrissie sighed. "OK. Keep quiet then."

They met Nick as he was walking quickly back to the hospital. He grabbed them both in a strong hug. "Thank God. You're OK. Margaret's with Theresa. The bastard and his two other thugs drove off with Jamal in cuffs. Nothing I could do," he said helplessly.

— 145 —

"Nick, what will happen to Jamal?" Penny asked.

"With any luck they'll just throw him out of the country." He didn't elaborate. "Look, we have to go around and tell the staff what's happened. Chrissie, go speak to Mother. She should be OK. She's been through worse than this."

So Nick knows her story too.

"Talk to the nurses and assistants. Be prepared for some of them to leave. Also one of you is going to have to take over the lab work."

Penny raised her hand. "I can do it. I know the simple stuff like blood smears and cross matching for transfusions."

"Excellent. Chrissie, what have I forgotten?"

"Nothing hits me right now. But first you and Penny should do rounds. I need you to look at the splenectomy patient in particular."

"OK. But then I have to go," Nick said. "I'm going to try to find out what they did with Jamal." After checking quickly on their patients, he said, "OK, Penny. You and Chrissie will have to deal with everything until Dan gets back." She felt a frisson of fear down her back. "I don't think those guys will be coming back here. And I know you'll be able to figure out the medical stuff between you. Yes?"

"Yes," she responded resolutely. "Go, Nick. Find Jamal. Please."

He touched her cheek and kissed her mouth softly. "I promise I'll be back. Hopefully for Christmas. Swear to me you won't do anything silly in the meantime." He looked at her. "You did really well back there today."

She just nodded and was unable to speak.

———

Dan was back at Kisimba by dinnertime. He began pacing up and down the room when he was told what had happened. His face was red with anger. He looked a bit more hopeful when he knew Nick had gone off to look for Jamal.

There was minimal conversation at dinner, and the somber meal was soon finished. Mother and Kathy took their leaves. Chrissie looked exhausted and went to her room. Penny and Dan were left alone in the dining room.

"Dan, what are we going to do?"

He sighed. "We carry on as usual and stay alert for whatever's going on. This doesn't bode well, Penny. I think we should plan on getting you out of here." She stared at him aghast, and he continued. "Maybe I should have put you on the plane with Emily." He rubbed his hand over his face.

"No! Dan, I don't want to leave. I can't..."

As though he read her thoughts, he said, "Penny, I'm not certain who's supposed to be in charge of you here. It seems to be a moving target. So, forgive me, but I feel I have to have a word with you about Nick Sottile."

She was taken flat-footed.

"Don't look at me like that. You have no idea what I'm going to say. Actually I'm having a hard time figuring it out myself." He took a deep breath. "I've known Nick for almost two years, and he's become a close friend. He's a fine man, Penny, and a damned good doctor. I bet you didn't know he's a war hero."

She shook her head and silently watched his face.

"He was awarded the Silver Star for risking his life to save others while he was a medic in Vietnam. And a Purple Heart for the bullet he took in his leg. You might have noticed it still bothers him sometimes."

"Yes," she whispered. She felt overwhelmed.

"He's never told me much about his wife, but the marriage seems to be over. And he's obviously working on something other than epidemiology here in Uganda. So he has his secrets. Given all that I want to be sure you know what you are getting into. It's clear you two have become...close. That's none of my business, but I think it

— 147 —

is my business to make sure you are safe here. I don't want to see you hurt. That's it."

She sat up straight. "Thank you, Dan. I can't tell you how much I appreciate your concern. I haven't quite figured everything out yet, but I do know I love Nick. I haven't even told him that."

"I think he knows. Everyone else does." He smiled. "All right. We'll play it by ear for now. Sleep well, Penny. Surgery same time tomorrow?"

"I'll be there, Dan. Good night."

She sat for a minute and willed herself to calm down. Then she got up and went into the kitchen for another drink of water. She heard the telephone ring in Chrissie's room and tensed. She feared the worst. *Have they found Jamal?*

When Chrissie called her, Penny ran to her room. The sister was sitting, beaming, and holding the phone. "It's Sue Campbell. She has some news she thought you might like to hear." She put her hand over the receiver and whispered, "Don't take too long. It's getting late."

"Penny? Penny? Are you there?"

"Hi, Sue. Can you hear me?"

The line was bad. It crackled and then went dead intermittently for a second or two. They managed to piece together the conversation with difficulty.

"I have news! I've started nursing again. We've been so short staffed here. Jim finally asked me to help. Isn't that terrific? I've always loved working with him, and we drive in and out together, so we're with each other so much more. Penny, are you still there?"

"I'm here. I'm really happy for you. You needed this. How is Jim?"

"He's well. Sorry. I've got to go now. Call me soon. OK? Take care, and give my love to Nick."

Penny sat with the phone receiver in her hand. *So much for secrets around here!*

— 148 —

22

SHE WAS QUIET and subdued when she walked into surgery at five thirty the next morning just as the sun was appearing over the horizon. Dan was already scrubbed and ready to go.

"Sorry I'm late," she mumbled.

"Penny, I've decided the most important thing for you to do today is familiarize yourself with Jamal's lab. Go over there and figure out what you have to do. I need you to be able to run tests today if necessary. Report back to me on the situation."

With his crisp instructions, he sounded almost like Nick.

"Yes, Doctor."

With a well-defined task to accomplish, she perked up. She had been in the lab several times but had never taken inventory. Jamal's precious microscope was encased in a plastic cover on one of the benches. She felt a pang of anguish and realized she would probably never see him again. Forcing herself to concentrate on the rest of the small space, she found a notebook filled with Jamal's meticulous handwriting. It detailed the procedures for various tests. It was almost like a recipe book.

"Blood smear for WBC count and differential." *WBC: white blood cells*, she translated mentally. *Where are the stains? Oh. There they are on the shelf.*

"Hematocrit." *There are the thin glass capillary tubes for measuring the percentage of red cell in the blood.*

"Blood smear and stain for visualization of malaria parasite. Blood group typing." This entry ended with the underlined words, "Reagents no longer available."

— 149 —

She continued reading. "Direct cross match of blood for reactivity between donor and recipient." *OK. I know that one. Better than nothing.*

"Gram stain for bacteria." She hunted for the reagents and noted the small bottles she located were almost empty. There were no new ones to be found.

That's it? This comprises the diagnostic lab? She thought of the sophisticated machines and tests available in the medical hospital laboratory in London, and she sighed.

"Get it together, Penny!" she muttered aloud. "You can do all this. You've done it a hundred times."

She wrote out a list of what the lab needed to remain functional and was ready to give it to Dan. She jumped when an assistant burst excitedly into the room. "Doctor Penny! A big box has been delivered!"

"Where did it come from?" she asked as she took a scalpel blade and cut the box open.

"From America I think."

"This is fantastic!" Then she looked inside. "Oh, no. What were these people thinking?"

Packets of oral contraceptives filled the box.

———

The sun was already high and hot when she got back to the hospital with her wish list in hand. Chrissie met her at the door. "Penny, get in here. Quickly. Dan needs you in surgery. Go!"

She ran over to the operating room. Dan told her to scrub immediately and take over from Margaret, who was anesthetizing a patient already on the table. To Penny's surprise Kathy was already standing opposite Dan and waiting to assist.

As she washed her hands repeatedly, Penny called over, "What's the story here?"

He replied tersely, "Nineteen-year-old. Gravida two. Thirty-two weeks pregnant. Placenta previa. Hurry!"

She sat at the head of the table and waited while Margaret put gloves on. Penny knew only too well what placenta previa meant. The afterbirth was lying over the uterine cervix. She assessed the patient's condition. "Pressure's low. Eighty over forty. Pulse thready, one hundred per. We need to get an IV going. Margaret? Can you start that?"

"Yes, Doctor Penny."

"Dan, I'm going to have to intubate her."

"Do it then." He was already making the incision over the woman's uterus. "Ah, Jesus. OK. Let's get the baby out. Then hysterectomy." He raised his voice. "Need another nurse in here!"

"Does Penny know what she's doing with this?" Kathy suddenly asked.

Dan didn't even look up. "Kathy, I will not have unprofessional behavior in this operating room. Penny, is the IV going?"

"Yes, Doctor. Dextrose saline."

"Good. Margaret, change your gloves. You will assist. Kathy, you may stay to observe if you wish. Penny, tube in?"

"Yes. Connected to the Ambu bag. Is there any blood we can give her?"

"No."

Dan quickly removed the baby, a girl, and handed her over to a nurse standing by with a blanket. Then they fought for the woman's life. As she continued to bleed profusely, Penny heard herself announcing, "No blood pressure or pulse, Doctor."

She continued to squeeze the Ambu bag and forced air into the patient's lungs. Dan performed cardiac massage, and Kathy cried real tears in the corner of the room.

Finally Dan sighed. "We've lost her. Thanks, everyone. We did what we could." He turned away and began to strip off his gown and mask. "Penny, could you suture her and make her look presentable?"

"Of course, Doctor."

She had never had to do this awful procedure, but then she thought of the woman's family and recognized the need to have the body prepared for burial. After she was done, she was getting ready to wash the body when Kathy said quietly, "Please, Penny, let me do that. And I'm sorry for what I said."

———

Dan had disappeared. Penny walked slowly back to the house and thought about how quickly life could be snuffed out. She had watched patients die in her own hospital and could never get used to seeing the life drain away from someone's eyes. Forever.

Chrissie met her in the hallway and squeezed her hand. "OK, Penny, we're off again. We have a house call to make."

She didn't mention the ordeal with the previous patient. They had to move on.

"A house call? There aren't any houses around here."

"You'd be surprised. The place we're going is only a couple of miles away. Take one of these baskets please. We're walking."

They set out into the bush. Penny flinched when she saw the house where the awful Norwegian had lived.

"Don't worry," Chrissie said. "They're long gone. They took off soon after your killer date with Peter."

Nick had been right. She was glad she hadn't taken that bet.

Chrissie continued. "The *shamba* is about a mile from here. The family is related to Luke, the first assistant. Apparently one of the wives is sick with a fever, and her baby is in a bad way too. I put together a bunch of stuff we might need."

"What is a *shamba*?" Penny asked.

"The word is often used to describe those thatch roof huts you see scattered around, but what it actually means is a small farm. A patch of land with several huts around it. You'll see."

KISIMBA

They soon arrived at the small outpost. A woman was wearing a plain blue skirt with her breasts bare. She sat outside one of the three huts and pounded on a pile of grain with a wooden staff. She looked up when Chrissie greeted her and silently pointed to the hut on her left. They headed toward it, and Chrissie called, "*Jambo*. Mrs. Akita? It's Sister Chrissie."

Someone inside the hut answered weakly. "*Jambo, Sista*. Come. Please."

Penny followed Chrissie into the hut, and she tried to adjust her eyes to the gloom. A woman lay on a rough blanket on the dirt floor. She was holding a listless baby, who wasn't making a sound. Penny drew in her breath sharply. This looked bad.

"Mrs. Akita, this is Doctor Penny. You look sick. And the baby too. What happened?"

In a mix of Swahili and English, it became clear the woman was unable to feed her baby. She bared her breasts. Penny immediately noted they were both engorged, and both nipples were severely cracked and crusted over. She asked, through Chrissie, if she could examine her, and the woman just nodded. Both fear and hope widened her eyes.

It was soon apparent the mother was running a fever, and her breasts were infected. The baby was dehydrated, and his little abdomen was distended. Another child, about two years old, sat against the wall and stared.

"We need to get them both back to the hospital. The other kid too," Penny said quietly.

The woman had obviously understood her words and began to weep and wail. "No, no! No hospital!"

Penny looked helplessly at Chrissie. "What should we do?"

"What would you do if they were in the hospital?"

"Feed and hydrate the children. Is the other one still being breastfed too?"

"Probably."

— 153 —

"Get the mother's infection under control. That's why she can't feed the kids. Where the heck is the father?"

"Who knows? Might have gone to market. The other wife obviously isn't interested in helping."

"OK. What did you bring with us?"

"Penicillin, antiseptic, gauze, formula, and clean water."

"How on earth did you know, Chrissie?"

"Long-distance diagnosis courtesy of Luke. Come on. Let's get started. Do you know how to make up the formula?" When Penny shook her head, Chrissie said brusquely, "First rule. Read the instructions. Get going while I get mum sorted out."

An hour later they had done all they could. The mother was tearful and grateful and clasped their hands. She tried to get up off the floor, and she said, "Please stay, *Sista*s. I have *matoke*. You would honor me to share it with us."

Chrissie gently eased her back on the blanket. "Thank you, Mrs. Akita. We will be very happy to eat with you once you are well. Now rest. We will be back when the sun is going down."

"We're going to have to keep an eye on her and the baby for the next few days," Penny observed as they began the trek back. "How do we play this?"

"We can come back together later today. Then you and I will take it in turns overnight. Do you want to go first or second?"

Penny told her she was happy either way.

"OK," Chrissie said. "You can go first at about ten or eleven. Then I'll do it at—let's see—three o'clock in the morning. Whoever's most awake at breakfast can nip over before surgery. We'll clear it with Dan."

Penny was a little leery about prowling around in the bush in the dark and said so.

"No problem. Joseph will go with us. He'll be our bodyguard."

"Good to know. What?"

Chrissie was giggling. "Sorry. It's just that you're beginning to sound like Nick. He says that all the time."

"Anyway, I have a couple of questions. First, what is *matoke*?"

"It's a food staple around these parts. It's made from plantains. She was offering it to us as a token of hospitality and respect."

Penny said, "But she has next to nothing herself. If it's such a common food, why don't we eat it?"

"Primarily because none of us is keen on it. It's disgusting. If these food shortages continue much longer, though, we might have to learn to like it. That and fried grasshoppers. What was the other question?"

"Is polygamy very common?" She didn't want to think about eating grasshoppers.

"Yes. It's a sign the man is rich enough to have two or more wives. Our Christian staff members don't practice it—at least not overtly. We try to discourage it but not very hard. It serves a useful purpose."

Penny was surprised. "Useful how?"

"When a man dies, his wife or wives can't survive alone. Usually a brother or nephew will take them in, even if the wife is old. By the way…" She paused and said seriously, "Theresa is pregnant."

"Oh, Lord. What on earth will she do?"

"She'll stay with Margaret here at Kisimba. We'll do the best we can. What a mess. OK. We're home. Let's track Dan down and let him know what's going on."

Penny hadn't realized how the morning had flown by. Dan was eating lunch in the dining room of the main house when they arrived. The women washed up quickly and joined him at the table as Zach was bringing in more plates of bread, some cheese, and tomatoes.

"That reminds me. I need to go to the market before Sister Clare gets back. Penny, do you want to come along tomorrow afternoon if things are quiet?"

"Certainly. Talking of shopping lists, I have one."

Penny passed the lab supply request over to Dan, who scrutinized it carefully. "I think this is doable. Some of it anyway. I'll call Jim Campbell and ask him for help. Sister Clare could bring supplies back with her."

"Thank you. What a great idea," Penny said. She was relieved.

"That's why they pay me the big bucks." His smile was wry.

Chrissie laughed. "Now *you* sound like Nick."

"Well, he does tend to rub off on one. So to speak." He glanced at Penny.

Penny fought a blush and thought curiously that Dan seemed unusually lighthearted, but she wisely held her tongue.

He continued. "How did it go with Mrs. Akita?"

Chrissie's mouth was full. She nodded to Penny, who told him about the morning's events and their plan to visit throughout the day and the coming night.

He gazed up at the ceiling and considered the options. "OK, but send Margaret in the morning. I'll need both you and Chrissie here. You finished eating, Penny? We still have rounds to do. We got a bit behind today."

23

IT WAS AFTER four o'clock when she and Chrissie started out again for the *shamba*. Chrissie changed Mrs. Akita's dressing and noted the inflammation seemed a little less severe. She decided to give her another shot of penicillin. Meanwhile, Penny fed formula to both children and added some *matoke* mush Zach had quickly cooked for the two-year-old. There was still no sign of the husband.

When they got back to the hospital, the muscles in her back and legs were screaming. She flopped down on the sofa in the sitting room and longed for a beer. Sherry would do. She looked hopefully at Chrissie. "Is Mother coming over for dinner?"

"Yes. Thank heavens. I need a little tonic!"

They were on the same page. Zach came in and handed Penny three airmail letters. *Three? Oh, no. When did I last write to Mum?*

"Do you mind if I read these, Chrissie? Just to make sure all is well. By the way, how does the mail get delivered here?"

"They send it from Kampala to Jinja. They hang on to it for a few weeks and eventually send it by bus and drop it off where we picked you up. Unless it looks like something valuable. Then it…vanishes. Anyway, go ahead and read. I think I'll take a quick shower. You might want to do the same. You look a bit grubby."

Her mother's letters were short due to the small size of the thin airmail page. The trivia of everyday life filled them. She was relieved to find nothing terrible had happened. All the letters ended in the same way: "Take care, be happy, and be strong. Much love,

Mummy and Father." She was surprised when a tide of homesickness swamped her. What would her parents think about her adventures so far? She decided they would hear the expurgated version, but she secretly hoped they would get to meet Nick one day.

Nick. She had managed to keep him from her thoughts throughout the long day, but he suddenly reappeared in her mind. She imagined him smiling at her with one eyebrow raised in amusement. With an immense effort of will, she stirred herself and got up to wash the red dirt off her body and hair.

Dinner passed uneventfully. David carefully carried the precious sherry bottle for Mother. They ran over the plans for Sister Clare's return the next day and then drifted off to bed. Penny changed into clean scrubs rather than a nightie. She knew she'd be up again in a few hours. At eleven o'clock, a tap on the door woke her.

"Doctor Penny. It is Joseph here. It is time for us to go. I will wait outside."

Joseph was clad in a long, loose white shirt over black trousers. He carried a big sword tucked into a scabbard slung around his hips. She had seen it before when he had casually sliced the head off a green mamba snake outside the hospital one day. The blade was about two feet long and ended in a wooden grip.

"What kind of sword is that, Joseph?" she asked as they set off into the bush.

He pulled it from its scabbard in a single smooth move. "It is called Seme. It is Masai." The double-edged wide steel blade glinted wickedly in the moonlight. "You will be safe while I carry Seme. Take this torch, Doctor. Shine the light on the ground where you walk. Do not fall."

As they made their careful way to the *shamba*, Joseph walked beside her. He constantly scanned their surroundings. He waited outside Mrs. Akita's hut while she tended to the mother and fed the baby, who was already looking a lot better and squalled heartily when she cleaned his dirty behind. The walk back was uneventful, and she fell back into bed. She was relieved she had another four hours of sleep ahead.

———

After lunch the next day, Dan informed Chrissie and Penny that if they were going to market, they had better do it soon, and they shouldn't linger there. "Sister Clare will be here by teatime I imagine, and I know she will want see to you all here."

The women dutifully drove away. After a while Chrissie said, "Penny? You haven't heard a word I've been saying, have you? Is anything wrong? Apart from missing Nick."

"Sorry. I was daydreaming." She took the opportunity to change the subject. "I'd like to look for some Christmas gifts if we have time."

"Don't bother with that. We don't exchange presents at Christmas."

"Oh." She was taken aback. "Why not?"

"Our gift is to the staff and patients at the hospital. We will cook and serve Christmas lunch to all who come."

"Well, in that case my gift will be to contribute. No." She held up her hand. "I'm serious. I've got a fair bit of money left. Please let me do it."

Chrissie reluctantly agreed as they pulled up at the market outside Jinja. It was busier than usual, and there were several stalls selling various crafts that caught her eye. They weren't here to barter today. Chrissie surveyed the noisy scene and headed for a large stall selling cans of food items and bags of dried edibles. She read the labels on the cans. "These are Russian. Let's find something from Europe or the United States."

She amassed a heap of canned pears, peaches, tuna, and sweet corn. Penny drifted over to another table and called, "Chrissie? How about rice and flour?"

"Yes. We always need those."

Penny soon filled her basket with large, heavy bags. Then she spotted a container of English custard powder in the very same yellow box her mother always bought, and Penny snuck it in with the rest of her selections. She could make that for the party—assuming they had milk. Next into her basket went orange marmalade from Spain, and she topped it all off with three tins of Christmas pudding with hard sauce. That was a classic British favorite. *How do these items end up in the wilds of Africa?* She could barely carry her finds to the stall owner to pay for them.

Chrissie looked over her choices and smiled. "Let's get this stuff back to the car before we go on. I can't carry any more."

Penny handed over the required amount of cash for her purchases and gulped at the price. She decided it was worth every shilling, though. They unloaded their baskets into the car and set off for round two.

"You go look around while I pick up fruit and try to find meat of some kind. Don't pay too much for anything. Always offer half what anyone asks and go from there. Get over the English reserve thing."

Penny headed for the stalls selling jewelry, scarves, and other local crafts. She hadn't missed shopping in the slightest until now, but today the array of items for sale fascinated her. *Everything's relative I suppose.*

A short man with Indian features arranged a small inventory of jewelry featuring black, smoky-gray, and pastel-colored stones on a cloth-covered table. She instantly thought of Jamal and felt anxiety for this vendor. She hovered over the display and picked up a ring. It had a simple design. A silvery material with a matte finish fashioned the metal band. An unpretentious setting enclosed a round black stone, which was carved with what appeared to be a jagged lightning bolt. She slipped it onto her finger. It was far too big, but she studied it. It was plain. It was real. She felt a power in it. She held it out to the Indian seller and asked for the price. He replied in impeccable English. "Madam, you have superb taste. That is an ancient African design. I carved it myself. However, it is made for a man. Would you like to see some of my creations for women?"

"Maybe in a bit. I don't have much money. How much for this ring?"

She felt uncomfortable as she engaged in the bargaining. Her mother would have told her to just pay what he asked. She would have reminded her how much more fortunate she was than he.

He said, "If you will excuse me, is this to be a gift for a gentleman friend? Yes? In that case half price. Who am I to hinder the path of true love?"

As he put the ring into a small bag, she looked over the rest of the table. Before long she had picked out a pendant in an ivory-colored stone carved with a primitive outline of a mother and child; a bangle intricately carved from some animal horn material, which gave her a twinge of guilt; a small leather-bound journal; and two pairs of silken slippers. One pair was small and one large. Their soft colors glowed in the sunlight. Her new Indian friend gave her a big discount without her even asking. As they made their way back to Kisimba, Chrissie asked suspiciously, "What were you up to back there?"

"Nothing. Just wandering around," she answered airily.

They got back to the compound and unloaded their purchases just in time. Sister Clare arrived at the main house with Joseph at the wheel. Once she had been handed a pair of aluminum crutches, she made a big to-do about getting out of the car under her own steam. Everyone crowded around to welcome her. She made the mistake of lifting one of the crutches in greeting and would have fallen if Joseph hadn't smoothly and inconspicuously steadied her.

"Hello, everybody. I'm very pleased to be home. Christine, come help me."

Thus the baton passed back from Chrissie to Sister Clare. Chrissie guided the boss to a firm chair in the center of the living room and called Zach to bring tea. Sister Clare addressed each in turn.

"Christine, we will meet together after tea to discuss recent unfortunate and tragic events and to go over the accounts. Where is Dr. Daniel?"

"Here, Sister." He had slipped into the room unnoticed. "Welcome back. I hope you are doing well."

"I am. Thank you, Doctor. You and I will speak after my meeting with Christine. I will need an update on all clinical matters. Mary Agnes." Her expression softened. "I'll call on you before dinner, and we can have a chat." She paused as she scanned the room. "As usual Sister Katherine is absent. Christine, please inform her I expect to see her at dinner and at prayers afterward. Then she and I will discuss the state of affairs in obstetrics." She took a slow sip of tea. "Then you and I will talk, Penelope."

Penny felt twelve years old again, summoned to the headmistress's office for cutting class and being caught smoking cigarettes at the far end of the hockey field. Judging from the expressions on other faces, she was not alone. Sister Clare set her cup back in its saucer, heaved herself to her feet, and took hold of her crutches. Her injured leg sported a smooth white cast, which she seemed to be ignoring totally. She suddenly bared her teeth in an unexpected smile as people rose from their seats. "What's the matter with you all? Cat got your tongues? You should be delighted I have returned so quickly. Look at the trouble you managed to get into while I was away. Christine, come with me please." Chrissie rolled her eyes behind the sister's back. "And don't you roll your eyes at me, young lady."

After the two had left the room, the rest of them sat in silence. Then Mother said, "I think I'll go back to my house and rest awhile. Maybe Zach could walk me back. Oh, I do miss Jamal so!"

Penny got up too and murmured, "Well, since I'm last on the schedule, I think I'll take a shower, if you will excuse me."

Dan followed her out of the room and caught up with her outside the kitchen. "Don't look so worried, Penny. She's been very sick and feeling helpless. She's got to get back into the swing of things. By the way, is there any wine left from your birthday party?"

She bit back a laugh. "I think so. It's probably in the fridge. I'll join you."

———

Over dinner they discussed preparations for the festival of lessons and carols on Christmas Eve, which was still a couple weeks away. They decided to cut the number of each from nine to five, but they couldn't agree on which to keep in the program. Sister Clare finally announced she would choose. Then she pinned everyone with a stare and said in a voice that brooked no argument that she would assign the readings to each of them at the table. Chrissie and Dan cheerfully accepted her decree. Kathy seemed about to argue but obviously thought better of it. Mother smiled happily and sipped her sherry. Penny hadn't spoken much at all. She was too busy trying to deal with the niggling worry she felt about her upcoming audience with the sister. It felt like going into an oral examination without having studied any of the material.

Prayers were over quickly and consisted mostly of Mother delivering a long paean to God for the safe return of Sister Clare. A tearful plea for Jamal's safety or if necessary his speedy acceptance into heaven followed. Penny felt her own tears welling up and hoped that, if there was an afterlife, Jamal would find his place in it.

As Kathy trailed after Sister Clare to her room, Dan woke Penny out of her reverie. "Let's talk about tomorrow," he said. "If it's anything like today, we'll be running ragged. Fortunately we have only two surgical cases, but they'll both be tricky."

"Who's on the list?" she asked.

"You haven't seen either of them. They came in earlier today while you were at the market. One is a middle-aged man with a chronic bone infection that has flared acutely. We're going to have to go in and expose the bone itself. The other is a boy with a tonsil abscess. I loaded him up with penicillin to try to get the swelling down overnight. The anesthesia will be difficult with that one." He sighed. "I'm hoping we might be able to get by with a needle aspiration of the abscess."

They discussed the pending cases for a while. Then Penny said, "I've been meaning to ask you something. I thought we'd be dealing with a lot of snakebites, but I haven't seen a single one."

"They certainly occur, but they rarely make it to the hospital. Remember, most of our patients come from a fair distance away. With a serious bite, the patient usually dies quite quickly or ends up in the hands of a local native healer who can't do anything about it anyway. Of course neither can we. We don't have any antivenins."

"Native healer? As in witch doctor?"

"Yes, but we prefer not to call it that. Native healers have their place. They handle insignificant problems and patients who would have recovered anyway. But sometimes the really sick people get worse, and when they finally get here, we have to deal with it."

Penny would have loved to continue their discussion, but at that moment she received her summons from Sister Clare. She hadn't noticed Kathy's departure and had completely forgotten about the upcoming ordeal. Dan grinned at her and whispered, "Good luck. I'll see you tomorrow at five thirty."

Sister Clare was sitting behind her desk with her hands folded on the scarred wood. Penny stood before her and braced for the worst.

"Sit, Penelope." Sister contemplated her seriously, took off her glasses, and rubbed the bridge of her nose. "What am I to do with you? On the one hand, I've received glowing reports on your enthusiasm, compassion, and skills, and you have dealt well with the recent emergencies. On the other, I am aware you have entered into a most inappropriate *friendship* with Dr. Sottile. I'm sure you must know he is married?"

"Yes, Sister. But he will be divorced soon," she added unwisely.

"Aside from the Church not recognizing divorce, it also frowns heavily on…intimacy…between people whom God has not joined. What do have to say for yourself?"

"I love him," Penny said quietly.

"Yes. I can see that." She sighed. "You are not a nun or one of my lay sisters, and you are not even Catholic, so the usual courses of action do not apply. But you are honest. I'll give you that. Are you sorry for what you have done?"

"No, Sister. But I do regret having caused you a problem."

The nun put her glasses back on. She seemed to have come to a decision. "Very well. We will speak no more of it. I'm certainly not going to send you home." She finally smiled at Penny, who relaxed a little. "You are far too valuable to us. I wish you could stay longer. Now tell me about poor Mrs. Akita and her baby. Shall we have some tea? Or would you prefer coffee?"

"I would like a cup of coffee please."

She was honest after all.

24

Nick was as good as his word and appeared without advance notice early on Christmas Eve morning. Penny and Dan were in surgery. She gave the ether, and he performed a relatively simple excision of a skin growth. Dan thought it was probably cancerous, but since the patient refused to go to Mulago Hospital, there was no way of finding out. He cut deep, left a wide margin around the tumor on the man's arm, and hoped for the best.

"Honey, I'm home!"

"If that's you, Nick," Dan said, "your timing is impeccable. We're just about to finish. We could have used you an hour ago."

"Don't be so unwelcoming, buddy. I bring gifts."

At that Dan lifted his head. "Like what?"

"Let's see. Ether, more IV kits, and sundry other stuff. A few vials of local anesthetic. As a special treat, I got some antitetanus antiserum. It has to be refrigerated, so I hope the power stays on. Also a few cans of ham for the Christmas party. Can I come in?"

"No, but thank you as always. Penny, wake up the patient please."

She was so excited she fumbled the ether and let a few more drops fall.

"Oh, for heaven's sake. Nurse Margaret, please take over from Doctor Penny. She seems to have lost her concentration."

"Thank you, Doctor," she managed to say as she flew out of the side door and into Nick's waiting arms.

After a long, thorough kiss, Nick held her away from him. "You're even thinner, babe. Should I be worrying about you?"

"No. We've been working long hours, and food is rather scarce again." She looked him over. "You look well. I'm glad you grew back the mustache. It suits you."

"It comes and goes," he replied. "What's planned for the rest of today?"

"Please tell me if you have any news of Jamal." She braced herself for the worst.

"I'm sorry, honey. I couldn't find any record of his arrest or anything else for that matter. Not in Jinja or Kampala. There's nothing more we can do I'm afraid." He sighed heavily.

They stood together silently and remembered the gentle, unassuming young man. "Do the others know yet?" Penny asked. "Theresa is taking this really hard. Margaret says she's not eating or sleeping, and she's certainly not working, poor kid. She just stands by the gate for hours and watches the road."

"I've informed Chrissie, Clare, and Mary Agnes. Chrissie is trying to figure out how to tell Theresa and Margaret. I'll talk to Dan later. In the meantime we have other things to think about. What time do the celebrations begin today?"

"There's nothing happening until this evening. After dinner we're having a candlelight service with carols, and then the staff and their families are going to hold a Christmas celebration dance. I have no idea what it'll be like. The only dance I've seen here was for the twin ceremony, and that was a bit naughty."

He pondered her answer. "OK. How about this? I want to give you my Christmas present first. It starts as soon as you've changed. Then we make tracks for the Majestic Hotel. We'll have a bite to eat and anything else that comes to mind. We get back here in time for the service. What do you think?"

"Wait a sec. Present?"

"Yeah. It might not be necessary, but it occurred to me. Do you know how to drive?"

"Sort of."

"That's what I was afraid of. I'm going to make sure you can drive my jeep if we ever need you to. Let's get you back to the house."

Penny changed, and then with Chrissie's blessing they climbed into the jeep. Penny was in the driver's seat.

"Let's go. Head for the road."

She looked at him helplessly. He sighed. "OK. This is a stick shift." He looked at her and raised a brow when she shrugged. "What? How do you get around in London?"

"I take the bus. I can't afford a car. I never really learned to drive. Although, I watched my dad while he was driving."

"God Almighty! I'm glad I thought of this."

The next hour was not pleasant. A fair amount of shouting was involved. Eventually Penny got the hang of it and was happy to get out of the vehicle as fast as she could when the lesson was over.

Nick sighed. "You wouldn't pass a driver's test, but you'll do in an emergency. Jesus, I need a beer."

———

On their way to the Majestic, they talked about events at the hospital. Then a thought struck Penny. "Did I tell you Sue called? She had lots of news."

"I heard she was nursing again. Anything else?'

"Yes. She told me Russian aid workers have overrun Kampala. Do you know anything about that?"

"Yeah. They're bringing in food supplies, grain, and so on. And farming equipment."

"Why the Russians? Aren't we helping the Ugandans?"

"Obote is known to be for communism. They're trying to get their feet in the door. Not just here in Uganda either."

KISIMBA

She mulled this over. Then she said, "Ha! I've figured it out."

"Do tell."

"You're not FBI. You're like James Bond! Secret Service!"

"One, I'm nothing like that Scottish dude. Two, you should consider abandoning medicine and going for a career in writing adventure novels."

He hadn't actually denied it. She just smiled at him and held her tongue. It felt so wonderful to be with him again. After a while she started humming under her breath and then sang, "You're just too good to be true. Can't take my eyes off you."

Nick burst in with the refrain in a horrible falsetto. "I love you, baby, and if it's quite all right—"

"Ah, how sweet. Don't give up your day job—whatever it is!"

He took her hand and held the wheel with his left.

"You told me to keep both hands on the wheel, Nick."

"I did indeed. I just hope and pray you'll never need to drive. Hey, how about this one?"

He began to sing Dylan's "Lay, Lady, Lay" in a deep, husky voice. He was only slightly off-key. After the first verse, he stopped singing.

"Go on. That was super!"

"I can't remember the words after that. How do you feel about the big brass bed?"

"It sounds very enticing. But can we eat first? I'm starving."

————

She ate a chicken sandwich while she watched Nick devour a steak. "Looks as if you were hungry too. I wonder where this place gets its meat. We never have anything like this. That is a *huge* portion."

"That's part of the reason I'm eating it now. God knows what we'll get back at the house. And I want to keep my energy up. Why are you giggling? Bad girl! Also, I'm bigger than you." He reached over and touched her bracelet. "I like seeing you wear this."

"I wear it all the time. Except in surgery. And clinic. And rounds. And I take it off when I go to bed. Or leave the compound."

"Which leaves maybe...ten minutes a day?"

"You exaggerate. Anyway, I have something for you." She rooted around in her bag and pulled out a tiny parcel wrapped in newspaper. "Apparently we don't exchange gifts at the hospital, and I wanted to give you this in private anyway."

"Newspaper. I'm never going to live that down, am I?"

"Nope. Hope you like it," she added. She felt suddenly shy.

When he saw the ring, his face lit up. He brought her hand to his lips. "Thank you. What's the stone?"

"I've no idea. Chrissie thinks it might be soapstone. But it was made here. I actually got it from an Indian man who carved the stone. The zigzag pattern means 'power' or 'strength.' I don't know what the band is made of. I hope it doesn't rust in the rain. Does it fit?"

"Perfectly. Look. Now we're well and truly pinned. Have you heard of pinning?"

"Yes," she said loftily. "A quaint little American custom denoting a social arrangement called 'going steady.' Practiced in high school. Aren't we a bit old for that?"

"How about this then? We have now exchanged symbols of our loving, committed, exclusive relationship."

His eyes were suddenly blazing hot, and she became almost faint with longing. They made it to the room without further words. The bed might not have been brass, but it proved most satisfactory.

Afterward they lay sated. Nick was dozing off when she wriggled out from under his arm and sat up. She took the opportunity to look at his flat stomach, long legs, and all parts between.

"Like what you see?" He was observing her with a sly smile.

"Not bad. I'm really envious of your legs." She traced the silvery scar on his thigh but didn't mention it.

KISIMBA

"Why? You have great legs."

"But I have to shave mine. You have hardly any hair on yours. Mmm, so smooth."

"I'm touched. Literally. That tickles. No one's ever said that to me before. Aren't you going to rest, woman?"

"I'm busy here. Do you mind?" Her fingers continued their journey. "Very pretty."

"Pretty?"

"Yes, but I'm afraid it's dead. Oh, dear. Did I kill it? Let's see if I can resuscitate it." She looked up at his comical expression and then dipped her mouth to him. "Don't worry. I'm almost a doctor. Oh, look at that! It's alive. It's a miracle."

"*Vieni qui, amore mio.* You are my miracle. Let's see if little Penny is alive...oh, yeah!"

This time Nick woke Penny. "Honey, I don't want to say this, but we need to talk. Seriously."

She was instantly alert and apprehensive. "What?"

"I'll be going away after Christmas lunch tomorrow. I don't know when I'll be back."

She was determined not to cry. She had known all along this would happen someday. *Why does it have to be today?* "I'll be leaving for England in less than a month."

"I know, baby. And I'll do my damnedest to get back before you go. I'll be mostly in Kampala, so in a pinch I should be able to come if anything goes wrong."

"What might go wrong? Do you know something we don't?"

"Nothing's ever certain. Just believe me when I promise I'll do my absolute best to be here if you need me."

"I need you now," she whispered.

"That I can take care of, sweetheart. Let's not waste the time we have. It's our first Christmas together, and I mean to make sure there'll be many more. Hold on to that thought."

They moved together slowly. They wanted to savor what could possibly be their last moment of intimacy. Then he whispered urgently to her. His breath was hot on her face. "Open your eyes, my darling Penny."

Their gazes locked, and their passion peaked.

25

THEY MADE IT back before five o'clock. The main house was buzzing with activity. Chrissie skidded to a halt as she was running past them. "There you are. Nice lunch?"

"Yes. Thank you. What's going on?"

"What do you think? We're preparing for the feast tomorrow. Go look in the kitchen and see if there's anything you can do to help."

Penny felt guilty about avoiding the work, and she peeked into the small kitchen where the action was focused. Nick was close on her heels. Zach was baking. Several loaves of millet bread were already cooling on the counter next to him. Kathy was chopping vegetables with determined swipes of her kitchen knife. Sister Clare, swathed in a huge apron, was standing over a pile of fresh meat, picking over it, and removing bits of bone and tendon.

Nick offered to take over. Sister Clare said with some asperity, "Doctor, I would not presume to interfere with your work if you were performing surgery on a person. How many times have you cooked a goat?"

Goat? Was it one of theirs? Penny was glad she hadn't gotten to know any of their small herd personally. "Is David OK with this?" she asked cautiously.

Sister Clare looked at her over her glasses. "Why not? The people here are far more pragmatic than we are about animals. They're just sources of food to them. This will make a tasty stew, but it's going to

— 173 —

take hours to cook." She waved them both away impatiently. "Find something useful to do."

"I was going to make a custard," Penny ventured.

Chrissie stuck her head in the door. "Already done. Didn't know when you'd be back. OK. Let's see. No. There's nothing left for you to do this evening. Go visit Mother or something." She winked. "Dinner, such as it is, will be at six, and the festival of carols will be at seven. And then the dance. Go!"

They found Mother dozing and decided to leave her in peace. They stood close together, watched the coppery sunset over the bushland, and then sat on the low wall at the rear of the compound in the hush of the evening. They held hands.

"No fooling around tonight." Penny strived for humor.

"Just as well. You wore me out."

After a few minutes, Penny said softly, "What will happen here? Does anyone know? Please tell me. Not knowing anything makes me feel...out of control. Especially since you won't be here."

After a long silence, Nick said, "I understand that. Let's face it. I've never been known for following the rules anyway. Penny, honey, you are the most important person in my life, and if I can help you to feel...I don't know...more able to cope with what might be coming, I'm willing to break those rules. But you must promise me this stays between us. OK?"

"I don't want to get you into trouble."

He laughed harshly. "Trouble? There's enough out there for everyone. Where to begin? Have you heard of Idi Amin?"

"Yes. He's one of Obote's high-ranking soldiers."

"True. To a point. Obote made him an army commander when he assisted in deposing King Mutesa, which put Obote into power. Amin built up the army and was made commander of all the armed forces. Then Obote got worried he was getting too powerful and put the brakes on. Last October he demoted Amin back to commander of the army. So there's a lot of bad blood between them.

"The United States took an interest for many reasons. This included the fact Obote had started leaning further toward socialism and was generally labeled as pro-communist. His government took over many of the private banks and businesses last year. That sort of thing, as you might know, really burns the national security-minded power brokers in the States. Meanwhile, Amin is touting himself as more conservative and pro-Western, and everyone seems to believe him. That includes the Israelis for some reason. For an ill-educated bully, he can be quite persuasive. So now they're all waiting for the other shoe to drop." He sighed. "Does that make any sense?"

"Not really. When do international politics ever make sense? How on earth did you get involved?"

"I guess it's the price you pay for being a patriot. I seem to keep doing that."

"You mean in Vietnam? When you were a medic? Did you have to fight?"

"No. I was too busy patching people up and seeing my friends die. And that fucking war is still going on. No one is winning. Everyone is losing. All we'll have in the end are ruined bodies and minds and thousands of gravesites on both sides. It's insane! I have this horrible certainty it will happen the same way here. With or without international intervention, the ones who will really lose are the Ugandan people and those who get in the way. Like well-meaning humanitarian white folks.

"I'm sorry, Penny. That probably didn't answer your questions. But it's the best I have right now." He checked the time. "Come on," he said wearily. "Let's go have a bite to eat before we go sing carols."

———

After a light meal, they all headed over to the chapel and took their usual places at the front. They started off with a rousing version of "Hark! The Herald Angels Sing." All the favorites followed—"We

Three Kings of Orient Are" and an exquisite rendition of "O Holy Night." Chrissie sang this and accompanied herself on the guitar. The readings that Sister Clare had selected were short. Penny had forgotten all about that aspect of the service and found herself at the pulpit reading from the gospel according to Luke. "And the angel said unto them, Fear not: for, behold, I bring you good tidings of great joy, which shall be to all people. For unto you is born this day in the city of David a Savior, which is Christ the Lord."

She had always thought this was the most stirring of the lessons and wondered why Sister Clare had chosen it for her. She returned to her seat in the pew next to Nick, and he took her hand with a smile. When the service ended, Mother Mary Agnes walked to the pulpit and proclaimed, "And now the Christmas celebration dance!"

The congregation cheered, whooped, and soon dispersed. "What should we do now?" Penny asked Chrissie.

"Take seats on the porch in front of the hospital. This is the staff's gift to us. You'll enjoy it. I promise."

Penny and Nick settled side by side into the chairs provided. They sat quietly and waited. Each was immersed in thought but content with their proximity. The drums began to beat and sing. They filled the night air with joy. *And what? A prayer? A hymn of praise?* Tonight the dancers were men and women all in white. They moved sedately and gracefully around and between each other. They touched hands, moved on, and swayed rhythmically. A sense of peace came over her, and she accepted it gratefully. Too soon the dance was over, and all present drifted off quietly into the night. Alone on the porch, Nick held her gently and kissed her, and then he walked away toward the guesthouse without speaking. She went to bed and slept deeply and dreamlessly.

If David hadn't woken her the next morning, Penny would have missed rounds. Fortunately there was little to do, and they were back in ample time for the Christmas morning service. There was no sign of Nick, and Penny began to panic. She thought he might have left in the night without telling her. However, he was waiting outside the chapel for her and walked beside her back to the house. When she smiled in relief, he said, "Penny, I'll never leave you without warning."

"How did you know what I was thinking?"

"I'm a gifted mind reader. Haven't you figured that out yet? C'mon. Let's help get this banquet out."

Tables in front of the main house were already groaning under the weight of a huge pot of goat stew, mounds of rice, sweet potatoes, *matoke*, and vegetables. The ham was sliced onto large plates, and Zach brought out the loaves of millet bread. Sister Clare handed Penny an apron and told her to start serving. She stood between Dan and Kathy and diligently spooned portions of the fragrant food onto the plates of their staff, patients, and their patients' families. She lost sight of Nick in the crowd. Then she felt a soft, warm breath on her cheek. "Good-bye, my darling Penny," he said.

When she turned he was gone.

26

THEY ALL PITCHED in to clean up, and then Sister Clare declared nap time. She sounded like a kindergarten teacher. Penny sank onto her bed and gave way to tears. She sobbed herself dry and then lay and stared at the ceiling for what seemed like hours. When David's head appeared beyond her window, she looked at her watch and was surprised to find only half an hour had passed.

"Doctor Penny, *Sista* Clare wish to see you," he whispered theatrically.

Shit! She didn't need this. She wanted to be left alone to wallow in her misery. "OK, David. Please tell her I'll be there in a few minutes."

She dragged herself to the bathroom and washed her face. Then she paused and returned to her room. She picked up the pair of slippers she had bought for Sister Clare at the market. She knocked on the partly open door of Sister Clare's room.

"What can I do for you, Sister?"

"I thought you could do with a cup of coffee."

"Thank you. That would help."

She sat and accepted the cup. Hoping to distract the sister from whatever she had in mind to say, she produced her package and handed it to her.

Sister Clare looked at her sternly. "You were told we do not exchange Christmas gifts, Penelope."

KISIMBA

"Yes. This is a thank-you gift for everything you have done for me."

"Hmm. Let's see what it is. Slippers?"

"I had no idea what one could give a nun. If I overstepped I apologize."

"Silly girl. They look so comfortable. Thank you. I look forward to wearing them when this wretched cast comes off." After a beat she continued, "You will be all right. You must know that. You are stronger than you think. And I have a gift for you. Not a Christmas gift but a belated birthday present. I understand you had quite a party."

She handed over a package from the table next to her with what looked suspiciously like a twinkle in her eyes. Penny opened it carefully and gasped. "Is this..."

"Yes. It is an old and very precious volume of the gospels. I believe we spoke of it. It is the one I carried with me when Mary Agnes and I escaped from the Congo. It is yours now. Look after it for me please. Now we should rest. I will see you at dinner, Penelope."

"Thank you, Sister. I'm honored to accept this."

As she left Sister Clare was surreptitiously dabbing at her eyes with her hankie. As she leaned against the wall outside Sister's room, Chrissie opened her door and whispered, "Come in here for a minute."

Penny sighed. *What is going on?* "OK. Give me a sec."

She popped back to her room, found the bangle she had bought, and returned to Chrissie's room. Chrissie handed Penny a small parcel. "Here. This is for you."

"I thought we didn't—"

"Yes, yes. I know. This is an early going-away present. Open it."

Penny exclaimed over the cotton wrap. It was made from material patterned with white feathers on a deep black background. It was like a negative image of the dress Chrissie had made for her birthday.

"How marvelous! Did you make this too?"

"Yeah. It was easy. Just had to hem the edges. Do you like it?"

— 179 —

"I love it. And I have something for you. This is to say thank you for being such a caring friend, Chrissie. I do hope we can keep in touch when I've gone home."

Chrissie admired the bangle and put it on. Then she began to sniffle and said, "Look, if you want to mope about Nick, you can always do it in here."

Penny decided that while she was up, she might as well visit Kathy. She tapped on the door, and she nearly lost her nerve when she heard Kathy say in her surliest voice, "Come in."

At least Kathy is unlikely to burst into tears. Penny took a breath. "Kathy, I'm sorry we've never really had a chance to get to know one another. I want to give you this, since I'll be leaving soon."

Kathy opened the small box and gazed without expression at the carving of the mother and child on the pendant. Then to Penny's dismay she began to weep. *Good grief! Another one?* She patted the older woman awkwardly on the back and had no idea what to say.

"Thank you, Penny. No one has ever given me anything like this."

All she could come up with was, "You deserve it. I know how you feel about your patients."

Then she beat a hasty retreat to her room. Now exhausted she lay down on her bed. She had completely lost the gift-giving urge. "To hell with it," she said aloud to the empty walls. "I'll finish it later."

27

S HE WAS SO occupied with her usual duties and the rudimentary lab work she had inherited, that despite her general melancholy, she found herself going for hours at a time without thinking about Nick. Then memories would come rushing back out of the blue to drain her spirit. However, the frantic pace of work had eased considerably. Every day there were noticeably fewer patients to see in clinic and hardly any admissions. The wards were less than half full. On the other hand, it soon became apparent the nursing staff was also significantly diminishing in number. Chrissie said they were slipping away during the night and never reappearing.

"Are they going home?"

"I hope so. There's no sign of them being...taken."

The drums were speaking in the night with increasing insistency, which didn't help to calm anyone's nerves. When she asked Zach what they were saying, he just shrugged uneasily and didn't answer. The New Year had come and gone with little ceremony. There was no word from Nick. On New Year's Eve, Chrissie and Penny had visited Mother, and they had indulged in a glass of sherry apiece. Penny had brought along the tiny pair of slippers she had found in Jinja and presented them to Mother with the excuse it was a gift to bring in the New Year. She had not been informed of any proscription against that sort of gift and felt quite proud of herself. Mother declared that she loved them and put them on right away. She turned her feet and admired the shifting colors of the material. They looked a little incongruous poking out from beneath her habit.

The following days passed at an excruciatingly slow pace. The number of patients slowed to almost a trickle, and Penny was finding it a challenge to occupy herself. The only unwanted excitement occurred when the power failed in the operating room, and they had to finish by the light of a large torch held by a nurse. She borrowed some textbooks from Dan and Chrissie and tried to devote herself to study. She did have final exams coming up in just a matter of weeks. Try as she might, though, she found it hard to concentrate and often ended up drifting around the garden picking vegetables with David and collecting eggs.

With less than a week to go before her trip home, their lives changed forever.

Penny, Dan, and Margaret were in surgery and finishing the only case of the morning. They all raised their heads when they heard shouting outside the operating room. Then three men stormed in and dragged Theresa, Margaret's visibly pregnant sister. One of her eyes was swollen shut, and blood was oozing from the corner of her mouth. They threw her to the floor, and her police officer brother grabbed Margaret from her seat at the head of the operating table where she was giving the anesthetic and pushed her to the ground. He was shouting so loudly spittle was flying from his lips. On reflex Penny moved toward the women. Dan grabbed her gloved hand with his. His voice shook just a little. "Doctor, we have a small problem with a supratentorial dysfunction here. We must calm the patient."

Penny stilled and recognized the phrase. It was unofficial medical code for, "Watch out! This one's bat-shit crazy."

The inspector yelled, "Silence! Both of you!"

He gestured to his two men to stand behind them. The one behind Dan cuffed him casually on the side of the head. Dan staggered but didn't fall. He looked warningly over at Penny, who had her own thug to deal with. Her mind frantically raced. She stood stock-still and hardly breathed as the scene played out. The patient on the table was still sleeping soundly.

Margaret and her sister lay weeping on the floor. Theresa pulled the loose folds of her dress around her. Their brother continued his rant in English. Presumably this was for the benefit of Dan and Penny.

"You," he spat at Theresa, "are the whore of a goat, and now you carry his filthy seed. And you!" He pointed to Margaret. "You are no better. You both deserve to die."

He slowly drew the pistol from his belt and aimed it at Margaret. In an instant Theresa pulled a gun from her dress and screamed unintelligibly. Anguish contorted her face. Her shot found its mark. A red bloom spread over her brother's chest, and he looked down at it in disbelief before he fell heavily. Time slowed. The other two cops rushed to his side in a panic. They pulled their own weapons and tried to decide whom to shoot first.

A tall, dark figure appeared silently behind them. Joseph had Seme in his powerful hand. He swept the flat blade against the back of the neck of one of them. He followed up with a fluid move that left the second on the ground. His neck was open to the bone. Then he ran his sword cleanly through the chest of the man he'd knocked out. He bent to confirm the inspector was dead. He didn't even raise his voice as they all stood silently and in shock. "Murderers. You kill my people. You kill my faith."

He spat deliberately on the face of the inspector and left the room.

No one moved for what seemed like an eternity. They just stared at the bloody corpses on the floor. Then Dan sighed. "All right, Theresa. Give me the gun. Was it Jamal's?"

She nodded and handed it over. He continued. "Margaret, take your sister back to your quarters. Penny, deal with the patient while I try to figure out what to do with these bodies."

She checked the patient's vitals, and then she found her voice at last. "We have to get rid of them. More will come when they realize they are missing. Where can we hide them? In the septic pit?"

"No. That's probably the first place they'll look. Let me think."

They didn't have to think for long. A nurse came in pushing a gurney. She studiously avoided looking at the carnage on the floor. She and Penny got the drowsy man loaded up, and the nurse wheeled him out. Then Joseph reappeared in clean clothes and said quietly, "Doctors, Luke and I will put them in their jeep and drive them out into the bush for many miles. We will...dispose of the bodies and leave the jeep some more miles away. We will return by tomorrow morning. It will be a long way to walk. Somebody must clean the floor in here."

Joseph was so calm and certain with his plan. He had taken command of the situation effortlessly. She wondered about his background. *Had he perhaps been a warrior or a tribal chieftain?*

Chrissie got back from her trip to the market where she had gone to find what food she could. She watched in white-faced horror as the remains of the police officers were carried out the side door where Joseph had pulled the jeep close to the building. No one else was in sight. Dan quickly explained what had happened and then left them to clean up. "I have to talk to Sister Clare and Mother," he said. "I'll be back to help."

The women got down on their knees and scoured the concrete floor from end to end and then back again. At least, they reasoned, one would expect to find traces of blood in an operating room.

———

While they were sitting at a dinner no one felt like eating that evening, the phone rang in the hallway. Sister Clare had moved it to a small table between her room and Chrissie's so there would always be someone around to answer it. Zach picked up and quickly came to the doorway. "*Sista* Clare, it is for you."

The sister talked for a while and then summoned Penny. "Mrs. Campbell has some unfortunate news for you. No," she hurriedly added. "Nothing about Nick or your family. Here. Talk to her yourself."

"Penny? Listen to me. The charter company you flew here with has been closed down. The owners and most of the employees have been thrown in jail. They're Indian," she added sadly.

Penny's heart dropped as she remembered the attractive hostess on her plane.

"Jim and I think you should get back here as soon as possible. I'll buy you a seat on British Airways or whatever's available. You can pay us back later. When you get to Kampala, take a cab to the house, and we'll take it from there. Can you hear me? Did you get that?"

"Yes, Sue. Thank you. I hope I'll see you soon."

She walked slowly back to join the others.

"What?" asked Chrissie urgently. "What's happening now?"

She told them what Sue had said and that she would be leaving the next morning. No one spoke for a while. Then Dan said, "I'm not sure this is the best idea, Penny. You might be safer staying with us. But...we do have to get you home."

"I suppose I should go and pack. Anyone have any ideas about how I can get to Kampala tomorrow?"

She thought her heart might be breaking, but she had to deal with it.

Sister Clare said, "If you are determined to do this, I suggest Joseph should drive you to Jinja, and you can catch a bus from there. It would be better if he took you all the way, but we might need the car, given everything that's happened. Are you certain you won't stay with us?"

"No. I'm not certain. But I do have to get back to England." Fighting to control herself, she left the room with Chrissie on her heels.

"Let me help you. Take the bare minimum. Wear that money pouch Sue gave you. I'll keep your other stuff safe and get it to you somehow. Oh, dear God. I wish this wasn't happening. I'm so worried about you."

"And I'm worried about you too. All of you. Chrissie—"

"Save it. For when we can get together again. It's been great having you here, Penny. We had a lot of fun, didn't we? And some not-so-fun times too. But we got through them, and we'll get through this."

She had almost finished packing when Dan tapped on her door. "Listen, Penny, I really don't like this plan. I think I'll come with you to Kampala to make sure you're safe."

She hugged him impulsively. "Thank you, Dan. But you are needed here. I'll have Joseph to look after me, and once I'm on the bus, I'm sure I'll be safe."

He touched her hand and left reluctantly.

28

For the first time in weeks, Penny couldn't sleep. Every time she closed her eyes, she saw blood and mayhem. The knowledge she had to leave the next morning plagued her. Finally she got up and turned on the light. *Maybe a few gulps of fresh air will help.* On impulse she rummaged around in her suitcase and found an unopened pack of cigarettes—one of the two Liz had given her at Heathrow Airport. She had tossed the other one away weeks before. For the first time since she had come to Africa, she found herself wishing she was back in London studying and having fun with her friends. Then she thought of Nick and realized above all she wanted to be near him.

She snagged a box of matches from the kitchen and crept out of the house. She hoped Buddy the mutt wouldn't wake up and alert everyone. She walked a little way from the porch and lit up. The first puff almost knocked her sideways. Then the soothing nicotine began to take effect. She jumped when the door behind her opened. Chrissie walked out, and Kathy followed closely.

"You naughty girl," Chrissie said. "I might have to report you. Let me have one of those."

Kathy sighed. "What the heck. I'll have one too please."

The three of them stood without talking. They puffed away with only an occasional cough. Then the light in the hallway came on, and the front door swung open again. Sister Clare stood in the doorway and glowered at them with her hands on her hips. "Penelope, I assume you are the instigator of this offense."

"Yes, Sister."

No one dared to move. Then Sister Clare sighed and said rather nostalgically, "I used to enjoy smoking. Many, many years ago. When you're finished, please dispose of the evidence properly. Good night."

"Good night, Sister," they chorused.

When the nun had returned inside and firmly closed the door, Chrissie began laughing a little wildly. Soon they were all giggling helplessly like schoolgirls, and they suddenly felt much better.

———

Despite her broken night, Penny awoke at five on the dot. She was alert and apprehensive. She heard voices from down the hall. *So I'm not the only one.*

Her mouth tasted like the bottom of a parrot's cage, and she quickly brushed her teeth and showered before donning a dress and joining everyone in the dining room. Chrissie called from the kitchen where she had a big pot of coffee brewing.

"Penny! Get in here and start scrambling lots of eggs. At least we have plenty of those. Do you think this ham is OK?" She looked dubiously at the curling slices on the plate. "It's been in the fridge, but we don't want to make everyone sick."

"Is that from Christmas? It came in a can, so it's probably loaded with preservatives. Should be all right if we fry it well. Are Joseph and Luke back yet? Where's Zach?"

"He was on pins and needles. I sent him and David to watch for the others coming. That's why we're cooking. Make a lot of toast too. Everyone's here."

They all fell on the food ravenously. They had not eaten much the previous day. Perhaps it was just part of the fight-or-flight reflex.

KISIMBA

Fill up now because you never know when you'll eat again. Penny remembered Sister Clare saying something similar a few weeks back.

"I do wish Joseph would get back," Chrissie said, voicing the worry on everyone's mind.

A minute later they heard David yelling and rushed to the door. Joseph and Luke were walking into the compound with Zach. They looked weary but unharmed, and they came straight through the door of the main house.

Chrissie shooed the men into the kitchen and bombarded them with questions. Joseph raised his hand and said firmly, "It is done. Now you must forget it. And please excuse us, but we are hungry and need to rest."

Sister Clare replied equally firmly, "Yes. And you will eat here. There is plenty for all of us."

She took three plates and loaded them with food. Joseph inclined his head and thanked her. Then he said, "We will eat here in the kitchen, Sister."

Then Dan called for everyone's attention. "Nick managed to get through on the phone last night. He was in Kampala and on the move again. I let him know what's going on here. He insisted we leave immediately given...the circumstances. I agree with him absolutely. He also said things are fairly quiet in Kampala, but there are those in high places who believe a coup is imminent. Even if it doesn't happen, we can certainly expect a return visit from the gestapo. Luke will be going with Margaret and Theresa, and probably Zach and David, to stay at the leprosy hospital. It's a long trip on foot, but they can stop at villages Luke knows along the way to rest. They should be safe there. So start packing up what you need. Now. We'll leave this afternoon." He turned to Penny. "Are you ready to go to Jinja with Joseph?"

"Yes," she said and sighed.

When Joseph brought the car around, he said, "Doctor Dan, I will return soon."

— 189 —

After a round of somber farewells, she departed from Kisimba with Joseph. Dan gripped both her shoulders hard and said, "Take care, Penny. Try to let us know somehow when you get to Kampala."

Then Mother Mary Agnes reached up and slipped a small crucifix around her neck. "My dear girl. I want you to have this. It has sustained me through some difficult times, and I think it will give you the strength and courage for what might lie ahead. God bless you, Penny."

———

"Thank you for doing this, Joseph."

"Yes, Doctor Penny."

It was all he said. There was no traffic on the road, either by vehicle or on foot. About ten miles from the hospital and halfway to Jinja, a green army jeep passed them going in the opposite direction. Then it turned around and sped up beside their car. The driver leaned over, shouted at Joseph, and waved a gun.

"Doctor, they are ordering us to stop. I cannot go faster than them in this car."

"They probably just want to check our papers or something."

They pulled up on the roadside. The man next to the driver stepped out of the jeep and strutted over to them. He was wearing a smart uniform and carried a short baton, which he smacked against his thigh. She assumed he was an officer. He spoke to Joseph, but all the while he stared at her. Joseph said, "He is ordering you to get out of the car, Doctor. Do as he says. Do not anger him."

She stood near the car with her legs trembling. One of the soldiers pulled out her bag and emptied it onto the ground. The officer said, "Pick up your passport, miss."

She complied silently and held it out to him.

"Where are you coming from?"

"The Hope Hospital in Kisimba."

He flipped through her passport. "And where are you going?"

"Jinja. And then to Kampala." Mindful of Joseph's warning, she kept her voice low and didn't meet his eyes. He studied her briefly, turned to Joseph, and shouted, "You! Go! Go back to where you came from. She stays here."

Joseph shook his head and sat like a rock. The soldier picked out a few of her belongings off the ground. This included her change purse, and he walked over to his officer to show him what he had. Then he leaned in, touched her breast with his big hand, and viciously tweaked her nipple through the cotton of her dress. She winced with the sudden pain. The officer impatiently batted the man's hand off her, stood threateningly over Joseph, who sat silently in the car, and continued to harangue him. Joseph finally began to speak at some length in his own tongue. A long silence followed. Penny thought sadly of Nick, her parents, and all her friends, old and new. *I love you all*, she thought and resigned herself to the worst.

The officer turned back to her and dispassionately looked her up and down. She stared back into his eyes. She was unflinching and just waiting for what was going to happen. Then he reached out, took hold of the crucifix around her neck, and studied it. She thought he was going to wrench it off her, but after a few moments, he just let it go. With a shrug he waved his men back to the jeep, and they took off. She stood and shook uncontrollably. Joseph picked up her scattered clothes and other items the soldiers had left on the ground.

He looked at her directly. "You are a brave woman, Doctor."

"No. I'm not! I was absolutely terrified. Joseph, what did you say to them?"

"I told them you are a child of God. A chosen one."

She thought of Dr. Hope back in the mission office in London and felt a deep regret she had made fun of him. "Thank you. Do you have Seme with you?" It certainly wasn't visible.

— 191 —

"Of course, Doctor. I would have used him if it became necessary. You are under my protection."

"What should we do now?"

"It is your decision, Doctor Penny."

The minutes passed in silence. "I don't know," she said finally.

"I know that if you were my family, I would take you back to Kisimba. Doctor, other cars are coming."

29

Out of the morning haze, another jeep was headed toward them at a dangerous speed. A car driven by an elderly native man followed. When Penny recognized the jeep, she was overwhelmed with relief and joy. *How did he find me?* Then both vehicles screeched to a halt over the rutted road, and Nick leaped out of the first one. His face was tight with anger.

"Where the *fuck* do you think you're going? How could you be so idiotic?"

"Don't you fucking yell at me!" Penny shouted.

White-hot rage and pent-up fear suddenly consumed her. They glared at each other.

"Get in the damn jeep!"

She stomped off and then stood by his vehicle. Her stomach churned. He walked around to Joseph and started bellowing at him. After a time he appeared to gain control and began to question Joseph at some length. She stood and watched while Joseph turned the car around and headed back down the road to the hospital. Nick strode back to her.

"How did you get through?" she asked.

He pointed silently to the jeep door, which now displayed a large red cross. He waited until she got in.

"Joseph told me what happened," Nick said. "Sweet Jesus, I could have lost you."

— 193 —

He pulled her into a rough embrace, and the tears she had been holding in finally rolled down her cheeks. His own eyes were brimming wet.

He held her while she cried and then said, "Come on, baby. Stiff upper lip and all that. Think of England!" He gave her his handkerchief. "Blow your nose. Pull it together now. We've got to get moving."

"I was going to catch a bus in Jinja to Kampala and then Entebbe. Sue called and said there were problems in in the city, and I needed to get out while I could. Nick, I didn't know how to reach you!"

"It's OK, honey. I'm here now. Listen. The airport is closed, and there's a lot of fighting going on back there in Kampala. I bought another car in Jinja." He pointed to the car behind. "We'll need it to get everyone out."

"What about the guy driving it?"

"His bike's in the back. Don't worry. I gave him a heap of cash for the old jalopy. What's the situation at the hospital?"

She blew her nose loudly and sat up straighter. She tried to concentrate on the here and now. "Most of the patients and staff have left. Everyone's packing to leave. I've only got this bag." She held it up. "Underwear, one dress, passport, etcetera."

"Your mom will be proud of you. I bet she went through something like this in the blitz. Right?"

She remembered the small suitcase her mother still kept in a small closet under the stairs at home and smiled reluctantly.

"Penny, did those men take anything from you? Did they mess with you? Do you still have your bracelet?"

She patted the money pouch under her dress. "It's safe. They took some loose change from my bag and that scarf Emily gave me for my birthday. One of them grabbed me here." She touched her breast gingerly. "He obviously meant to hurt me, and he did. Joseph saved me. He just sat there in the car and refused to leave."

KISIMBA

"Thank God," Nick replied grimly.

"Nick?"

"Here we go. Yeah, honey?"

"You're wearing a gun." The hefty-looking weapon was holstered at his hip.

"Can't get anything past you, can I?"

"But you're a doctor. How can you have a gun? And it's so big!"

He shot her a quick grin. "Ya think? Is that a compliment?"

"No! How come I've never seen it before? Is it a Secret Service thing?"

"You never asked. Anyway, I don't usually carry openly. Today seemed like a good day to have it handy."

"I really don't believe in guns. Except maybe for hunting."

"And I'm not too wild about killing animals for sport. I think you'd change your mind about guns if you were ever in a situation where, God forbid, someone was trying to kill you. Now are you done? We've gotta get going."

He jammed the car into gear and sped down the deserted road. Just a few miles out from the hospital, a military jeep swung into their path from the left and braked sharply. "Ah, shit! Penny, is that one of the guys who stopped you?"

She was so scared she could hardly speak. "Yes. I think so. He's one of the men who was with the officer."

"Stay put. Don't move."

She didn't question him and just sat rigidly in her seat. He quickly removed his holster and stuffed the pistol behind him into the waistband of his pants. Joseph had already disappeared ahead of them. Their second car with the native driver pulled up a good distance behind them.

Nick got out of the jeep and walked slowly toward the soldier. "Can I help you?"

The man marched past him. "No stupid officer save you this time, child of God." He roughly pulled Penny out onto the dirt road

— 195 —

by her arm. She realized he was the soldier who had mauled her. "I come back for you, pretty lady."

Her heart stopped. Nick turned and continued toward him once more. "C'mon, man. You don't want to do this."

The man was sweating profusely. "And who do you think you are, filthy white man? I kill you first," he said, and he started to reach for his weapon.

Penny twisted away. Nick pulled his weapon, fired as he walked toward him, and hit him squarely in the chest three times. The sound of the gun rocked her. The beast fell flat onto his back and panted for breath. Nick stood over him. His face was a cold mask, and he put the last shot cleanly between his eyes.

Her ears rang. Nick knelt and took the forty-five automatic from the holster on the motionless body. "I learned in 'Nam you can never have too much firepower. I'm sorry, Penny. I wouldn't have put you through that if there were any other way."

She touched his shoulder. "I'm glad you killed the bloody bastard."

He searched her face for a moment. "OK. Now we have to move before he's found. Let's haul ass."

As they traveled the last distance to Kisimba, they saw two more soldiers. They were covered with blood and lying on the side of the road. "Christ! They must have argued over you."

He jammed on the brakes, retrieved another two weapons, briefly inspected them, and passed them over to Penny.

———

The house was in a state of chaos. Sister Clare and Chrissie were giving out conflicting orders, while Dan stood in the center of the living room and tried to control everyone. He looked relieved when he saw Nick. "Good to see you, my friend. I was hoping you'd come. Penny, you all right?" He seemed satisfied by her nod.

KISIMBA

"Wouldn't miss this party for the world," Nick said. "Listen up, everyone. Here's the situation. Idi Amin has taken over. Obote is in Singapore at some conference. The army has occupied Entebbe International Airport, and there are no flights in or out. There's a fair amount of shooting in Kampala. The railroads have been closed. The phone service is almost nonexistent. Soldiers have been...seen on the road to Jinja. We have to leave. And soon."

Nick's voice was strong and confident. The only sign of stress was he was twirling Penny's ring around on his finger. Everyone was quiet and taking in the information.

"We have three vehicles. Yours, mine, and one I bought in Jinja. We'll need them all. You have to change clothes. Chrissie and Kathy, wear nurse's dresses. Dan and Penny, put on scrubs. Any white coats here?"

"No, Doctor," said Sister Clare.

"Too bad. Sister, you and Mother change into something comfortable but nunly. Actually, Sister, you'll do. Mother, I want you to lose the wimple. Wear one of those light veils."

Everyone nodded obediently and began moving in different directions.

"Hold up. I'm not finished." Nick placed a large envelope on the coffee table. "These are CDC badges. Everyone has to wear one—including you, Joseph."

"Is that legal?" Penny asked.

"Probably not. Does it matter?" He laughed sardonically. "Joseph will drive the mission car. By the way, hide the sword, man. Dan, you get the new car. It seems to be running well." He handed guns to both of them, which they accepted without comment. "Everyone pack appropriately for a short visit by our CDC team to the Lady of Light mission in Kenya. Nothing else except small items of real importance to you. Questions?"

— 197 —

"Guess that means I can't take my record player, huh?" Chrissie said. "Can I take my guitar?"

"Yeah. We can swing that."

"Thanks. I can't wait to see my fiancé again. I think he's still in Nairobi."

"Any news of the Campbells?" asked Sister Clare worriedly.

"I haven't been able to get through to them. I'll try again later."

"Nick, dear," Mother piped up. She was pink with excitement. "I'm so happy we're going to Our Lady of Light. They have a small convent there. Can I bring Buddy?"

He paused and then said with a gentle smile, "We'll squeeze him in somehow. But he has to behave. Now let's get this show on the road!"

As Chrissie left the room, she remarked, "Big gun, Doctor."

She smirked at him. He gave her a bow with nothing but humor in his expression. "Thank you. Always nice to be appreciated. Get moving, everyone. Penny, go change."

As she donned her scrubs and repacked her bag, Penny thought of how, despite everything, Nick had taken charge so effortlessly and calmly. He was like a senior surgeon beginning a complicated operation. For the first time in hours—even days—she felt grounded.

———

Nick supervised the loading of people, belongings, and the dog. Then Kathy got out again and said defiantly, "I'm staying. I can't leave these people."

A chorus of protests and pleas sounded. Nick strode over to her and held up his hand like a traffic cop. "Kathy, get in the freaking car."

He glared at her. His shoulders were tight and did not give an inch. She scowled back at him, and then her face crumpled. She got back in next to Joseph.

Nick walked over to Luke, who was talking to Joseph. "Do you know how to use a gun?"

"Of course, Doctor. I thank you." Luke took the weapon Nick offered and stuck it into his pants.

And so they left. Penny sat beside Nick in his jeep. The other two cars followed closely. Her chest hurt so much she thought she might be having a heart attack. Despite her intentions and against her better judgment, she looked back at the compound. Margaret, Theresa, Luke, Zach, and David were waving farewell from the front steps of the hospital. No patients were in sight. Although, she knew a few of the very sick were still on the wards.

"I'm so scared for them," she whispered.

He gripped her hand hard. "I know. I'll do what I can."

When she glanced over, his face was grim. This frightened her even more. "Nick, what will happen?"

"I really don't know. The immediate goal is to get you all to Kenya."

"And then what? You whisked us out of Kisimba so fast I didn't have a chance to ask."

He finally smiled at her. "We have a little while before we reach the border, so let's talk plans. First, you go with the others to the Lady of Light mission. The sisters seem to know the place. You should be safe there. Stay with them for a night or two, and then take off for Nairobi. Joseph will go with you. Dan might also decide to go back to England, and it sounds as though Chrissie will be hunting down her man. By the way, don't get any ideas about Dan. I'd hate to have to beat up a friend."

"How could you...oh. OK. I'll try to restrain myself. What do I do in Nairobi?"

"Go to the British High Commission and tell them what happened. Ask for repatriation. They nearly always agree, but it's a lot easier if you have money." He reached into his pocket and pulled out a fat envelope. "Here's a few thousand bucks. Three to be exact.

— 199 —

Dollars are worth more these days. Use it to get back to England. Dan too if he goes. Keep the rest safe for me until I can find my way back to you. I'm about tapped out, so please don't lose it."

She stared at the envelope aghast. "I can't take that."

"The hell you can't. Do you really think I'm going to risk losing you for the sake of a few bloody pesos? I withdrew the cash days ago. Just in case. Now let's talk about what happens once you're back home."

"OK," she managed against the painful lump in her throat.

"You graduate medical school. That's in a few months, right? During that time, all being well, I'll have finished business here, gone back to the United States, finalized my divorce, and seen my family. Then I hotfoot it to London." He fished for his wallet and removed a card. "My folks' address and phone number are on the back. Once I'm out of here, they'll probably know how to find me. More to the point, I need your address and number. Find some paper and write it down. And your parents' information too. In case you get some crazy bug up your ass about taking off somewhere."

Penny felt better having something to do and started rooting around in her bag for paper and pen. The news Nick was planning to come to London filled her with hope and certainly helped her regain some equanimity.

"OK. Here you are," she said, and she handed over the small folder that contained her now-useless plane ticket. "Nick, may I ask you something?"

"Works for me. Makes the situation feel almost normal."

"You never spoke about coming to England or really anything in the future."

"Is there a question in there somewhere? Don't bother. I have the answer." He slowed the jeep, and the rest of their caravan pulled up behind them on the roadside. He turned to her and took her face gently between his hands. "I had hoped for something a bit more romantic than an escape from a political coup, but you'll have to put

— 200 —

up with it. Penny, my darling, I love you, and I intend to spend the rest of my life with you, watch our children grow, and cherish you forever. If you agree of course. Although, I can't imagine why you wouldn't, given all the advantages I obviously have to offer. Being soon unemployed, in debt, and so forth. What do you say?"

"Yes please," she whispered. "I love you too. Forever."

Despite the fear and real threat they all faced, the world outside seemed to disappear. It left only her and Nick in one perfect moment as they held each other. After a long pause, he said, "Good. We're nearly in Kenya. If you have anything else for me, say it now."

"Will you be OK? I need you to come find me again."

"I'll do my very best. I promise."

"Where do I get the proper proposal?"

"Yorkshire? Paris? Rome? Take your pick. You'll have a while to think about it. I've got one for you. How many kids do you want?"

"You are absolutely impossible! OK. I'll play. Minimum two. Maximum twelve."

"I can go with that. You'll be the one having them. Now hush while we get through the checkpoint."

He got out of the jeep and shook the hand of the soldier at the border crossing. They obviously knew each other. He must have traveled this way before. She could see him gesturing toward her and the two cars behind, and it looked as though some money changed hands. The man saluted Nick and raised the barrier, and they all drove through. On the Kenyan side, they weren't even stopped—just waved on. Nick drove slowly a few miles up the road and then pulled the jeep to a halt.

"This is where you get out, baby." He came round and opened her door. "You're driving with Dan. Let's go."

She stood by the car while Nick said his farewells to everyone. When he bent his head to kiss Mother Mary Agnes, she said in a remarkably firm voice, "Nick, you are an angel. God bless you and keep you safe, my dearest boy."

— 201 —

Then he came back to Penny's side and opened the car door. He leaned in. "Dan, take care of my girl here."

"Will do, old friend. Watch out for yourself."

Nick and Penny came together in a last embrace. He said, "Good-bye, my sweet Penny. *Amore mio*. I'll be seeing you."

"And I'll be waiting. Good-bye, Nick."

She was suddenly aware the drums were silent.

PART 2
REUNION

30

Penny sat silently in the back of the car. Dan was at the wheel and carefully following the car in front of them, which Joseph was driving. Dan and Chrissie occasionally exchanged a few quiet words. Penny leaned her head against the window and vacantly stared out at the landscape. It looked no different from that of the country they had just left. She felt deadened by grief for those they had left behind and the overwhelming sense of loss knowing she might never see Nick again. Emotionally spent she slipped into an uneasy sleep and only awoke when the car stopped.

"Come on, Penny girl. We're here," Chrissie said gently.

They parked in front of a large white two-story house. It was set off the ground and surrounded by verandas. A young girl in a white habit was standing by the front door. She waved when she saw them and disappeared inside. Moments later what appeared to be a welcoming committee came out of the house and gathered on the wide steps. A tall, stately nun with a decidedly authoritative demeanor stood at the center of the group. All the women were dressed in long black habits—except for the girl in the white one. They wore short veils with black bands.

The travelers climbed out of the cars, and Buddy shot off toward some nearby bushes and lifted his leg. Joseph helped Mother Mary Agnes forward. Sister Clare was close behind her on crutches. Chrissie whispered to Penny, "That's the mother superior. Don't let the stern look put you off. She's really very kind."

The mother-in-charge, as Penny mentally labeled her, walked down the steps and kissed both sisters on each cheek. "Sister Mary Agnes, I'm so glad to see you safe. Thanks be to God. Sister Clare, you can tell me later why your leg is in a cast. You must both be tired."

Mary Agnes smiled happily. Apparently her demotion in title did not bother her at all. She said, "Oh, no, Mother. Just being here has perked us up. I'm sure you remember Sister Chrissie."

Then she introduced Dan, Penny, and Kathy to the mother superior, who smiled benignly at them.

"Everyone, welcome to Our Lady of Light. I am Mother Frances. I hope you will find peace during your stay with us. We will discuss your plans later. I suggest you retire to rest until vespers at five thirty. Sisters Mary Agnes and Clare, I have had rooms readied for you in the nuns' quarters here upstairs. Doctor Greenleaf, you will be staying in the men's guesthouse. You will have it to yourself. Miss Drayton, you, Christine, and Katherine will be in the women's guesthouse. Christine will show you all the way. Milk and sandwiches will be brought to you. The evening meal will be served after vespers. You are invited to join the community to eat. We don't stand too much on ceremony here. Joseph, Dominick here will show you to your quarters. We'll have to find somewhere appropriate for that little dog. Him, I did not expect.

"You are welcome to go wherever you would like in the compound—except, of course, the sisters' quarters. You may attend services in the visitors' section of the chapel. There is a schedule of daily offices and mealtimes in your rooms. Do you have any questions?"

"Yes, Mother," Dan said. "May I ask how you knew we were coming?"

"A Dr. Sottile called to let us know. Now, you may all retire."

Penny felt a certain degree of relief to know everything had been arranged for them. She almost expected Mother Frances to remind them to brush their teeth before bed. She also felt her heart lift a little when she heard Nick had called ahead. At least she knew he was safe—for now.

They pulled their few belongings from the cars and followed Chrissie. Mary Agnes and Clare were led inside the convent house. As they slowly walked through the large compound, which was bustling with activity, Chrissie pointed out the different buildings. "That, as you can tell, is the chapel. The small building next door is where Father Philippe lives while he's here. I hope you get to meet him. And that..." She pointed to a small wooden building painted a cheerful sky blue. "That's the school."

A bunch of children were running around and shrieking with laughter while a young nun with her habit tied up to her knees chased them around in an energetic game.

"The long building over there is where the African nurses live," Chrissie said. "And over there is the hospital. Dan, you and Penny will probably want to check that out. They are much better equipped than we were at Kisimba."

She fell silent and bowed her head for a moment. Penny struggled to hold back tears as Dan gave her a reassuring pat on her shoulder. Kathy was looking around avidly at the colorful scene and spoke for the first time in hours. "I really like it here. It's a happy place."

"It's certainly a busy place." Chrissie pointed to a group of nuns wearing long white aprons over their habits. "They're nursing sisters. Others are teachers. And everyone takes turns cooking and cleaning—not to mention doing the laundry and ironing. Have you any idea how long it takes to iron for thirty-odd nuns? They have very few houseboys. It's just Dominick, whom you saw back there, and another man. I can't remember his name. Well, here we are. Dan, you're over there. Ladies, follow me." Take-charge Chrissie was back.

Dan said, "I'm going to catch a few winks. Can you make sure I'm up in time for vespers?"

"If I wake up in time!" She laughed.

The guesthouses were bigger than those at Kisimba. There were two bedrooms, a bathroom, and a small sitting room in the women's house, and Penny assumed the men's quarters were the same. Chrissie decreed she and Penny would share one of the bedrooms, and Kathy looked relieved. As promised Dominick soon delivered a pitcher of milk and a plate of what proved to be cucumber sandwiches. They sat down and ate the simple meal, took turns in the bathroom, and then retired to their respective rooms. Penny undressed and donned the one nightie she had brought along.

"Chrissie? I brought three dresses: the *kitenge* one you gave me, my blue one, and the white cotton one my mum made. Which do you think would be most suitable to wear here? And what should I do with these scrubs?"

"If you're worrying about clothes, you must be feeling better. Leave those for the hospital, and wear the white dress here. Makes you look very innocent!"

"Oh, Lord." Penny blushed. "Don't start that."

"Did you bring your shorts? They would be the most comfortable to travel in when we go to Nairobi."

"We? Are you coming too? Oh, I'm so glad, Chrissie. Can I borrow a T-shirt to go with the shorts? I seem to have forgotten to bring any."

"Of course I'm going. I can't wait to see Alan. It's been so long, and letters are no substitute for the real thing. I haven't decided yet what to do after that. Yes to the T-shirt. Now sleep, girl. Whether you realize it or not, you're exhausted."

———

"Wake up, sunshine!"

Chrissie's voice penetrated her sleep, and she struggled awake. She yawned. She could hear water running in the bathroom. Kathy was obviously up already.

"Do I have time for a shower?"

"No. Just wash your face and get dressed. We don't want to be late!"

"Yes, Mum," she muttered.

Penny stood with her friends in one section of the chapel as the nuns filed in. Their heads were bowed, and their hands were folded in front of them. The service was fairly brief. She had had no idea what it would involve. Everyone remained standing as Mother Frances led the office, which consisted of the nuns singing in Latin, a short reading from the Bible, and then a chorus of the *Magnificat*. Penny felt more at peace than she had for a long time.

Then Mother Frances addressed the congregants. "Sisters, we have guests this evening. They have come to us from Uganda for sanctuary. I know you will welcome them into your hearts. Sister Clare and Sister Mary Agnes, whom many of you know, have already asked permission to stay on with us. I have, of course, consented. Let us pray for the safety of the Ugandan people and the friends and loved ones who remain there."

There was silence for several minutes. Penny's days of belief had long passed, but she found herself thinking, *Oh, please let the people at Hope Hospital make it through this. And look after Nick and the Campbells.* As an afterthought, she added, *Thanks.*

"Praise be to God," Mother finally said and wrapped up the service.

They waited until the nuns left and then followed them.

"That was really heartwarming," Penny said outside the chapel. The sun was just setting.

"Yeah. It's one of the best aspects of religious life," Chrissie said. "I couldn't do it full-time or forever, though. I want to get married one day and have kids. Now let's head for the dining hall. It's in the main house."

"That reminds me," Dan said quietly. "Will Mother let us use the phone? I really want to call Emily."

"I'm sure she will. Penny, you should probably call your parents, and I need to see if I can get in touch with the Campbells and then try to reach Alan. Kathy?"

Kathy shook her head but smiled. She was quite attractive when she wasn't wearing her habitual frown.

Supper was served buffet style in a large room set with long tables. Sister Mary Agnes waved them over. "I saved places for you. It might be frowned upon, but we wanted to talk to all of you. Didn't we, Sister Clare?"

"Yes. We do."

She looked a little strained, and Penny wondered if her leg was hurting her. Dan obviously was thinking along the same lines. "Sister, I'm going to take a look at that leg of yours tonight. I'll hand you over to a doctor here tomorrow. I'm looking forward to meeting everyone at the hospital. Doesn't the medical staff eat here too?"

"Yes. Usually. They must all be busy. A few of the sisters are missing too." Sister Clare surveyed the room. "Go and get in line, or there'll be none left for you."

The nuns were helping themselves from large bowls of spaghetti and meatballs, hunks of crusty bread, and salad. Penny's mouth started watering. Then she realized neither of the old nuns was standing.

As she was about to open her mouth, Chrissie preempted her. "Sister Mary Agnes, may I bring you a plate? And you, Sister Clare? Penny will help me."

"Thank you, dear girl," replied Mary Agnes. "Just a small helping for me please."

"And a rather bigger portion for me. Thank you," said Sister Clare.

— 210 —

They stood in line behind the nuns. Chrissie whispered, "Thank heavens. They're bringing out more. I was worried they'd run out before we got our own. I'm really hungry."

Eventually they filled plates for the two sisters and then rejoined the queue and helped themselves. At their table the group was in quiet discussion while the nuns around them chattered and laughed lightheartedly.

"Obviously there's no vow of silence here," Penny said.

"Only at lunch when they listen to a reading," Chrissie replied. "So, everyone, what are your plans?"

"As Mother Frances said, Mary Agnes and I have decided to stay on here. At least for the present," Sister Clare said. "It's a lovely community, and once I'm mobile again, I believe I can be of real use."

"I've decided to return to England," Dan said. "I'll travel with Joseph and Penny to Nairobi."

"I'm coming with you too and will meet up with Alan, if I can find the man. What about you, Kathy?"

"I haven't decided yet. I want to talk to Mother Frances first."

It was the first substantial meal they'd eaten since Christmas, and Penny made herself stop before she overdid it. They all stood when Mother Frances joined their table. "Sit, sit," she said pleasantly.

Penny took her first close look at the woman. She was solidly built but carried the weight well on her tall frame. Her skin was as clear and unlined as that of a much younger woman, and she had a lovely smile.

"I can see you enjoyed your supper." She laughed.

"Very much. Thank you, Mother," Chrissie said. "May we help clean up?"

"No. Not tonight. Don't worry. I'll find plenty for you to do tomorrow, Christine." She looked around the table. "Is there anything I can do for you before compline?"

Dan replied, "Yes, Mother. Penny and I would like to examine Sister Clare's leg, if we may. I think perhaps she's overdone it today."

— 211 —

"Certainly. You may see her in the small parlor. Also there's a telephone in there, if anyone wishes to make a call." She rose and said, "Compline is at nine thirty."

She then moved to sit at another table and talk to the nuns there.

Dan rose from the table. "OK. Let's do it, Sister Clare. Penny, you coming?"

31

SISTER CLARE LED them to a small, comfortable room, and Penny shut the door. She narrowly missed Buddy, who snuck in behind them. Dan helped the nun sit in an armchair, and Penny dragged over an ottoman. Together they carefully lifted the sister's cast-encased leg onto it. The woman winced slightly but didn't complain when Penny gently lifted the habit up to her knee.

"What is your impression, Doctor Penny?" Dan asked with a slight smile.

She easily slipped back into medical mode as she knelt on the floor and carefully examined their patient's leg. Satisfied with her findings, she got to her feet. "Sister Clare is clearly in some discomfort. However, there is no swelling, temperature change, or color change in the tissue below or above the cast. I recall from Dr. Campbell's report that the tibial fracture was a clean transverse break with minimal displacement. If my math is correct, it is over six weeks since the cast was applied, but some time had elapsed between the fracture and treatment." She hesitated.

"Well? What do you suggest?" Dan asked her.

"I think we should perform X-rays, if they have a machine here, and check for misalignment. If all is well, the cast should stay on for several more weeks. A brace is probably not indicated at this time. Sorry, Sister."

Dan regarded her thoughtfully and then said, "I agree. We'll get that done in the morning. How does that sound, Sister?"

"I would have much preferred to have the thing removed. Thank you both anyway. Now if you could help me up…"

"Hold on, Sister. When did you last take any aspirin?"

She waved him off. "Can't remember. Sometime yesterday I believe."

Dan opened his black bag and found a small packet, which he handed to her. "Take two of these with a glass of milk tonight. Please ask the doctors for more when necessary. It isn't a sin to take pain-killers when you need them."

A nun was waiting outside the parlor to help Sister Clare to her room. Buddy headed off purposefully to the rear of the house. He seemed to know his way around already. At least they wouldn't have to worry about him.

"Dan, why don't you call Emily now?" Penny said. "I'll wait in the hall."

He looked at his watch. "England's about three hours behind us here, so it's still quite early over there. I won't be too long. Assuming I get a connection quickly."

Penny joined Chrissie in the hall and sank onto a hard wooden bench. "Dan's calling home. Do you want to go next?"

"No. That's OK. It'll be much easier for me to get through to Nairobi. Tell me about Sister Clare."

The time passed quickly as they talked quietly. When Dan came out of the parlor, he looked much happier. "Em is thrilled we're safe and that I'll be going home soon. I can't wait to see them all. I think I'll go and stretch my legs before compline. Penny, your turn."

She was connected to the operator in England almost immediately, and in a few more minutes, she heard her mother's gentle voice.

"Hello, Mummy. It's me." She started to sniffle a bit.

"Penny! How are you, pet? It's wonderful to hear your voice."

"Mum, did you hear about the coup in Uganda?"

"Yes, dear. We're so relieved you are safe in Kenya. When do you think you'll be coming home?"

— 214 —

KISIMBA

"How did you know I was here?" Penny asked.

"We had a call very early this morning from a charming American man called Nick. He told us he got you and your friends out of Uganda. He also told us…" She dropped her voice and whispered. "He said he intends to marry you. What on earth have you been up to?"

"It's a long story, Mum. I can't stay on the phone long. I'm calling from the convent where we're staying for a couple days."

"A *convent*? Oh, my. Hold on. Your father's hovering over me."

"Now then, love," came her dad's gruff voice.

That was his normal greeting to her. He was a man of few words, but she knew he loved her dearly.

"Hi, Dad. I hear you got the news I'm OK."

"Aye. That young chap, Nick, rang us early—really early. Startled your mother a bit, he did."

"How are you both? Is it snowing there in Yorkshire?"

"Course it is. It's January. Can't complain. So, how long have you known this Nick?"

"Oh, a few months," she said vaguely. "I think you'd like him, Dad. He's a doctor." She thought that might allay his suspicions.

"Hmph. Well, at least I know you're all right for cash. *Doctor* Nick told me he'd given you money for your ticket home."

"It's just a loan, Dad, and it's for me and another person who's coming back to England. Don't worry about it. Please."

After a pause he said, "Well, then. You take care of yourself now. I'm proud of you, lass. I hear you've been doing great work over there. Hang on. Your mother wants to say cheerio."

Her mum got back on the line. "Don't mind him. You know how he is. Please call again when you get back to London. Stay safe, pet."

"Bye, Mummy." She hung up, a real smile on her face. *That must have been some conversation they had with Nick!*

She opened the parlor door to find Chrissie prowling around impatiently. "All yours," she said.

— 215 —

"Thanks. Why are you so pink? Everything OK?"

"Yeah. I'll tell you later. Maybe. Shouldn't we give them some money for these calls? We must be running up quite a bill."

Distracted from her piercing assessment of Penny's face, Chrissie answered, "I'd love to, but I don't have much in the way of cash. Do you have any?"

Chrissie raised her eyebrows when Penny told her about the money Nick had given her. Penny said it was for all of them to use if necessary.

"Blimey! That man thinks of everything. Remind me when we leave here to give the mission a parting thank-you gift. I know they'll appreciate it. What are you going to do until compline?"

"Take a long shower. It seems like weeks since I've had one." *Was it really only this morning I left Kisimba with Joseph on the near-disastrous trip to Jinja?*

"OK. See you back at the house."

Penny walked slowly through the balmy evening. Her mind was curiously at rest. She smiled as she heard faraway drums beginning to sound the news of the day, but they didn't speak about her anymore.

―――――

Compline was a simple, soothing service with a psalm, a private prayer, and a hymn. It ended with the *Nunc dimittis*. It was over in less than twenty minutes.

As the four visitors made their way back to the guesthouses, they discussed plans for the next day.

"The nuns get up at five thirty," Chrissie said, "but we can sleep in, and I think we should. Lauds is at seven, and breakfast is at eight, so we'll have to wait a bit for coffee. By the way, Penny, you don't have to attend the offices if you don't want to."

"I'd like to. Anyway, it seems only polite."

"Penny and I have to see to Sister Clare," Dan said. "According to the schedule, work begins at nine o'clock, so I think we should take her over to the hospital then."

"Right. I need to wash out a few things. What about you, Chrissie?"

"Kathy and I have been assigned to clean up after breakfast, so you two got out of that. But don't worry, Penny. You'll be helping with preparing and serving lunch. For some obscure reason, Dan, you've been excused from manual labor," she said with some asperity.

"Splendid. I knew there had to be some benefits to being a male. I must remember to tell Emily."

Chrissie ignored him. "We also have to figure out the trip to Nairobi. Kathy, have you decided yet if you'll be coming with us?"

"I'll know by the evening. I'm meeting with Mother Frances tomorrow afternoon."

They had arrived at the guesthouses. Dan bid them a good night and left them for his quarters. When the women approached their house, a man rose from the porch.

"*Sista*s, it is me."

"Joseph!" Penny exclaimed. "Is everything OK?"

They hadn't seen him since their arrival.

"Yes, Doctor Penny."

"You should go rest, Joseph. You've had a long day too," Chrissie said. "I hope they found you somewhere comfortable?"

"Yes, *Sista*. But I will sleep here tonight. I gave my word to Doctor Nick I would watch over you." With an unusual glint of humor, he added, "I am not alone. Seme is with me."

"Have you eaten?" Kathy asked.

"Yes, *Sista*. And I have a blanket."

He looked at them impassively as they thanked him and entered the house.

———

Early the next morning, Penny stepped out and took a lungful of the sweet, fresh air. Joseph had departed, and in his place on the porch was a jug of coffee and another of milk. She took them inside and announced, "The coffee fairy visited!"

"Thank you, Lord," Chrissie said fervently, and they helped themselves. "This should keep us going until breakfast."

They filed into the chapel behind the long line of nuns and took their places. During the service Penny spent most of the time thinking about the events of the previous day and wishing the feelings of horror and grief would lessen—if only a little. She had to get her mind on the days and months ahead.

Breakfast was a cheerful affair. Several nuns greeted them and asked about their plans. After they had finished hearty helpings of scrambled eggs and toast, Dan and Penny met Sister Clare outside. Chrissie and Kathy began clearing the tables and carrying the dirty dishes into the kitchen. The nun was obviously feeling better and insisted on walking on her crutches over to the hospital. Dan said, "I got a chance to talk to one of the doctors yesterday afternoon. Ah, there he is."

A handsome Kenyan man was striding over to them. Dan introduced him. "Sister, Penny, this is Dr. Oduya." He explained their plan to the doctor.

"That sounds most reasonable, Doctor Greenleaf. Please follow me."

He took them to a large room that patients already filled.

"This is our clinic. We are fortunate to have the room for it."

He opened a side door to a small examination room, and they got Sister Clare on the table. Dr. Oduya asked politely if he could assess her condition and then carefully examined her leg.

"Do you have X-ray facilities, Doctor?" asked Dan. "I would like to see what's going on in there."

"Of course. I will arrange it immediately."

KISIMBA

When they were alone, Dan remarked, "This seems to be a very fine hospital, Sister. They'll take good care of you here."

"I'm sure they will, but it won't be the same as having you and Penelope on hand."

Her words reminded Penny she would be leaving the next day. She murmured, "I'm really going to miss you and Sister Mary Agnes."

The nun patted her hand and said briskly, "Now, now. You never know when we might meet again. I'll pray for you. I believe you will be an excellent doctor, Penelope."

Dr. Oduya returned with a young man pushing a portable X-ray machine. "I thought this would be more comfortable for Sister Clare than moving her around the hospital," he said. "This is Simon, our technician. Let's leave the room while he takes the X-rays."

In the hallway Penny asked, "Doctor Oduya, may I ask where you trained?"

"At the University of Leeds Medical School in England." He laughed at her expression. "I take it you know it."

"I certainly do," she replied. "I grew up in Yorkshire."

"I thought so. I recognized your accent. Which school are you attending?"

She told him, and they chatted until the door to the examination room opened and the technician pushed out the clumsy machine. "The films will be ready shortly, Doctor," he said.

The X-rays showed Sister Clare was healing well, and Dr. Oduya asked her to come back to have her leg checked again in two weeks. Then he wished Dan and Penny a safe journey and departed.

They escorted Sister Clare back to the main house and saw her safely inside. Dan suggested they should take a stroll before she had to present herself for kitchen duty. They walked in companionable silence for a while and ended up fairly close to the guesthouses.

Penny stopped and said, "Dan, I'm just going to run in for a minute."

— 219 —

She took off, and he nodded amiably. She was out quickly and rejoined him. As they resumed their meanderings, Penny said, "I had a marvelous time working with you, Dan. You're a superb teacher, and I learned so much from you. Thank you for everything."

"It has been a real pleasure. I'm sorry we had to cut it short. You've gained so much confidence since you arrived. I'm proud of you. Just don't go doing things you aren't supposed to yet!" He smiled affectionately at her. "Remember to let me know how you're getting on. Who knows? We might end up working together again in the future."

"That would be fantastic. I have something for you, Dan. I hope you will use it."

She handed him the leather-bound journal she had bought for him at the Jinja market. It was still wrapped in plain paper.

Dan opened the rough package curiously. "Penny, you didn't have to do this!"

"I know. Just promise me it will be the first one you use when you begin your surgical fellowship. Wherever that might be."

"I will. And you must promise me you will pass your finals and go on to do big things. I hate to be blunt, but so many female doctors—the few there are—give up medicine when they have husbands and families. Please don't waste your talent, Penny. I'll tell Nick the same thing when we next talk."

"I promise, Dan. I'll never leave medicine. And I know Nick would agree if he were here." Her breath hitched a bit.

He caught her in a quick hug. "He'll be back, Penny."

32

WITH LITTLE CEREMONY Dan, Chrissie, Penny, and Joseph left the next morning after breakfast. They had reluctantly said their farewells to Sister Clare and Sister Mary Agnes. Kathy had decided to stay on at Our Lady of Light to figure out if the religious life was right for her. Mother Frances had accepted two crisp one hundred-dollar bills graciously and wished them a safe journey and fulfilling lives.

The drive to Nairobi seemed endless, and no one was in the mood to talk. They found a small, relatively inexpensive hotel near the center of the city and checked into two adjoining rooms. Penny worried what Joseph would do, but he assured them he would find a place to sleep and would join them in the morning. He appeared to be confident enough of their safety that he could leave them to their own devices. They decided to clean up quickly and meet for dinner in the small hotel restaurant. While Penny was in the shower, which consisted of a rather thin trickle of lukewarm water, Chrissie grabbed the phone.

When Penny emerged from the bathroom, Chrissie was talking excitedly to her fiancé. She ended the conversation as Penny hovered uncertainly.

"I can't believe it. Alan lives quite close to here. He's going to join us for dinner." Chrissie collapsed on one of the beds. "What am I going to do? I look like something the cat dragged in. Oh, Penny, I haven't seen him in months! You have to help me. What am I going to wear?"

"Didn't you pack a dress?"

"No. And I'm not going to wear a nurse's dress either."

"You could wear the *kitenge* dress you made for my birthday."

Chrissie perked up at the thought, and then her face fell. "I dunno. I'm a bit...bigger than you. You've lost so much weight it might actually be too loose on you. You look downright willowy," she said rather enviously.

"Come on. Try it on."

Chrissie wriggled into the dress. It was decidedly snug around the hips but showed off her bust splendidly. She peered critically at her reflection in the long mirror on the wall and muttered, "I look like a prossie."

"You do not. You're just not used to wearing real clothes. And I want it back after tonight. Anyway, a prostitute would be showing a lot more leg. I think you'll knock Alan's socks off."

"Well, OK. Thanks." Finally convinced, Chrissie took it off carefully. "I'll hop in the shower now."

In the restaurant Chrissie took a seat facing the door and waited anxiously as Penny and Dan talked about going to the British High Commission the next day. He had discovered it was only a short taxi ride away from the hotel. Since they had no idea what the process would entail to get them out of Kenya, they decided they would get there early. Chrissie suddenly leaped up from the table and almost ran to the door. She dodged the patrons and servers who were in her way.

Alan looked as serious as he did in the photo Penny had seen, but when he spotted Chrissie, his face creased in a huge grin, and he put his arms around her and hugged her tightly. Penny watched misty-eyed as he bent and whispered into her friend's ear. Chrissie blushed and then dragged him by the hand over to their table.

"Penny, Dan, this is Alan."

"I think we suspected as much." Dan chuckled as he and Penny shook his hand.

"Very nice to meet you both. Actually outstanding—considering what you've all been through." He put his arm around Chrissie again.

"Hope you two don't mind if we leave you," she said. "We've got a lot of catching up to do." She blushed again, much to Penny's amusement. "I'll try not to wake you when I come in."

Dan said, "No problem. We quite understand."

Penny whispered wickedly, "Behave yourself!"

Left to their own devices, Dan and Penny ate an unremarkable meal and then decided to go for a walk. She was struck by how noisy it was. She felt like the country mouse in the town. When she mentioned it to Dan, he grinned and said, "Wait until you get back to London. Now that's a big city."

As they wandered down the crowded street and peered into store windows, she was startled when Dan grasped her elbow. "Keep walking," he said. "I think we're being followed."

"Oh, crap. Here we go again," she grumbled.

A minute later Dan called out without turning, "Joseph? Is that you?"

"Yes, Doctor."

Penny spun around. "Joseph, is everything OK? What are you doing here?"

"I am keeping my word to Doctor Nick."

"Oh. Thank you. I do hope you're not planning on spending the night outside the hotel."

"No. But I will, of course, if you wish me to."

"I think she'll be safe, Joseph," Dan said. "Did you find a room for tonight?"

"Yes. I will return tomorrow morning to drive you to your High Commission. I have found out where it is. *Lala salama*, Doctors."

He slipped away into the darkness of a side street.

Penny turned to Dan. "That man is amazing. I owe him a lot. Actually I probably owe him my life. How did you even know we were being followed?"

"When you grow up in a rough neighborhood in Liverpool like I did, you learn to look over your shoulder."

After a pause Penny said, "Dan? Could I ask you a question?"

"Certainly. Your questions are always interesting." She caught the gleam of his smile.

"Only yesterday I was wishing the sadness would go away. If just for a while." She hesitated.

"And now?"

"It's easing. And this evening was fun. It was great to see Chrissie so happy."

He stopped and turned her gently to face him. His hands rested on her shoulders. "Are you feeling guilty?" She nodded mutely. "Well, don't. It's quite normal. We can't keep grief going indefinitely. We'd go mad. What's done is done, and we have to move on. Penny, you're a strong woman."

That word again!

"And I know Nick will do his damnedest to find you again. Now, enough of this! If Joseph is still lurking around, I don't want him getting the wrong idea." He kissed her cheek lightly.

She smiled. "Right. Thank you, Dan. I think I'll go get some sleep. We have a big day tomorrow."

Chrissie crept into the room at about three in the morning. She stubbed her toe on her bedside table and muttered what sounded like a rather rude word. Penny said sleepily, "So, how was it?"

"None of your business, girl. However, you were right about the dress. Now go back to sleep."

———

Joseph was waiting by the car when they left the hotel again after breakfast. It was promising to be another hot day. Penny was wearing her white dress. Dan looked very professional in a shirt and tie with his slacks. They had decided Dan should carry the cash since he was "the man." They drove down a wide street, turned off on a dirt road, and parked in front of an unpretentious building.

"This is it?" Penny asked.

It was a three-story, white stucco structure surrounded by grass and a few straggly trees.

"Yes, Doctor Penny. I will wait here."

"It looks like a high school," Penny said. "I expected something a bit more...imposing."

Once inside they joined a queue of mostly white people lined up in front of a small desk. Dan said, "We were right to come early. This is going to take time."

Surprisingly the line moved quickly as people were given numbered slips of paper and settled in chairs lining the large room. When they reached the desk, the young woman didn't even look up. "Names?" Having noted them, she asked, "Nature of business?"

Dan answered for both of them. "Repatriation."

She sighed, handed him two forms for them to fill out, told them to sit on the left wall, and then called, "Next!"

They found themselves with a large number of anxious British nationals. As they waited they chatted with those around them and heard their stories. Many had fled Uganda. Their experiences varied from the mundane to the horrific. Penny deliberately shut herself off and daydreamed. She was astonished when their names were called.

"Come on, Penny. That's us."

They were pointed toward a small cubicle where a young white man in a cheap suit sat at a desk piled high with papers. The nameplate before him said "Mr. Eric Stapleton."

"Names?" he asked.

"Dr. Greenleaf and Miss Drayton. UK citizens," Dan answered crisply.

The man looked up at them. "Are you married?"

"Yes," replied Dan.

"No," Penny said.

Mr. Stapleton surveyed them with a small smile. "Well, which is it?"

"I am married but not to this lady. She is a medical student entrusted to my care."

"Where's your wife?" He had a flat Midlands accent.

"Emily and my two children left Uganda some weeks ago and went home to Harrogate to stay with her parents."

"Hmm. And you, Miss Drayton. Where are you from?"

She told him the name of her medical school in London and produced the letters detailing her elective in Kisimba. The man read everything carefully and examined their passports.

"OK. I'm going to approve this. You are by no means the first to come here in the last few days. Can you pay the fee for the repatriation?"

"I believe so," Dan said. "How much is it? In dollars?"

Mr. Stapleton consulted a worn sheet of paper. "US or Canadian?"

"American."

"One hundred fifty apiece."

"We can do that," Dan said.

And cheap at the price, Penny thought.

"OK. Hang on a tick here."

Stapleton pawed uselessly through the folders in front of him, picked up his phone, turned his back on them, and spent about ten minutes talking to some unknown person on the other end. He made notes in a meticulous script. He looked pleased when he swiveled in his chair to face them again.

"I think you'll be happy with this," he said. "Dr. Greenleaf, I've got you on a plane to Manchester this afternoon at four o'clock. It will cost you another three hundred dollars. OK?"

"Yes!" Dan looked ecstatic. "What about Penny?"

"She's booked to Heathrow tomorrow morning at nine. Four hundred dollars."

Dan opened his wallet and counted out ten one hundred-dollar bills, which Stapleton tucked into an envelope and put it in a manila folder. Then he stamped their passports with an official-looking seal. "You're done. Best of luck to both of you." He stood and shook their hands. "See the young lady outside. She'll give you your tickets."

"I can't believe it was that easy," Penny said as they made their way outside to meet up with Joseph.

They were both a bit dazed. Dan said, "Probably because they've been flooded with requests. I'm sure a lot of expats fled Uganda. It probably takes much longer if you're just some kid who ran out of money. Penny, I have to get ready to leave. Will you be all right?"

"You know I will. Now we have to go back so you can pack."

At the hotel Penny made a quick call to her mother to let her know she'd be on her way the next morning.

———

They said their farewells to Dan at the hotel. Joseph would drive him to the airport. Chrissie hugged him tightly as he spoke softly to her. She gave him a tearful smile and wished him well. When it was Penny's turn, she held out her hand to him. He disregarded it and wrapped his arms around her.

"Penny, it's been great knowing you. I'm going to miss you. You have our address. Please keep in touch."

"I promise I will. *We* will."

"Tell Nick thanks for the loan. Tell him I'll pay him back."

She ignored his words and held him close. "Go. I hate saying good-byes. Give my love to Emily and the kids. You're a lucky man."

33

CHRISSIE CAME WITH her to the airport. Joseph had appeared early to drive them there. If possible he was even more taciturn than usual. At the curb Joseph handed her bag to her and then stood impassively and watched her.

"Joseph, what will you do now?" Penny asked.

"I will return to Uganda. I have to help my people."

She struggled to find the right words to say to the proud man standing before her. Finally she said, "I am so grateful for everything you have done for me—for all of us. I'll never forget you, Joseph. Thank you. Stay safe."

He bowed his head slightly. "It has been my honor, Doctor Penny. I will think of you often." Then he turned to Chrissie. "I will wait for you here, *Sista*, and drive you back. Then I will leave the car with you."

He turned away from them. The conversation was over.

Chrissie walked to the departure gate with her and chattered in an attempt to keep the mood light. "Now don't worry about Joseph. I'll give him the money as we agreed. You have Alan's address. We'll be getting married as soon as possible. I'm sorry you won't be here for the wedding. Please let me know what's going on with you, and give my best to Nick when you see him. Oh dear. We're all scattering to the winds, aren't we? Dammit. I didn't want to cry. I'll leave you now. Be happy, girl."

Penny found a seat and collapsed miserably into it to wait for her plane to be announced. *Jesus!* Her emotions were all over the

KISIMBA

place again. A harried-looking young white woman walked by and dropped her bag on the seat next to her. She was obviously pregnant. Penny guessed about twenty-four weeks. She was carrying an infant in one arm while she dragged a toddler behind her. She looked around helplessly and then focused on Penny.

"Miss?" she said tentatively. "Please could you help me? I need to change Donnie here, and I can't just put the baby on the floor."

"No problem," Penny said. "I'll hold him for you."

She cuddled the sleeping infant in her arms. Then it was time to leave Africa.

34

T HEY LANDED AT Heathrow in a torrential rain. She shivered in the bitter cold as they disembarked. It was only a short walk to the arrival gate, but by the time she got inside, she was cold and sopping wet in her thin cotton dress. *Why on earth didn't I think to bring a jacket?*

"Penny! Penny! Over here!"

She looked over the crowd awaiting their families and friends and was delighted to see Liz bouncing up and down and waving to her. Her roommate's greeting was typical. "God! You look like a drowned rat! What happened to all your clothes? It's still winter here, in case you'd forgotten. Here. Take my jacket. I've got a jumper on underneath."

"Nice to see you too, Liz. Thanks. How did you know I'd be coming in?"

"Your mum called me. Now let's get your luggage, go to a bar, and get you dry before we take the train back to London. Come on. Get your behind in gear!"

Penny suddenly realized Liz had a lot in common with Chrissie. They would have probably fought like crazy women. They ended up spending more than an hour in the warm, smoky bar. They drank wine and caught up with their news. Liz and Diane had had a good time in Canada. They had also had a lot of time off, which they had used to study for finals as well as play. Not having seriously cracked the books for months, Penny felt a twinge of panic.

KISIMBA

Then Liz turned her razor-sharp attention on her. "You look different. What's going on?"

"I haven't had a haircut for ages, and I got a bit of a tan. That's all."

"No. It's more than that. For one thing you've lost a lot of weight. Have you been sick? You look healthy, even if you are thin. And you look…I dunno. Older somehow."

"Well, thanks a lot! Older? What on earth are you talking about?"

"Keep your hair on. 'Older' was the wrong word. More mature, maybe. Less girlie."

"Give over. I'd smack you if I wasn't so tired. Can we go home now please?" The idea of their flat was suddenly very appealing.

"In a minute. I've got some extra cash. I'll spring for a taxi. It'll be quicker. Hmm. Did you meet anyone interesting over there?"

"I met lots of interesting people. Don't you want to hear about the hospital and the patients I saw?"

"OK. You're blushing. Am I good, or am I good?"

"You're impossible. That's what."

She sighed. Liz was relentless when she fixed on something. She was going to be a terrific diagnostician. During the taxi ride home, which took nearly an hour, Liz grilled her mercilessly. She finally divulged a little information about Nick.

"Thirty-two? Is he married? All the best ones are at that age." There were echoes of Chrissie again. "Did you sleep with him? Do you have a photo of him?"

"Liz! What a thing to ask. But yes. I have a few snaps. I have to get them developed."

"OK. I get it. Hope I get to meet him someday." Then she turned serious and added, "I really do want to hear how you got out of Uganda. I was worried sick about you. I've been following the news, and it's getting worse over there every day." After a pause she continued. "You have a few days to relax, but you'll have to check back in by Friday. They've rearranged our pediatric rotations. *Again*. You'll be

— 231 —

going to Canterbury with Diane next Monday. I'm stuck in London, but at least I'll be able to sleep in my own bed. You'll be in some god-awful residency house for three weeks."

Penny's heart sank. She really didn't feel like any more traveling for a while. *Oh well*, she thought. *Shit happens.* She paused. *Oh. Now I'm even thinking like Nick.* She took a much-needed bath and fell gratefully into bed. From across the room, Liz continued to chatter until Penny drifted off into sleep.

She awoke to the burbling sounds of the radiator kicking in. It was another cold, rainy day. Bundling herself into a thick robe, she found she was already missing the warm Ugandan climate. The house was quiet. Liz and Diane were long gone, and Marie, their nurse flatmate, was ensconced in her little room with a large "Do Not Disturb" notice stuck to the door. She was obviously still working nights.

Penny made herself a cup of instant coffee and ate a bowl of cereal while standing at the sink and trying to figure out what to do with her day. The first priority was to get out her winter clothes and check them for moth holes. Then she had to make a trek to the Laundromat. Since she had brought so little back with her, that wouldn't take long. *I should buckle down and begin studying. Maybe tomorrow.*

She paced the small kitchen restlessly. A call to her mum and dad was in order to let them know she was back in England in one piece, but they'd both be at work. She'd do that this evening. Then there were the rolls of film to develop. That thought perked her up a bit. She was looking forward to having some pictures of Nick. *Nick!* She'd call his parents in Seattle and find out if they had any news of him.

She found the card with their number on it and hurried to the telephone in the sitting room. Then she hesitated at the thought of calling complete strangers living thousands of miles away. They would probably hang up on her. She mentally rehearsed what she was going to say and then determinedly called the overseas operator. The call went straight through. This took her by surprise. She was used to the long waits for connections in Uganda.

A man with a brusque voice answered the phone. "Sottile residence."

Penny's mouth was suddenly dry. "Hello? Is this Mr. Sottile?"

"Yes. May I ask who's calling at this hour?"

"This is Penelope Drayton in London. I met your son in Uganda. Oh dear. I have no idea what time it is over there. I hope I didn't wake you."

"Penny? Don't worry about it. Nick did tell us you would be calling." His voice faded as he spoke to someone who must have been standing beside him. Then he said, "Are you still there, Penny? Nick's mother wants to talk to you."

The woman sounded quite excited. "Hi, Penny. This is Louisa Sottile. I'm so glad you called. How are you? Where are you calling from?"

"I'm well. Thank you, Mrs. Sottile. I'm sorry it's so late. I was hoping you could tell Nick I'm back in London. Have you spoken to him since all the trouble started? Is he OK?"

"He called yesterday from a place called Jinja. The line was terrible, and we didn't have long to talk. He said he was on his way to Kampala. He also asked me to send you his love if you called. He told me about you weeks ago, Penny. I am so looking forward to meeting you."

She suddenly felt lighter than air. "Me too, Mrs. Sottile. Do you mind if I ring you again for news?"

"Of course not, honey. Please give me your number too."

She dictated it and then said, "Well, I'd better let you go now, Mrs. Sottile."

"Please call me Louisa. Good night, Penny."

— 233 —

Suddenly filled with energy, she raced around in the rain doing her small chores. While she was waiting for her clothes to finish drying, she popped in to a small hairdressing place next door. They managed to fit her in, and on Penny's firm instructions, the hairdresser, who seemed rather unhappy, lopped off several inches of curls.

On her way home, she picked up a bottle of wine and some cheese to go with dinner. Back in the flat, she examined her small selection of winter clothes and was surprised and a little miffed to find all her skirts were very loose. A female student was required to wear a white coat, skirt, blouse, and stockings in the hospital, unless she was in surgery. She sighed when she realized she had no presentable hose and thought wistfully of how easy it had been to wear scrubs and go bare legged all day at Kisimba. She'd have to go shopping again. She also had to deposit what was left of Nick's money in the bank. She certainly didn't want all that cash lying around.

She set off once more for the small shopping area near the flat. The rain had turned into an icy drizzle. She stopped first at her bank and cashed her remaining thirty pounds in traveler's checks. Then she waited until someone was free to open a new account for her. The assistant manager raised his eyebrows when he saw the pile of one hundred-dollar bills but didn't ask any questions. She had to wait while he confirmed the current rate of exchange, and she was surprised at the much smaller number of pounds the dollars would buy. Her own balance was getting fairly low. She'd have to watch her spending, or she'd end up borrowing from her parents again. At least in a few months she would be finally earning a salary as a house officer. That was assuming she passed her final exams.

With her financial business complete, she headed for the supermarket where she bought a couple pairs of hose and a tired-looking Scotch egg for lunch. On her way back, she passed a clothing store she knew carried inexpensive items, and she stopped when she saw a large "sale" sign in the window. Rationalizing that she definitely needed some new clothes, she went in and looked through the skirts.

The only one she found that she liked was a straight, black skirt that hit the middle of her calf. It fit perfectly. She wouldn't be able to wear it at the hospital, but it was a steal at two pounds, so she bought it.

Back home again she was startled to realize the morning had flown by, and she was hungry and very tired. The jet lag was beginning to get to her. She quickly ate her egg and went back to bed.

35

DIANE AND PENNY caught a fast train to Canterbury on Monday morning. Diane was full of questions about Hope Hospital and the patients she had seen there. Diane was the complete opposite of Liz. She avoided parties and spent most weekends with her family who lived just outside London. She was more interested in Penny's work than her love life. She was clearly envious Penny had been given so much responsibility and couldn't believe she had become skilled with ether anesthesia. "Not that you'll ever use it again," she said, "but still."

She was also impressed Penny had taken over the running of the lab. Then she said, "I hope you've written all this down."

"No. Why?"

"You'll forget it if you don't. You should make a start on it soon."

The idea had a certain appeal. They had brought lots of textbooks with them so they could study if they had time, but writing a journal of her (medical) experiences in Africa would be fun.

The three weeks spent in Canterbury were torture for Penny. She quickly found out hospital pediatrics was not for her. Most of the inpatient children were really sick or dying of horrible diseases, and every night she went back to the student residency house feeling depressed. She and Diane dutifully attended ward rounds and outpatient clinics, but they weren't permitted to do anything meaningful, so they had quite a lot of free time. They visited the cathedral and walked around the town, but there was really nothing else to do. Penny finally got out the books and began studying in earnest for her finals.

She also spent some time scanning the major papers for news from Uganda. Her heart sank when she learned the first two casualties of the coup had been two Catholic priests at Entebbe as they were waiting for their flight home. The army had taken over the airport and imposed a curfew in Kampala at night. Thousands of people had been rounded up and executed in the first days of the new regime. That included hundreds of soldiers thought to have been supporters of Obote. The horrific accounts she read of the mass murders and other atrocities sickened her.

She was outraged to read in the early news reports that Britain had formally recognized the new government and its president. *What the hell?* However, it soon became clear Amin was going to rule as an absolute dictator. He suspended all elections, and he and his cronies started running everything themselves. The civilian population was in a constant state of fear of the army troops and the special security forces Amin had quickly created. Many people were taken from their homes and never seen again or just shot in front of their families. Some villages had been burned to the ground, but she couldn't determine which ones. There were stories in which the corpses were thrown into the Nile River every night for crocodiles to eat. The special forces targeted the general population as well as teachers, doctors, nurses, priests, and journalists—many of whom were foreign.

She feared so much for the fates of Joseph, Margaret, and the others. She realized sadly she would probably never know what had happened to them. At least Entebbe International Airport had reopened, so there was hope Nick and the Campbells were safe.

Liz was in the kitchen when Penny and Diane walked in the door of their flat.

"Penny, a letter arrived for you today. From *America*!"

From her tone one would think it had been sent from Saturn. Penny grabbed it and retired to her room to read it in privacy.

My darling Penny,

I suspected as much. You've been abducted by aliens. I hope you have been returned in one piece.

I'm back in the States. I'm in Florida—at least for a while. I've been trying to get through to you for many, many days at the number you gave me. Finally, last week someone named Marie answered and grudgingly informed me you are some place called Canterbury. I bought a guide to England and determined it has a cathedral but not much else. What on earth are you doing there? I should have known you would take off to parts unknown. At least it's in England, according to the guide book anyway.

Please call my mom again as soon as you get this. She told me she likes you just from talking to you. Let her know where you are. I'll be moving around again soon, so I can't give you a direct number.

All my love,

Nick

Penny read and reread the letter, and her heart burst with joy. He had made it out of Africa! He was safe! She ran into the kitchen. "We're celebrating tonight!"

Liz said, "I take it your Nick is back in America. Thank God. You've been driving everyone nuts! Now you can settle down and concentrate on passing finals. Meanwhile, I have a bottle of wine waiting and ready to go!"

KISIMBA

Between doing her next rotation in anesthesia and reading textbooks every night until she thought her eyes would bleed, the time passed quickly. She thoroughly enjoyed the rotation. It was conducted mostly under the watchful eye of a senior registrar who was very interested to hear of her experiences with ether in Uganda. They worked primarily with two surgical teams of doctors and house staff. She already knew most of them. This included one senior houseman whom she had dated briefly. Alex had tousled blond hair and very blue eyes. All the women agreed he was exceptionally handsome, and he knew it. He had a reputation for his pursuit of female companionship, and Penny had heard he'd been caught sneaking out of the nurses' residence building one night. She regretted she had ever gone out with him—especially that she had gone to bed with him on one very unsatisfactory occasion. He had quickly moved on once that had been accomplished. She couldn't for the life of her remember what she had ever seen in him.

One afternoon during a tea break between cases, he cornered her and looked her up and down with his famous smile. "Penny, I've been meaning to say how marvelous it is to see you again."

Right! "Hello, Alex. How are you?" she asked politely.

"Fantastic. Thanks. I've been offered a surgical registrar position here, so I'm on my way to success. Listen, I can't believe how different you look. You're so...slender. I think we should get together again sometime. I'll call you."

"No. Thank you. I'm studying for finals, so I don't have any free time. Now excuse me, but I need to visit the loo before we start the next case."

She walked away and clamped her mouth shut to prevent the escape of a few choice words such as "arsehole."

As much as she liked giving anesthesia, she found she really wanted to get her hands on a surgical case again. She tried to imagine

— 239 —

becoming a surgeon one day but realized regretfully that would be unlikely. There were very few females in any field of surgery, except perhaps gynecology, and it was a popular choice with her male classmates. She had enjoyed being one of very few women in her class but was now seeing the disadvantages of it.

Her last rotation was another in internal medicine. She breezed through it, even though the hours were tough, and she had to spend one night a week on call in the hospital. She was pleased to discover she had actually learned a great deal on the vast subject, which calmed her nerves about the rapidly approaching examinations.

Like an express train out of control, the first day of finals was then upon them. She would spend the week taking written tests in medicine, surgery, obstetrics, and gynecology. Friday would be free, and then the exams would continue over the following week. The tests in medicine would include everything from cardiology to psychiatry, and the surgery exams would be just as bad. Questions would range from urology and orthopedics to abdominal and cardiac surgery. They would have four hours in the morning and another four each afternoon to write answers in essay form.

They stood amid a throng of students and waited for the doors to the huge testing room to open. They listened to the nervous chatter. Some students were convinced the more pages one wrote, the higher the grade would be. Penny, Diane, and Liz had decided to use a different technique—write quickly but legibly and underline key words in red ink. They hoped the examiners would tire of plowing through so many papers and concentrate on finding the important stuff.

The doors opened promptly at eight o'clock. They took their seats under the watchful eyes of several proctors. A test booklet and a notebook for answers were on each desk. Once all students were seated, the dean of their school strode in and greeted them cheerfully. He was a handsome, down-to-earth man—a dermatologist by specialty. "I fully expect you will all excel in these examinations of everything you have learned in the last four years. Now settle down and take a few deep breaths. You may begin."

Penny carefully wrote her name on the answer book and opened the test. There were six questions. *OK. About forty minutes per...make that thirty-five. That way I'll be able to look over my essays at the end.* She jotted down the times by each question so she could keep track and read the first one. She nearly laughed aloud. "Describe the etiologic agents, presentation, clinical course, complications, and treatment of malaria. Discuss the problems of and solutions to treatment in areas of limited access to modern care. Include pertinent, recent research and findings."

She speedily polished that one off. The next one made her groan. "Discuss the diagnosis and management of schizophrenia." She racked her brain to come up with enough impressive jargon to fill her answer.

Some questions were very straightforward. Others were less so. The worst at first sight was a bit odd. "Compare the renal function of humans and the desert rat. Discuss how a chronic glomerulone-phritis would impact each of these species." *Who the heck comes up with these things?* She decided to concentrate on writing a thorough treatise on kidney failure.

Fifteen minutes before noon, she was reading her responses and adding a few more red underlines. Then it was over. The three flat-mates rushed to their lockers to get the sandwiches they had made for lunch. They had to start again at one o'clock. As they chewed and sat on the floor in the hallway—all the chairs had been taken—Diane said, "You lucked out on that malaria question, Penny. You came down with it in Africa, didn't you?"

Penny smiled as she remembered waking from her delirium to find Nick sitting on her bed. "Yes. That was lucky," she said. *In more ways than one.*

They chatted some more about the test. The "rat question" had baffled them all. Then it was time to take a pee and start again. By four o'clock they were drained, and they caught the bus to go home. *At least the first day is over.*

By comparison Penny found the last three days of written tests fairly easy. Although, she was too nervous to take anything for granted. They still had the second week of exams coming up. They all slept in late on Friday and then spent the day with mundane tasks they had ignored during the week. After supper Diane announced in a tone that brooked no argument that she was going to bed. Penny was tired, but when Liz suggested they should pop down to the pub for a quick drink, she agreed. She needed to get out and think about something else. On a whim she put on her new skirt and paired it with a silky ivory blouse she had had for years.

They walked to the pub only a few streets away. It was a popular haunt of students and doctors who lived in the area. Penny groaned when she saw Alex sitting with two young women at a corner table.

"What's up?" Liz asked, and then she followed her line of sight. "Oh, Mr. Macho. He hasn't been bothering you, has he? Just ignore the creep. He seems to have both hands full anyway."

Penny laughed and noticed three girls from their class at a corner table. "Look who's over there. Let's join them."

They settled in, and the conversation inevitably turned to discussion of the week's exams. She was beginning to wish she hadn't left the peace and quiet of the flat. She wanted to let her mind go blank until she started to prepare for the upcoming week of torture. Then she felt a hand on her shoulder and looked up. *Damn!* It was Alex.

"Evening, ladies." He swept his eyes over them. "Is it all right if I take Penny away for a minute or two? Penny?"

He held out his hand, which Penny ignored.

Liz said sharply, "Buzz off, Alex. We're busy."

"I'm so sorry. I wouldn't have interrupted, but this is important."

Penny looked over at Liz and shrugged. "OK. Just for a minute."

As she rose from the table, Alex caught her hand and drew her to the opposite end of the pub into the corridor leading to the bathrooms.

"What's so important then?" she asked.

"This is," he murmured throatily, and he pulled her into his arms. "You are hard to find these days."

"I'm in the middle of exams. What did you expect? Anyway, I told you I'm not interested."

He tightened his hold. "I know when no means yes," he said softly, and he bent his head to kiss her. One hand began easing up her skirt.

"Let me go, you twit! Get your hands off me."

She knew she was OK in the crowded pub, even if Nick wasn't on hand to rescue her. *What would he do?*

She gave him a level look. "You really don't want to do this, Alex."

"Oh no? Watch me."

So that didn't work. She turned slowly in his arms so she was leaning against him. He pushed his erection against her back, and she said in as sultry a voice as she could muster, "OK, sweetie. How about *this*?"

She lifted her high heel and stomped down hard on his instep. He yelled out in pain and outrage, and she returned to her friends. She was so ticked she didn't immediately register the applause that greeted her. Obviously Alex's antics had not gone unnoticed.

"Well done, girl," said Liz. "Do you want to go home?"

"No way. Why the hell should I? We don't have to get up at dawn tomorrow."

It was a most satisfactory end to the week.

36

THE SECOND WEEK of testing was nowhere near as strenuous. There was, however, a certain amount of travel involved. They were all assigned to medical school hospitals throughout the city, other than their own. Some students from other schools in the University of London system had to go to theirs. Since they were all taking the same tests, the switch was deemed necessary to avoid the possibility that a student would have the advantage of knowing a particular patient. Sending the students out to unfamiliar schools also ensured unfamiliar faculty examined them. It all seemed a lot of hassle, but they agreed it was probably fair. Penny set off with her A–Z map of the London streets in hand to a hospital on the other side of the city, while Liz and Diane were both headed for another.

Monday morning consisted of "spot diagnoses." The students lined up in several rows outside a large room filled with people who were sitting around the edge of the room talking to each other, drinking tea, and eating pastries. There was an almost festive air to the scene. Penny knew these were patients with chronic diseases who came back year after year to participate in the fun in exchange for refreshments and a small monetary compensation. They were all holding signs with numbers on them. When the students entered the room, they were directed to particular patients. Then they waited for examiners to join them.

Penny scanned the motley collection of volunteers as she headed for number fourteen, a forty-plus woman with a cheerful smile. Her examiner joined her quickly and introduced himself as Dr. Pinder. He was a pleasant young man who reminded her of Dan. He told her to examine the patient's hands and asked for her diagnosis.

"I believe this patient has rheumatoid arthritis."

"You are correct. Thank you, Mrs. Reed. Let's move on."

Penny nodded her thanks to the lady and walked to the next patient with the doctor. He asked the man to stand up. She immediately noted his limbs were very short, but his head and torso were of normal size. He obviously had achondroplasia, a form of dwarfism.

Dr. Pinder said, "Good morning, Mr. Bryant. Would you like to ask this candidate your favorite question?"

"Yeah, Doc. OK, lass. If I were a dog, what would I be?"

She looked at him blankly.

"Come on, love. Don't be shy to tell us."

Think. Short limbs. Normal size torso and head.

"A dachshund?" she said tentatively.

"Good on yer, girl. You got yourself a smart one 'ere, Doc," he said and laughed.

As they moved away, Dr. Pinder said, "OK. Let's find someone a bit more challenging for you."

The next two were indeed tricky. Both had heart murmurs, and the second was presented with an electrocardiogram to assist her. She apparently made the correct diagnoses because they moved on without further comment. After several more easy ones, her examiner looked at his watch and said, "One more. Over here. Mrs. Braithwaite, this student is going to examine you. Is that OK? Are you getting tired?"

"No, Doctor," she said.

Her mouth barely moved. Penny looked at her face without touching for a while. She was very pale, and her skin was smooth. However, her mouth was partly open, and she seemed to be having some difficulty breathing.

"May I see your hands, Mrs. Braithwaite?"

The lady held them out, and Penny took them gently in her own. The skin was cold and felt like marble. She struggled to find the name of the disease. It was really rare. "Thank you," she said and turned away to walk a few paces from the patient.

"Well?" her interrogator asked with interest.

"I believe it's scleroderma, but I've never seen a patient with it before."

She was trying to contain an excitement she knew was totally inappropriate under the circumstances.

"Glad we could be of assistance." Dr. Pinder smiled as he shook her hand. "You did well. Best of luck with the rest of the week."

———

Penny left the building in high spirits. She had ample time for lunch before the next ordeal, so she walked away from the hospital and found a café where she ordered a turkey and cheese sandwich and a coffee. She sat back to relax. That proved impossible, and as soon as she had eaten, she decided the best thing was to walk off the adrenaline rush. She arrived back at the unfamiliar hospital a few minutes before one o'clock.

The schedule for the afternoon included two inpatients whom she would examine and then discuss with an examiner. Her first patient was a relatively simple case of emphysema. The second one completely threw her for a loop. She met her examiner outside the cubicle. He didn't look at her but consulted a chart and said, "Proceed."

She took a breath and tried to make the best of it. "This patient is a fifty-nine-year-old woman. She is well nourished and in no acute distress. Her presenting complaint is..." She swallowed hard. "Nothing. She also denied any symptoms pertaining to all her systems. Unfortunately she declined to be examined." The doctor was still studying the chart he held and was expressionless. "Purely on observation I determined her speech was slow, and she appeared to have a swelling in her neck. Her demeanor is impassive. Her eyebrows are sparse. I apologize, Doctor."

He finally looked at her. "OK. Let's go back in there."

He stood by the patient's bed and said, "Mrs. Johnson? It's Dr. Boone. How are you feeling?"

"I'm fine, Doctor. Just a little weary."

"OK, We'll let you rest now. By the way, what did you think of this young lady here? Was she nice to you?"

"Yes, Doctor. She was really kind."

Her eyes drifted closed, and Penny and the examiner slipped outside again.

"I take it from your presentation you think she might have a thyroid dysfunction."

"Yes, Doctor."

"Well, she doesn't. But that wasn't the point. The most important thing was you interacted with the patient well. Thank you. You may go."

Still unsure of the outcome of the test, she left the hospital and headed back to the apartment.

———

Everyone was rather subdued at dinner that night. None felt they had performed adequately. Then Liz recounted how one male student had been summarily removed for sitting on the bed of an attractive young female patient, which lightened the mood. The next day involved examination of a pregnant patient in the morning followed by an oral exam in both obstetrics and gynecology in the afternoon. This time all three had been assigned to different hospitals. They went to bed early.

When she entered the room of her patient the next morning, Penny was feeling more confident. The first whispered words out of the patient's mouth were, "I'm having twins!"

She suppressed a smile as she took a detailed history and examined the patient. She was in her element here. They finished well within the hour allowed and sat chatting while they waited for the examiner. When he arrived he said dryly, "Sorry to interrupt, ladies. Miss Drayton, please present your patient."

The afternoon orals went without a hitch. Both examiners seemed rather mellow after their lunch and asked simple questions. She found she was quite disappointed. *Oh well.*

Wednesday was also uneventful. It consisted of oral exams in medicine both in the morning and afternoon. Then disaster struck on Thursday.

The two examiners in surgery were both gray-haired and formidable. They seemed to be looking at her rather disapprovingly as she sat across from them. Dispensing with niceties, one of them selected a big glass jar from a table behind him and asked, "What is your diagnosis?"

She peered through the murky yellow fluid at the large chunk of tissue inside. It looked at least a hundred years old.

"This is a section of intestine, sir."

He turned to the man beside him. "We have a genius here. Continue."

"I'm sorry. I have no idea," Penny said. Her heart was in her mouth. She was seeing all her dreams slip away.

He said irritably, "Come on, young lady. At least tell us which part of the intestine we are looking at."

From there it went from bad to worse. Finally her tormentor lost interest and waved his hand at his colleague to continue the interrogation. The second examiner folded his hands as though in prayer and brought the fingertips to his mouth as he studied her. "How would you approach a case of an acute splenic rupture?"

She relaxed a little. She could do this. As she spoke of the presentation and surgical intervention required, the examiner interrupted, "What if you don't have enough units of blood on hand?"

— 248 —

Thank you, Jesus. "Well, I would order plasma at the very least. As a last resort, one could perform autotransfusion."

They both became alert. "And what would you know about that, may I ask?"

She replied boldly. "I have performed the procedure in just such an emergency during my elective in Africa."

They were all ears. She described in detail the case of the boy who fell out of the tree, the surgery, the unusual transfusion, and the patient's subsequent uneventful recovery. Then she discussed the attendant risks as she had with Dan, and she sat back to await a further onslaught.

The first examiner said dourly, "Well, Miss Drayton, you might have just redeemed yourself. You may go."

Her possible reprieve alleviated her worry a little. She thanked them and slipped out of the hospital before anyone could stop her. She quickly packed a bag and said good-bye to Diane, who was the only one in the quiet flat. Their exam results wouldn't be out for at least a week, and she had decided to spend the intervening time with her family.

37

S HE HAD A restful trip to the Yorkshire Dales. It was made even better by the fact her mother had taken the week off from her work to spend it with her. They had long talks in the garden at the back of the small bungalow. Mostly they talked about Nick as her mother puffed on cigarettes. Penny indulged in one or two herself. She gave a carefully censored version of their meeting and courtship, which made her mum romantically misty-eyed. Although, a couple times Penny felt her shrewdly appraising her and realized her mother was probably not as innocent as she seemed. She also told her about the other people she had met and worked with and the marvelous experiences she had had in the hospital. She omitted the awful confrontations with the police and the army. Her mother didn't need to know about those.

Inevitably the conversations came back around to Nick. One evening they sat together and sipped sherry. (Every time the bottle appeared, Penny thought of Mother Mary Agnes.) While they waited for her dad to come home for supper, her mother said, "Penny, pet, you're a grown woman, but I have to say something. Your Nick sounds wonderful, but you haven't really spent that much time with him. Are you absolutely sure you want to marry him?"

"Yes, Mummy. He's the one. I want to spend the rest of my life with him. I don't know what I'll do if we don't find each other again."

"That's good enough for me. Let's hope that happens…and soon. Now let's go and set the table. I hear the car."

She also spent some one-on-one time with her father. He tried to teach her some of the finer points of the photographic arts with limited success. Both parents had studied the pictures of Nick with interest. Her mum seemed very taken with his appearance—especially in one photograph where he was smiling into the camera with the Owens Falls behind him.

Her dad made a disapproving sound and then proceeded to chastise her on the folly of taking thirty-two photographs of sunsets. The only picture he really approved of was one she had taken of the Narimembe Cathedral in Kampala. He praised the composition and the use of light. She hadn't the heart to tell him it was just a quick snapshot she had taken without any particular care. However, since she had the negatives with her, he selected a few photographs, and together they set up a temporary darkroom in the cellar as they had when she was a kid. They played with various methods of printing until he was satisfied with the results. She had to admit they made a marked improvement.

All in all it was a splendid visit, and she enjoyed having her mum fuss over her and make her favorite meals. They went grocery shopping together, and one day they took the bus into Leeds and got her some new clothes. They visited Penny's two godmothers, and she also met up with an old friend from high school who had become a teacher.

When she arrived back at the flat, Liz and Diane greeted her with excitement. The exam results had arrived in the mail. Both women had passed. Diane had received a commendation in medicine. Liz handed Penny her letter, and she took it with trepidation.

"I'm too nervous to open it," she finally said. "Here. One of you do it."

Penny turned away and crossed her fingers. Liz shrieked, "Yes! You passed. And you got a commendation in obstetrics!"

They danced around the kitchen in delight. Now all they had to do was confirm their house jobs. Liz had been approved for a position in medicine at their hospital and Diane for one in Surrey close to her parents' home. Penny had been accepted at their sister hospital in South London, Saint Luke's, for a position in surgery. They were due to begin in two weeks.

As the knowledge of the impending changes in their lives sank in, they calmed down and began to make their plans. First they had to assign their shares of the apartment lease to other students. That wouldn't be a problem. Affordable housing was relatively scarce. Then they had to pack up their belongings and prepare for their moves to the doctors' residences of their respective hospitals. By common consent they decided to forego attendance at graduation. By all accounts it was a ghastly affair that took hours. The total graduating class for the university numbered in the many thousands. In the meantime, though, they were going to let their hair down for at least that night and celebrate.

The day before they went their separate ways, a letter arrived from America.

> Atlanta, Georgia
> Dearest Penny,
> You are driving me crazy. I may not survive this unending search for your whereabouts. My mother tells me you are done with your finals and are waiting for your results. She also gave me the letter you wrote two weeks ago, which brought me back from the brink. Thank you. In the meantime you have again taken off—this time to visit your parents. This is, of course, understandable. However, by the time I got this news, you were gone from their home and on the move again. There was no answer when I called your apartment. I can

only pray that either you tell *someone* where you are or, at the very least, you have mail forwarding in England.

However, I'm not really complaining…much. After all, I've been moving around a lot myself. I'm currently in Atlanta for a few days and then possibly off to New York, but I don't know for certain yet. We'll figure it out eventually. All I know is I miss you and want to be with you again.

Darling girl, I long for you more with every passing day, if that is possible.

(A detailed description of his intentions followed and brought a fiery blush to her cheeks and nearly stopped her heart.)

Until then I'll wait as patiently as I can. I will love you always.

Nick

———

Eager to begin her new life as a real doctor, Penny arrived at Saint Luke's Hospital two days before her official start date. She wanted to settle in to the residence and find her feet. They had also turned in their apartment keys, and she had to sleep somewhere. The three women parted sadly with many promises of keeping up with each other. She knew they would. They had lived together for four years and had become as close as sisters.

She climbed off the bus at a stop conveniently positioned outside the large wrought-iron gates of the hospital. She had performed several of her rotations at Saint Luke's, which belonged to her medical school hospital a few miles down the road. It was a small complex of handsome Victorian buildings set back from the road and surrounded by several acres of mature sycamore trees. The red brick glowed in the sunshine. Welsh slate comprised the roofs, and intricate, cream-painted dentil molding laced the eaves. Small towers with steeply pitched roofs provided perches for the ubiquitous pigeons. Carved frames surrounded tall windows. These were also painted cream. She loved the place and hoped to stay there for the next house officer position after this one.

The wards were located in two buildings at the rear of the complex and had long covered porches overlooking the parkland behind them. Those patients who could walk or could be taken outside in wheelchairs loved to congregate there when the weather was clement. They were also permitted to smoke there, unless it was medically forbidden, which was mostly the case.

The hospital itself had a long and varied history. Built in the late nineteenth century as a workhouse infirmary, the army commandeered it soon after the onset of World War I. Thousands of soldiers, including some American troops, had passed through those gates. Once the war had ended, Saint Luke's became known as a "fever hospital" because many patients with tuberculosis were treated there. The porches had been added to the wards in order to afford the patients the healing benefits of fresh air. Fortunately it survived World War II with only minor bomb damage, and no one was killed. After that war was won, it was converted to a general hospital.

Penny stopped by the porter's lodge—a small building just inside the gates. The day porter, Albert, set down his paper and came to the door with his hand outstretched. "Penny, love! It's good to have you back. I suppose I'll have to call you Doctor Drayton now. Congratulations. I knew you'd get there."

She smiled into his twinkling eyes. He was in his sixties with a comfortable paunch and a deep, calm voice that would have been ideally suited to a late-night radio music host. "Hello, Albert. It's great to be back. And you must please still call me Penny."

"You're on, ducks—except when the boss is around."

They both knew he was referring to the hospital matron, a fierce woman who took no guff from anyone and especially doctors.

"Here's your keys," Albert said. "This one's to the front door of the residence. The other is your room key. You're in a quiet room at the back on the second floor. Very nice view it has. And this 'ere's your pager. Don't turn it on till you start. Time enough for all that. You don't have a car, do you? No? That's good. We're a bit tight for parking right now."

"Thanks, Albert. Is Maude still running the dining room?"

"That she is. I know she'll have you fattened up in no time. You're all skin and bones! You're not sick, are you? Do you need any 'elp with them bags?"

"I'm very well. Thanks. Don't worry. OK. I'll be off then. I'll see you later."

Penny was smiling as she sought out her room. It felt like coming home again. She was very pleased with her new accommodation. It was spacious with a big window looking out over trees, grass, and a small pond. In addition to a single bed—already made up— there was a decent-size closet for clothes, a small chest of drawers, a bedside table, and a desk and chair under the window. A sink stood against one wall. Towels were provided. She felt as though she had fallen into the lap of luxury. She dropped her bags on the bed and wandered out into the hall. The women's bathroom and shower were conveniently next door, and a telephone hung on the wall halfway down the corridor. Above the phone was a large loudspeaker connected to the hospital public address system.

As she sat on the bed and tried to decide if she should start unpacking, her stomach let out an anxious growl. She checked her watch and realized it was time for lunch, and she didn't want to miss it. She quickly took out her framed photograph of Nick, positioned it carefully by her bed, and placed her small carving of the African woman on the desk. Then she headed out again.

There was quite a crowd of doctors and students in the dining room. In addition to the tables, there was a fair-size sitting area with a large television against the wall next to a keg of beer and a small refrigerator. She had forgotten that little detail. *How civilized.* Calls of welcome greeted her, and she chose a seat next to some people who had been in the class above her. She noticed she was the only female in the room. A stocky man with a shock of red hair got up from his table and came over. "You must be Penny Drayton. I'm Paul Padgett, one of the surgery registrars here. We'll be working together quite a lot. I hope you're ready for the fray."

He had a soft Welsh inflection to his voice but a no-nonsense manner. She stood to shake his hand.

"Well, I'll let you eat," he said. "I'll be seeing you."

"Thank you. I'm looking forward to it."

A very large woman wearing an apron and a tight gray permanent wave bustled at top speed over to her table. It was Maude, one of her favorite people in the world. "Is that my Penny?" she said. "Penny, love, come give me a hug. So you're a doctor now! You must be starving. What's the matter with you? You're so thin! What can I get for you?"

"Hello, Maude. How are you? I'll have to tell you all about my adventures once I've eaten. What's for lunch?"

Lowering her voice to a conspiratorial whisper, Maude said, "You don't want it, deary. They sent over liver and onions, and I don't like the look of it, to tell you God's honest truth. I don't know why this lot..." She waved expansively. "I don't know why they eat that rubbish. How about I make you a nice Welsh rabbit with some fried potatoes?"

"That sounds fabulous. Won't the others object?"

"Tough," Maude said. "This is your first day. I'm going to feed you proper. Sit!"

As she ate Penny ignored the envious looks she got from her lunch companions. Happily stuffed she sat back and tried to decide what to do with her afternoon. If she needed to buy anything, she would have to do it that day. The next day was Sunday, and most stores would be closed. She couldn't really think of anything apart from toiletries. All her meals would be taken under the maternal eye of Maude, and she didn't have to make a rent payment or cough up her share of electricity. She was beginning to feel quite affluent.

A dark-haired, earnest man sat down next to her. "Hi. Are you the new surgical houseman?"

"Yes. I'm Penny. Who are you?"

"The name's Mark. I'm a second-year registrar in medicine. I'm moving out tomorrow into married quarters." He blushed. It was quite endearing.

"Congrats," she said. "What can I do for you?"

"I was wondering if you'd like to buy a television. It's a black-and-white set and only two years old."

She envisioned herself on her time off watching a movie in the seclusion and comfort of her new room. "How much?" she asked cautiously.

"Ten quid. It cost fifty new," he added hastily. "And it has a sharp picture. Do you want to come check it out?"

"This isn't a version of 'come up and see my etchings,' is it?" His face reddened again, and she felt terrible. "I'm sorry. I was just teasing."

"You can't be too careful these days. So, do you want to see it?"

"Yes please. Let's go."

They walked back over to the residence. Mark was careful to leave the door to his room wide open. She made an instant decision and accepted the deal. He carried the TV up to her room, set it carefully on the desk, turned it on, and fiddled with the aerial. The picture was indeed crisp and the sound OK. She handed over ten pounds, which he accepted gratefully. On his way out he pointed to the picture of Nick. "Is that your boyfriend?" he asked.

"That's my fiancé, Nick," she said with a surge of pride.

She left the TV on while she unpacked. A silly sitcom was playing, and she listened with half an ear, and then the news came on. Images of carnage in Vietnam filled the small screen, and she watched for a few minutes. She was horrified thinking about what Nick had been through. She turned off the set. She didn't want thoughts of blood and death to plague her. There would be enough of that at work.

Two starched and crisply ironed white coats had been placed on her bed with a card informing her to leave her used coats by the door every Friday or earlier if they were too soiled. She tried one on and groaned. It was obviously made for a large male. It hung almost to her feet and fell in voluminous folds around her. She ran back to the dining room where Maude was clearing the tables.

"What on earth are you wearing, ducky? Oh, those idiot women in housekeeping. They think all the doctors are men. Leave it 'ere. I'll deal with it. We got to have you looking spiffy on Monday, don't we?"

"Thanks, Maude," she said in relief. She could just imagine the amusement her appearance would have caused on the wards. "I'm going out for a bit. Where's the nearest supermarket? I just realized I never looked around the area when I was on rotation here. Do I have to take a bus?"

"No, love. Just turn left outside and go down the road a bit. Maybe a half mile or so. There's a little shopping center on your right. It's got a post office an' all. Don't go to the butcher, though. He'll steal you blind. What am I saying? You don't need to buy yer food. I'll feed you what you like. Go have a brisk walk now. It'll settle yer lunch."

Penny set off into the sunny afternoon. She had high hopes for this house job. First, though, she had to buy some more airmail letters and write to Nick. After her quick stop at the post office, she passed a flower shop and on impulse bought a big bunch of dahlias for her room. In the supermarket she stocked up on personal necessities.

On her way back, she checked her watch. It would be a perfect time to call her mum and catch up. She also wanted to call the Sottiles in America. She had finally figured out that Seattle was eight hours

KISIMBA

behind London in time zones. *Uh-oh. Six in the morning over there.* She'd wait a few hours before she made that call. Mum first.

"Hello, Mummy. I'm all settled into the residence and thought I'd give you a call."

"How are you, pet? Listen, tell me again which hospital you're working in. Your young man keeps calling, and I never made a note of it."

"It's Saint Luke's, Mum. Did Nick leave a message for me?"

"Several. He asked me to write the last one down. Where did I put it? Hold on."

Penny waited anxiously and paced the length of the telephone cord up and down the hallway.

"Here it is, dear. Are you ready?"

"Yes, Mum." She wanted to shout "please get on with it" but restrained herself.

"Wait a minute. I can't find my glasses. Oh, here they are. I keep leaving them on top of my head. Maybe I should get one of those chains so I can hang them around my neck."

"Mummy, please read me the message."

"I'm getting there. It says, 'Please tell your lovely daughter that if she doesn't tell you—meaning me—where exactly she is these days, he will set the Secret Service on you—meaning you.' Hmm. That's a bit odd. Don't you think? What on earth did he mean?"

"I'll explain it another time." *Not likely!* "Was there anything else?"

"Let me see. Yes. He said to tell you he loves you more than life itself, and that if I'm anything at all like you, he can't wait to meet me." Penny smiled as her mother let loose a girlish giggle. "Now tell me about your job. Have they set you up in a comfy room?"

Relieved to be back in safer territory, she told her mother all about it and reassured her she was healthy, eating well, and happy. She ended with a promise to call in a week.

Later that afternoon she tried to call Nick's parents, but there was no answer. After a substantial dinner of shepherd's pie and peas, she went to bed. She was suddenly exhausted.

————

At one in the morning, the PA speaker in the hall woke her. "Code blue. Ward three. Code blue. Ward three. All available doctors respond please. Ward three."

She automatically stumbled out of bed, dragged on slacks and a T-shirt, and donned the ridiculous white coat. When she arrived at the scene, several people were already in the process of attempting to revive a man who had gone into cardiac arrest. She stood out of the way and waited to see if she might be needed. After about thirty minutes of heroic efforts, the registrar called a halt and wearily asked for the chart to note the time of death. It was Paul, the surgery registrar she'd met earlier. He looked over at her and did not immediately recognize her. Then he said brusquely, "Penny, what the hell are you doing here? You haven't even started yet."

"I heard the code and came out of reflex. Sorry."

"No problem. Sorry I snapped at you. That patient was going home tomorrow." He ran a hand over his face. "You want to get a coffee?"

"Sure. Why not?"

She knew what it was like to lose a patient. Someone to talk it out with helped. As they walked over to the nurses' dining room, which stayed open all night, he suddenly chuckled and asked, "What the heck are you wearing?"

38

PENNY HAD NEVER been so exhausted in her life. Her feet and back were killing her. Her call schedule during the week was one night on and one off with Sunday and Monday off on alternate weekends. Being on call at night meant she worked the entire day starting from seven in the morning. Then she worked the whole of that night and all of the following day. She rarely saw her counterpart, Joe. He was a flamboyant young man who had trained at Bart's Hospital. They were given two weeks of holiday time during the six months of their house job. This life certainly wasn't for sissies. Nevertheless, as far as she was concerned, a huge plus was that she got to wear scrubs all day and most nights.

There was no set routine. Theoretically she and Paul started the day with ward rounds, but they were often in surgery and had to fit in rounds when they could. Many patients were emergency cases. They were either referred from the main hospital or brought straight in by ambulance. It depended on how many beds they had available. Unlike the medical and obstetric services, they had no out-patient clinics. Consulting attendants who had seen their patients at the medical school hospital performed elective surgeries, and whoever was available would assist. The work was intense, but she did enjoy the variety of emergencies they saw. However, she often found herself in the operating theater for hours on end. She would flex her calf muscles to keep the blood flowing and try not to fall asleep on the patient.

In addition to her own work, she also had to supervise the activities of two or three medical students on their surgery rotations. As she assisted them in their tasks when they got stuck, which was often, she had to answer their constant questions and quiz them on their knowledge. She gained a new respect for those who had shepherded her through the same process and soon discovered she enjoyed teaching. It was frequently quite entertaining—to say the least.

She sometimes envied the medical registrars and housemen. At least they got to sit while they dealt with their patients. In contrast the obstetrics team was constantly on the go. *Maybe I should consider specializing in dermatology.* There were very few skin emergencies that got them up at night. On the other hand, the thought of looking at an endless parade of rashes didn't much appeal to her. *Perhaps psychiatry?* She would be able to sit and listen to her patients, look wise, and then fiddle with their medications. *No. That's not for me either.*

After dinner each evening, those surgical doctors who managed to make it on time for the meal tended to nod off in the comfortable chairs in front of the big TV in their dining-cum-sitting room. The exception was on Friday nights. Everyone congregated to watch *Star Trek* then. If they weren't on call, they'd drink beer. They were all addicted to the show and began to call their parent hospital the "mother ship."

When they missed meals, Maude was usually on hand to fix something for them, and it was often a lot tastier than the food sent over from the hospital kitchens. In a pinch they could always use the nurses' dining room. After ten o'clock at night, everyone could eat there—not only nurses on break but house staff, registrars, and orderlies. Most of the time there was usually only one of the kitchen staff on duty to fill and refill a giant urn of coffee and make mounds of scrambled eggs and toast. Nothing else was available, but it was delicious, free, and much appreciated when they needed a predawn boost. Penny was eating much more than she had been and had definitely put on a few pounds. Maude's fried potatoes were irresistible.

KISIMBA

She gradually adapted to the life during the first weeks. She learned to take naps whenever and wherever she could, and on her nights off, she turned off her pager with relief and went to bed immediately after dinner to fall into a comatose state. Her social life was nonexistent. Then a letter arrived in her mailbox, and she nearly cried with sheer happiness to see Nick's distinctive, bold handwriting on the envelope.

My dearest, darling Penny,
It amazes me it could be so hard to locate someone on such a tiny island as England. I was about to get on a plane and scour the country town by town. Now I know where you are, though, and I'll be with you soon.

I've been talking to your mom on a fairly regular basis, and she reminds me a little of you. I learned from her you had passed your finals and graduated. I'm so proud of you. I knew you'd breeze through it. By the way, your account of how you wowed them with your description of the splenectomy and the autotransfusion really tickled me. I'm sure the old dudes would have been even more entranced if you had told them what you'd been doing a few hours earlier. I trust you didn't.

Your mom also informed me after a few nudges that you have started a job somewhere in London at a hospital called Saint Luke's. Sounds Catholic. I'll figure out where it is. Don't worry. It's great you have a National Health Service over there. Maybe one day they'll get around to setting up a system like it over here. Although, I'm not holding my breath on that one. On my part I've been traveling from coast to coast in the United States and getting my life in order. I'll fill you in on all that in due course.

I want to get some bad news over with first. I didn't want to tell you before because it would have upset you right at the time you were taking your exams. Jim Campbell was killed

— 263 —

in Kampala at Mulago Hospital. Details later. Sue is OK, and I was on hand to make sure she got out on a plane to the United Kingdom. She now lives in some burg called Luton. We'll look her up when I get there.

The good news is I am now free to make an honest woman of you, if you are still so inclined. I certainly hope so. I might just do it anyway when you're not looking.

I've still got some business to wrap up, so I'm not sure when I'll be in London, but it won't be long. I'll be seeing you.

With all my love, Nick.

39

Penny struggled to stifle a yawn and noted the time on the patient's chart. It was 3:08 a.m. She hadn't slept for twenty-two hours, if she didn't count a half-hour catnap in a chair in the doctors' sitting room.

"Morning, Mr. Jenkins. I'm Dr. Drayton. I know you're in a lot of discomfort, and we're going to help you with that in a jiffy. But first I need to find out a few things about you. May I ask how old you are?"

"I'm eighty-two, young woman. How old are you?"

"Now, Mr. Jenkins, you know it isn't polite to ask a lady how old she is."

"Are you even a doctor? A little flibbertigibbet like you?"

"I am indeed. Mr. Bigelow, please present Mr. Jenkins's history."

Tim Bigelow, a third-year medical student, cleared his throat and recited authoritatively. "Mr. Jenkins is an eighty-two-year-old white male who presented in acute distress due to urinary retention over the past six hours. He reports no previous similar history and has been in otherwise fair health. He does have a history of hypertension, but his pressure today is one hundred twenty-eight over seventy-five."

"That's it, Mr. Bigelow? Has he ever consulted a urologist?"

"Yes, Doctor. I forgot. He was told he has an enlarged prostate."

"Well, that helps us a little. Has the registrar seen him?"

"Yes. He told me to catheterize him."

— 265 —

"I take it you were unsuccessful, and that is why you called me."

"Yes, Doctor."

"OK, Mr. Jenkins, we'll get you sorted soon," Penny said. "Let me just examine you. Mr. Bigelow, where is the fresh cath kit?"

"Er...I'll get it right away, Doctor."

The poor man's bladder was palpable almost to his navel, and he winced when she pressed lightly on it.

"Hey, watch it there, love! So you're going to try to shove a tube up me too? That young lad couldn't do it. Bloody prostate!" he muttered.

Just then the pager clipped to her green scrub pants buzzed loudly. "Someone answer that for me please," she called.

The student came back from the phone. "You're wanted in the nurses' dining room. The porter said it's important but not urgent."

The dining room? How odd. At least no one is choking to death in there, or they'd have sent me running.

She took off her white coat, gloved up, lubricated the rubber catheter, and slipped it in before the patient even knew what had happened. He groaned mightily with relief as the urine poured out in an apparently unending stream.

"You're going to feel a lot better now, Mr. Jenkins. I'll leave you in Mr. Bigelow's capable hands."

"Ta, Doc. You're a bonny lass, ain't ya?"

In the hallway Tim Bigelow said admiringly, "That was smooth, Doctor. Have you done a lot of those?"

She answered as she was writing her chart notes at the nurses' station. "You might not know this, but the first time I cathed a male was three months ago. Female students are only allowed to do it on female patients. Talk about archaic! And now as a house officer, I have to do it when the male students miss." She grumbled to herself. "See you later. I'd better go and find out what's going on downstairs."

She popped into the loo, washed her hands, and retied her ponytail. It had started to loosen and let messy curls hang around her

KISIMBA

face. When she saw her reflection in the mirror, she shuddered. She looked terrible. Then she walked down the stairs to the nurses' dining room in the basement. She could certainly use a caffeine jolt.

She looked around the large room and tried to figure out why she'd been called. A group of nurses were huddled at a table and eying the only other occupant in sight. Her heart skipped several beats when she realized who it was. She stood motionless in the entrance and drank in the sight of him. Her hands were shoved deep into the pockets of her white coat to hide their trembling.

Nick was wearing dark pants, a white shirt with the top button undone and the sleeves rolled up to his elbows, and a blue tie loosened around his neck. His suit jacket was slung over the back of the chair next to him. His CDC badge was clipped to the lapel. He sat with one long leg balanced negligently over the other knee. He was reading a newspaper with a cup of coffee beside him on the table. His tanned face and arms looked almost exotic under the harsh fluorescent lights, and his black curls were longer than she remembered. Despite the hour his cheeks were smooth, but he had shadows under his eyes.

He looked up and stared straight at her. One eyebrow raised, and his mouth curved into a smile. He dropped the paper on the table and stood as she walked toward him.

"Good morning. You must be Dr. Drayton."

"And good morning to you too, Dr. Sottile. What can I do for you?"

"I'm sure we'll be able to come up with something," he murmured, and he drew her into his arms and kissed her rather chastely right there before the audience of five delighted nurses. "Hi there, baby. You look just the same as the day you left. Please tell me those aren't the same scrubs."

"Nick! When did you get in? How did you get here? How long can you stay? Where—"

He silenced her with another kiss. "You're babbling, honey. I just flew in. Landed about two hours ago. I came straight here from the

— 267 —

airport. I was kinda hoping you could find me a place to sack out for the rest of the night. I'm wiped. You look beat yourself. Sit. Let me get you a coffee."

She fell into a chair at his table and gratefully accepted the cup. She was suddenly tongue-tied as he took her hand in his. "You're wearing the ring," she blurted.

"And you are *not* wearing the bracelet. Am I to assume the worst?"

"You know I can't...OK. You got me again." Her pager sounded, and she nearly screamed. "I'm going to stomp on this bloody thing and flush it down the toilet," she muttered. "I have to answer it. Don't you dare move."

She ran to the phone on the wall. Another emergency admission had come in. The "mother ship" had sent it over.

"I'm sorry, Nick. Typical Saturday night. But I'll be off duty at seven, and I don't have to come back in until Tuesday morning."

"Not bad. You young docs have it easy these days. So, can you find me a bed somewhere? Then at least one of us will be awake later on."

Penny pulled a bunch of keys from her pocket and handed him one. "You can have mine. I'll show you where the doctors' residence is. Try not to wake anyone up by snoring too loudly."

"I don't snore," he said indignantly, and he picked up his jacket and a small leather bag. They left the dining room.

"Oh no? How do you know? You're asleep when you do it."

They were laughing like teenagers when she showed him the building and directed him to the second floor. "There's a men's bathroom two doors down from my room."

"How quaint. Don't have much in the way of security here, do you?"

"This is England, Nick. Enjoy. Anyway, I bet the porter logged you in at the gate. They probably wouldn't have let you in so easily without your ID. I'll see you in a little while."

KISIMBA

She stood on tiptoes, kissed him fiercely, and then took off again into the night.

————

Penny quietly opened the door to her room with her spare key and crept inside. Nick hadn't bothered to close the curtains. He had just stripped down to his snug black briefs and crashed. He lay on his back in a tangle of sheets with his arms flung out and his feet dangling over the end of the small bed. She gazed at him and wondered how she was going to be able to lie down next to him without waking him up. She made sure her pager was turned off and that she had locked the door. It was now Sunday morning, so she knew the cleaning staff wouldn't disturb them. She closed the curtains against the gray August day.

Feeling suddenly shy she undressed quickly, put on a short cotton T-shirt, and then cautiously lay down on the very edge of the bed. Nick turned in his sleep and enfolded her in one arm. He tucked her bottom into the curve of his body and rested his hand lightly on her breast. A wave of deep contentment flooded her, and she fell into slumber. The sound of her door opening and the marvelous aroma of fresh coffee woke her. She opened her eyes drowsily. Nick was already fully dressed in well-fitting jeans and a light tan sweater. He sat on the bed and carefully put the big mug down on the side table. Then he held a napkin-covered bundle under her nose.

"Fantastic. Bacon. Thank you. I'll love you forever."

"I'd heard you English women were easy. Whoa! You still hit like a girl fortunately."

"Where did you get it?"

"I found my way to the doctors' mess and looked helpless. Maude took pity on me when I told her I'm a friend of yours. She's very fond of you. Calls you her 'lady doctor.' Wait a minute. 'Lady' as in the only female doc around here?"

— 269 —

"Why else do you think they stuck me up on this floor at the end of the hallway? At least I have the women's bathroom to myself." She took a huge bite of her sandwich and held it out to him. "Mmm. This is delicious. You want a bite of my butty?"

After a pause he said, "You know what? I really have no idea how to answer that. You naughty girl."

In one swift move, he flipped her over onto her front, pulled down her panties, and nipped her on her bottom. She let out a shriek. When she rolled back over, she held her arms out to him. He backed away.

"Nope. We have to go check into the hotel."

"Hotel?"

"If you think we're going to spend the next two nights in this bed built for a midget, you're very much mistaken. I've booked us into a plush place not far from the American embassy. I'll need to register with them anyway. Have you any idea how to get to Grosvenor Square? Maybe you should drive. I'm not used to driving on the wrong side of the road yet." He smacked his forehead theatrically. "What am I thinking? I'm not letting you drive anywhere."

"You have a car?"

"How else do you think I got here?"

"Taxi?"

"Hell no. We need to be able to get around. I'll check out the address while you wash your face and go pee. Pack a toothbrush and whatever. And you'll need a jacket. It's raining. I like it here. It's cool and wet like Seattle."

He stood and started flipping through an A–Z map of London.

"Where did you get that?"

"Your friend Albert loaned it to me. I'll need to get my own copy." She took a last gulp of coffee and then said, "Albert? The porter?"

"Yeah. Great guy. He was telling me all about his time in World War Two. He was seconded to an American unit. Loves the Yanks.

KISIMBA

I gave him the phone number of the hotel just in case, God forbid, there's some mass emergency, and they need to get ahold of you."

Nick had been casting his usual spell on everyone it seemed.

"I really need a shower."

"You can do that later at the hotel. Ah! Found it. Looks easy to get to. Come on, lady. I need lunch. This jet lag is playing havoc with my diurnal rhythm."

40

Nick drove carefully through the rainy London streets in his rented Ford, and they arrived at their destination in less than thirty minutes. It was, as he had promised, an upscale hotel. *Very nice.* She wondered how much it had cost. As they sat in the dining room and perused the lunch menu, she asked him.

"An arm and a leg," he said. "Which reminds me, do you have any of that money left?"

"Of course," she said indignantly. "I opened a new bank account and put it in there. Almost two thousand dollars. Of course, it was quite a bit less than that in pounds."

"That's a relief. We're going to need it until I get paid."

She let that one slide and figured he would tell her in his own sweet time. He ordered a ham and cheese omelet, and she opted for a bowl of vegetable soup. She was still full after her bacon sandwich, which had been quite substantial.

"Baby, we need to talk."

"No," she wailed. "You only just got here!"

"What? No. I'm not going anywhere. Let's start again. How much longer do you have to go with this internship?"

"Until December. Then I have to find another one. I think I'd best do one in medicine and then probably another in obstetrics."

"Peculiar system. Why not choose what you want to do and go straight into it?"

KISIMBA

"Because I need experience in everything else first. Though, I have to tell you, my time in Kisimba has really made a difference. What are you planning to do after this visit?"

"I managed to con the CDC into renewing my fellowship, and they've assigned me to the London School of Hygiene and Tropical Medicine in Bloomsbury. It's right up my alley. They're even going to pay me. And no guns involved. I swear."

She stared at him openmouthed as his words sank in. "You mean we'll be here together for more than one or two days? Oh, Nick."

"Yeah, honey. I'll get an apartment somewhere near your hospital, and we'll take it from there. Does that work for you?"

All she could do was nod silently.

"Excellent. Finish your soup. I need a nap."

By the time they got to their room, she could barely walk. She knew full well what they were going to be doing next. Nick closed the door firmly and turned to her. He slowly undressed her and caressed her skin as he exposed it. When he lowered his mouth to her breast, he whispered, "Ah...*perfetto*."

She could hardly breathe. Then he quickly removed his own clothes. When he freed himself from his briefs, it was quite clear he had only one thing on his mind. He picked her up and laid her gently on the big bed. His gaze was smoldering. He spread her thighs, knelt between them, and touched her. "Oh, baby, you're so wet." He groaned. "It's been far too long." Then he muttered in frustration, "What did I do with my damn wallet?"

"Don't stop now. Please. Oh please."

"I gotta get a..."

"No, you don't. I'm on the pill now."

He stilled. "Since when?"

"Since I knew you were coming back to me."

"Oh, Jesus. I don't know if I can hold on—"

"I don't care, Nick. I need you. Now."

She cried out from the sensation as he slid powerfully into her. In just a few moves, he climaxed with a shout, and after he finished thrusting, he collapsed on top of her. She held him tightly with her legs wrapped around him. She murmured her love as he pulsed inside her. Finally he rolled to one side and took her with him. She cradled him in her arms. She felt overwhelmed.

After a while, she started to move against him. "Nick, I'm soaked."

"Mmm."

"What about the sheets?"

"They'll do the laundry, baby. Don't worry.'

After another pause, she said, "That was incredible. What would be the volume of that?"

"Holy Mother! You're a doctor. You figure it out. About eight months' worth," he mumbled.

"I have no idea, but it seems like a lot." She moved her hips against him and whispered, "Can we do that again please?"

"Oh, honey. I'm sorry. I was too quick. You missed, didn't you? Turn around."

He curved his body around hers and slipped his hand between her legs. Soon his clever fingers worked their slow magic. "There you go, *cara mia*. Now please can we sleep? We have all the time in the world ahead of us. The rest of our lives."

———

Nick surfaced first and woke her by rubbing her tummy as though she were a cat.

"What time is it?" she purred sleepily.

"Teatime. They do something called a cream tea here."

"I hate tea."

"How can you not drink tea? You're a Brit. I'm glad to hear it, though. I don't like it either. It must be an omen."

KISIMBA

"I wouldn't say no to a cup of coffee. But what I would really like is a shower. I'm extremely sticky—especially my bits."

"Your bits? Oh, OK. Yeah. You certainly are. You go ahead while I find us some coffee, and then I'll clean up too. Would you like to walk over to the American embassy with me this afternoon?"

"I'd rather stay here and get in the shower with you. Anyway, it's Sunday. They'll be closed."

"The embassy never sleeps, my darling. Just because they won't let the riffraff in today doesn't mean they aren't open. Don't you want to see the guards in their splendid marine uniforms?"

As they talked Penny had been doing some detailed explorations under the sheet as he lay with his hands clasped behind his head.

"A tempting thought," she said. "After we shower. Oh, how about that? It's what you want to do too."

"You're going to wear me out, girl, and then what're you gonna do?"

"Come on. You're still relatively young and fairly fit." She grinned.

"Two insults in one sentence." He lifted her in his arms and carried her to the bathroom. "You'll pay for that, baby. But if I wash your bits, you have to wash mine."

"Deal."

Because they lingered in the shower, it was too late for tea anyway. Nick shaved and then dressed quickly while she was still trying to untangle her wet curls. She studied his reflection in the mirror over the dressing table. He sat behind her on the bed and watched her with his hands clasped loosely between his knees.

"Nick, how come you always look so gorgeous?"

"Huh?"

"You never have a bad hair day. You always manage to be clean and fairly tidy, even in scruffy clothes. You have an incredible body, but I've never seen you exercise."

"I was in the navy."

— 275 —

"It's more than that." She snorted. "You don't pick your nose or fart. And you have impeccable manners for an American."

"Hey, wait up! What do you mean 'for an American?'"

"You do hold your cutlery in a strange way when you eat. Where was I going with this?"

"I have no idea, but it's fascinating."

"Yes. I remember. You are an amazing lover, and you are very... well endowed. Believe me. I should know. I've probably examined more men than you have, so I've got a real basis for comparison. Patients I mean. Of course, they didn't have erections at the time. Most of them, anyway. Oh dear."

"Would you like me to give you a hand out of that pit, or are you going to keep digging?" Nick was grinning, and his eyes were dancing.

She waved off his words. "I do like that you are circumcised. It's much more attractive than...you know. In any case there have been several studies recently that have shown...Nick! Are you listening?"

"Yes, ma'am." He gasped as he tried valiantly to stop himself from laughing. "Please go on."

"Thank you. And even though you snore, it's usually fairly quiet. More of a little whistling noise like a hamster. And even though you eat like a flipping horse, you never gain weight."

"Let's get off the hamsters and horses and get back to my sexual attributes. That was fun."

Penny turned around on the chair and looked at him directly. "You're smart, kind, and funny. You are also a superb doctor, from what I've seen. You came to my rescue when I needed you on several occasions. Although, I must say you dillydallied around getting here to London!"

"OK. I'm getting mixed messages here."

"Only because I'm trying to be honest, which sometimes requires...never mind. I suppose I'm trying to tell you that I think

KISIMBA

you're almost perfect. Oh, you're naked again. When did that happen?"

"Don't worry about it. You were a tad preoccupied." He eased her robe off and laid her back down on the bed.

"I thought we were going out to see the pretty marines," she said.

"We will. In a while. First I think it's time to tell you the truth about myself." He positioned himself and spoke as he moved against her. "Once upon a time, many years ago, a hardworking couple who lived on a small farm in...um...Iowa or somewhere like that found a little baby boy in one of their barns. They had no idea where he'd come from, but they decided to keep him and tell everyone he was theirs. They'd always wanted children, but it had never happened. They loved him very much, and he grew up to be a fine young man. That would be me. Although he developed an unfortunate tendency to wear a cape and tights—which did, however, display his magnificent package to great advantage—he went about rescuing damsels in distress and doing other heroic deeds, and he made quite a name for himself."

He gave her a stern look as he slipped neatly inside her. "No giggling. This is a serious story."

"Oh, Nick, you're wonderful, but you're not Superman."

"Exactly, honey. Now, since we seem to have started again, let's finish."

41

SHE DECIDED TO wear her *kitenge* dress in honor of the occasion with a light black raincoat in case the heavy clouds let loose again. They headed out into the dreary afternoon and walked toward the area where Nick thought the embassy should be. However, on the way they passed a small pub and decided to stop for a drink. Penny asked for a glass of wine, and Nick had an ale. He eyed the huge dimpled mug when it arrived and said, "This'll get the kidneys going. No wonder women don't drink beer over here."

Penny said, "I can't wait any longer. Tell me what's been happening with you."

"You've been astonishingly patient. Most unlike you. Where to begin?"

"How about when you left me in Kenya? What did you do?"

"Not much. I got to Jinja without any problems and found a working phone. I called the Lady of Light mission and told them you were all on your way there. Then I tried calling your parents and actually got through. I was worried they would have seen the news from Kampala, which they had. So I reassured them you were safe and would be home soon."

"Just like that? Whom did you talk to? My mum or my dad?" She didn't disclose the fact she had already heard about that call.

"Your mom first. She was a bit shaky but took the news well. Then your father got on the line. Oh, boy. He doesn't have a shotgun, does he?"

— 278 —

"No. Why?"

"As soon as he knew you were OK, he gave me the third degree. I think it might have been because I admitted to being American. Once he had my family history, details of my education, and the reasons I was in Africa, he asked how we had met. I figured he was going to inquire if my intentions toward you were honorable, so I decided to preempt him and told him flat out I was going to marry you."

"Blimey! Actually that sounds like my dad. He's one of those people who always comes through in a crisis. A bit like someone else I know."

"Whatever. He said he wanted to meet me. Then your mom got back on and started talking about weddings. I guess we should visit soon. If you promise to protect me. By the way, would you like to have the proposal now?"

"Here? In this noisy pub? I think not. Anyway, the floor looks none too clean."

"You're probably right. These jeans are fairly new. If I'm going to get on my knees, I'd rather do it on carpet. Just not in your folks' living room, if you don't mind."

Penny chuckled and then was suddenly serious. "So, did you get back to Kisimba? I was really worried those corpses would be found and the army would take it out on the people at Hope Hospital."

"I did. There was no sign of them. I'm guessing the natives stripped the bodies of their belongings and carried them off into the bush. The place was almost deserted. All but a handful of patients and staff had left. I made sure the patients were stable and could get back home safely, and then I sent everyone else away. Margaret and Theresa had already gone with Luke. Zach and David agreed to leave when I did. I told them to take what food they could find and anything else they wanted. Zach asked if he could have Chrissie's record player. He was very fond of her. Poor little David cried nonstop. I gave him all the books you guys had been teaching him from. It was really heartbreaking."

— 279 —

Penny's own heart was hurting again. It was hard to believe the Hope Hospital was no longer.

"When I left I picked up the remaining medical supplies, drugs, and Jamal's microscope, and I took them with me to Kampala. I figured the hospital would be able to use them."

He stopped short, and she could read the pain in his eyes. "What happened in Kampala, Nick?"

"I was too fucking late to save Jim Campbell. That's what happened."

After a long silence, she said, "Please tell me. I need to know."

"Yes. You do." He stared into his beer. "OK. The city was in chaos. Soldiers were roaming the streets, and many of them were totally out of control. There were violent robberies, rapes, and random killings everywhere. The day before I got there, a bunch of them stormed into Mulago Hospital and searched out the white doctors and nurses and anyone else they didn't like the look of. Apparently Jim was on one of the wards. They just walked in and shot him in the head. He died instantly."

She stared at him in horror. She was unable to speak.

"Sue was at home. She'd gotten sick and couldn't go to work that day. I was the one who had to give her the news. God."

One part of Penny's mind watched them from a distance. She was in shock, and Nick was pale and drawn. They were sitting in a warm, comfortable pub so far away from the Africa she had grown to love.

"What then?" she said finally. "Finish it."

"Their houseboy...what was his name?"

"Thomas," Penny answered quietly.

"Yes, Thomas. He said he was ready to give his life for Sue, and I believed him. We took turns guarding the house. Eventually everything quieted down, and Radio Uganda reported the airport had reopened. I used my...connections, and I got her out on a plane to England. A few days later, I left too." After a few more minutes, Nick stood and said, "Penny, do you mind if we leave? I need to walk."

KISIMBA

It was raining again quite heavily. She didn't care. She welcomed the cool water streaming down her face and washing away her tears as she remembered the man she had come to admire and respect and who had been cut down in cold blood as he went about the work he loved. They walked silently and hand in hand through the quiet Sunday evening.

———

After a while Nick said, "Well, let's get the rest of the nasty stuff out of the way."

"Nasty? Please no. More bad news?" Her heart was pounding again.

"Not for us. Although, I'm not sure how you'll take it. Peter Nygaard and his associate turned up dead a few days after Amin took over. They must have been on the wrong side of the coup when the shit hit the fan. Their bodies were found along with hundreds of others floating in the Nile. Their throats had been cut, and they'd been castrated."

Nick was right. She didn't know how she felt about it. The thought of such horrible deaths sickened her, but she was also aware of a dark satisfaction deep inside her. He was watching her closely as she stopped in her tracks. She rubbed hard at her eyes and walked into the safe circle of his arms.

———

Later they stood at the gates of the American embassy. Nick strode up to one of the two guards and said briskly, "Evening, marine."

The man was a boy really. He stood at attention and looked past Nick. "Sir, the embassy is closed, sir."

"Relax, Corporal. We'll be back tomorrow. Good night."

"Sir."

— 281 —

"That went well," Penny said with a small chuckle. "Did you really think they'd invite you in for a brandy?"

"Nah. I did it for fun. I just needed to make sure I knew where this place is. We can come back in the morning. I want to get the paperwork started for getting you a visa to the United States. That reminds me. If you're going to take the ECFMG, you should probably do it soon while all the material's fresh in your head."

"I have absolutely no idea what you're talking about."

"The Educational Commission for Foreign Medical Graduates such as yourself. Their exam is required in the States to get licensed over there, if that's where we end up."

She stopped in her tracks. "Hold your horses. Aren't you jumping the gun a bit?"

"You're right," he replied. "I haven't told you the rest yet. Sorry. Do you want to go back to the hotel or keep walking?"

"Walking. I need to work up an appetite for dinner."

Nick collected his thoughts. "Where was I? Right. So I made it to Florida and met with Vicky. She's doing OK and has a steady boyfriend. I went to divorce court. I gave her everything. It was the best I could do. It wasn't much anyway. She seemed happy with it."

Penny studied his face. He seemed undisturbed, so she kept quiet.

"I nearly forgot the other important thing. Tomorrow we have to go to the bank and sign me on to the account you opened. I'll have my salary deposited there too."

"Nick, it's your money."

He stopped her and put his hands on her shoulders. "Sweetheart, that's not the way I am. It's ours. I just need to be able to write a check now and again. How much are you making anyway, if you don't mind my asking?"

"Seventeen hundred sixty pounds."

"Hey, not bad. I'll be getting about two thousand bucks. We should be able to live quite well on that."

"Nick, that's my salary per year."

"You're kidding! Well, no one will be able to say I married you for your money. How on earth do you manage?"

"My room and meals are free, and I don't have time to shop."

As they walked on, the sound of dreamy music floated out to the street from a dimly lit building that looked from the outside like a small nightclub. "Do you like dancing, Nick?"

There were still so many things she didn't know about him. He stopped again and swept her into his arms. Her hand automatically reached for his while the other rested at his waist.

"I'll have you know," he said with a mischievous look in his eyes, "that I am an exceptional dancer."

He neatly spun her around and then took her off guard by dipping her almost horizontal. She was shrieking and laughing when he pulled her upright again.

"OK. I believe you. Also I admire such modesty in a man," she said breathlessly. "Seriously, though." Nick groaned. "No. Seriously. We need to find out more about each other."

"OK. Two questions each. I'm getting hungry. You first."

She said, "Only two? All right. Favorite movie?"

"*Casablanca*," they chimed in unison.

"Favorite opera composer?"

"Puccini," she said.

He answered, "Verdi."

"Close enough," he said. "Your turn again."

"Your position on women's rights?"

He was deep in thought, and he took both her hands and held them in a firm grip behind her back. "On top."

He laughed, and she struggled to free herself. Still holding her helpless, he murmured, "Last one and then we eat. How do you feel about making love on a rainy Sunday evening?"

"Yes please," she whispered.

"Not right this minute. Calm down, girl."

Walking again they wandered into a residential section of town, and they came upon a small restaurant. The sign announced "Mamma Menotti's." Nick slowed his pace as they were passing.

"Italian. Let's take a peek. Eh, *marone*! I smell Marsala sauce. This OK with you?"

Penny realized she was very hungry. "Yes. This would be lovely."

The place was full, but they managed to get seats at a small table near the kitchen. Nick ordered a bottle of Chianti, and they sat back to study the menu.

"What the hell? Half of this is Indian food."

"Goody. I love curry."

"This is truly bizarre. Oh well. Let's try it."

He ordered veal Marsala and scowled at her when she asked for chicken tikka. The complimentary appetizer consisted of tomato and basil bruschetta and a bowl of chickpea dip with naan flatbread. He ate most of the spicy peas and bread, and she managed to grab one of the bruschetta. He continued his story while they nibbled.

"So then I made it to Seattle and spent some time with my parents and saw my sisters. Rosemary is pregnant and huge. I'm finally going to be an uncle. Mom told me she had talked to you a few times and had let you know I was alive and kicking, but she didn't know where you were. I had to get that information from your mom. Jesus. Carrier pigeons were more efficient."

They smiled contentedly at each other. Nick took her hand and ran the delicate silver links of her bracelet between his fingers. The food arrived, and it was fragrant and delicious. They took bites from both plates, and Nick decided he liked Indian food—so much so that he ate most of it.

He poured the last of the wine and said, "Are you ready for the rest? It took a while to do, but it's quick to tell."

"Yes. I have so many questions."

KISIMBA

"What a surprise. I went back to Atlanta and wrote up my report. They didn't seem to know quite what to do with me. So I went to Virginia and...hung around for a while."

She nodded wisely. "Uh-huh. The Double Oh Seven bit."

"No. Oh, whatever. A little mystery in a relationship might be healthy. I thought about going for an infectious diseases position up at NYU but didn't want to leave you hanging here. Someone would have certainly tried to steal you away. So when the CDC came up with the gig at the Tropical Medicine School, I jumped at it. And here I am. Did I miss anything?"

"How do I know?" she asked reasonably. "It was your odyssey."

"Odyssey. I like that." He placed his napkin on the table and finished his wine. Then he knelt before her. The people at the nearby tables stopped talking and eating and stared.

"This seems like the right place. Penny, *cuore mio*, will you marry me?"

She slipped to her knees beside him. "Of course I will, Nick. I've been waiting all day. I was about to ask you!"

They kissed and were oblivious to the cheers and applause around them.

When he helped her to her feet, Penny looked around. She was dazed. The hovering server shook Nick's hand enthusiastically and said, "Our congratulations, sir and madam. The manager asked me to tell you the wine is our gift to you. May you enjoy long life and happiness."

Nick pulled a fistful of bills from his pocket. "Thanks, buddy. Will this cover it?"

The man counted it quickly and then handed over a five-pound note. "Too much, sir."

Nick promptly gave it back to him. "This is for you."

They started on their long walk back. He began to sing "Lay, Lady, Lay" softly. She was startled and stopped and stared at him.

"What? It wasn't that bad."

"I was just singing that in my head. How did you know?"

"It must be telepathy. How convenient! I'll be able to send thoughts to you through the airwaves. 'Hi, honey. I'm on my way. Do you have my dinner ready? Are my slippers warming by the fire?' It'll be like having our own private phones to carry around." When she narrowed her eyes at him, he hastily continued. "Actually you were humming the melody. You just didn't realize it."

Then she asked, "Nick?"

"Yeah, baby?"

"It's been quite an adventure so far. Where do we go from here? And do I get a ring?"

"Well, first we celebrate our engagement when we get back to the hotel. Assuming we can find it. And I'm glad you mentioned the ring. I forgot about it in all the excitement." He pulled a small velvet-covered box from his pocket. "This was my grandmother's. My mom gave it to me for you. If you want to choose another, that's OK with me, but this one's yours anyway if you like it." He took out the ring and slid it onto her left ring finger. "A bit tight. We can have it sized."

Penny gazed at the square diamond set with a sapphire on each side. "Nick, it's so beautiful. It's exquisite. Thank you, and your mother too." She smiled and felt overwhelmed. She turned her hand to make the stones sparkle in the light of the streetlamps. When he enfolded her in his embrace, she said, "Then what? Will we live here or in America? Or go back to Africa?"

"Who knows?" he said. "We'll just have to figure it out as we go along, my love."

GILLIAN M. MERCURIO is the pen name of an English-born physician. Early in her career she worked in a bush hospital in Uganda, an experience that inspired her first novel, Kisimba.

Mercurio spent most of her professional life in academic medicine and has published widely in scientific literature.

Now retired from medical practice, Mercurio currently lives in Las Vegas, Nevada, with her husband of thirty years.

Made in the USA
San Bernardino, CA
21 July 2016